Len E Hooke

RIP – CRIMSON

AUSTIN MACAULEY PUBLISHERS™

LONDON • CAMBRIDGE • NEW YORK • SHARJAH

A CIP catalogue record for this title is available from the British Library.

ISBN 9781788233507 (Paperback)
ISBN 9781788233514 (Hardback)
ISBN 9781788233521 (E-Book)

www.austinmacauley.com

First Published (2018)
Austin Macauley Publishers Ltd.
25 Canada Square
Canary Wharf
London
E14 5LQ

The author lives in Orpington with his wife and young son. He worked as an office manager, and later as a psychic, hypnotherapist, healer and a life coach.

Other Works by the Author

RIP – Synergy

Prologue

Synergy

This is what God intended.

It made some sense in what the entity had said about doing God's bidding, and having no choice in that. I had no freedom to choose not to take this action; I just followed the signs set up for me by God. Of course, God did not tell me this would happen; but there could be no other reason that I was given this mark on my hand. I was to use it to destroy the one thing strong enough, determined enough, to challenge God. And what of my Guardian; was he just doing as he was told, or was he also in on the scam?

My doubts intensified, to the degree that I had half a thought to remove my hand. But the wish to do what was right throughout my life, even at the expense of myself, took over, and my hand stayed rooted inside the shimmering, shaking form of the entity. My mind convinced me that I could smell burning as the heat inside the pod intensified. The screeching of the entity drilled into the core of the being that I had become and I started to understand that the screams were not of pain, but of despair. The entity knew what was happening and the likely outcome, and it was this realisation that caused it so much torment.

I lost all sense of who and where I was. My whole being was aflame. *'I'm sorry. I'm really sorry,'* I muttered in my mind. *'Turn it off, turn the damned machine off!'* I screamed out, hoping that my Guardian would hear my desperate plea.

And a face showed above me, only one.

I felt so weak now, so empty. I gazed out, peering through the frosty cover that topped the pod inside which all my energy was ebbing away. The screams I heard became weaker. They were sorrowful and sad instead of angry. I continued to try and peer through the top of the capsule. The face I thought I could see was so faint. I gathered up every ounce of energy and focused my gaze.

I could barely make out my father. I had not seen him for 33 desperately lonely years.

He smiled, for the first time since he died.

I blinked three times.

Part One

The Plan

Chapter One

Judy banged with increasing force against the solid white door, the booming sound echoing down the enclosed cement-floored hallway. She placed her face against the door's cold surface and peered into the spyglass at its centre. The passageway was empty, three doors shut and one slightly ajar. The internal hallway inside was dark, lit only by the natural light that squeezed through the small gap under each closed door and the opening in the other. Her sense of panic grew.

'Come on you creepy bastard, open the door!' Judy muttered as she rooted around inside her shoulder bag.

She grabbed the cold dark key, inserted its shaft into the lock and turned it very gently to the left, and then to the right, repeating the turns until the mechanism clicked three times. She pulled the door hard toward her, before pushing forcefully against it with her right shoulder.

The door swung open violently. Judy removed her key and shut the door. She left her bag in the hallway and rushed towards the first of the closed doors.

As she gently pushed the door open her sight fell upon a single chair backed up against the wall to her left, an old wooden wardrobe, two drawers below a set of double doors, of which one door stood slightly ajar. Deep purple curtains were drawn shut, the thin material struggling to restrain the searing white light of a bright mid-afternoon sun. The black-painted metal end of a bed came into sight. Moving her gaze further around the room, she saw a pair of black socked feet, splayed slightly, and unmoving. Judy pushed the door hard and it swung all the way open, banging into a door jamb placed on the right side.

Judy moved briskly to the side of the bed.

My body lay prone, hands straight by my side palms down. My head lay slightly to the left side, facing my visitor.

It was then that Judy noticed the silence in the room, thick and all-pervading. She darted forwards and placed an ear against my chest searching for any sign of a heartbeat. She found none.

Judy pulled as hard as she could at my left arm, using all her might to drag me onto the carpeted floor. My body fell with a muffled thump. Judy frantically pulled me onto my back. She dropped her head to my chest and listened once again for any sign of life. There was nothing.

'Oh my God, what have you done?' she asked nervously.

Judy clasped her two hands together and pushed firmly into the middle of my chest. She counted a single digit and then pushed again, this time harder.

She counted in between frantically desperate pushes.

'Come on you stupid fucking idiot, do you think it is meant to end like this? You selfish bastard, come on, don't waste my time you motherfucking, goddamned, useless piece of psychic shit, come on!' she shouted out.

Urging herself on, she pushed through the pain that seared up her arms and into the base of her back. She pushed hard again, and again Judy took a deep breath, held it, and then bent over and blew with all her might into my mouth. She then pushed hard, one more time on my chest.

An almost imperceptible exhalation escaped my lips. Judy pushed hard again. I jumped up and into a sitting position, clashing heads with Judy as my unexpected movement caught her by surprise. I coughed hard and then gulped in the most refreshing, wonderful lungful of air. Whatever it was that I breathed out left a wet cardboard flavour in the roof of my mouth that smacked of bitterness. I coughed again, straightened my arms and placed my hands palm down on the bedcover.

Chapter Two

'Hey,' I looked at Judy with tear-stained eyes, 'that was one hell of a kiss.'

Judy reached around my back and pulled me close to her.

'Watch it!' I said, 'I only just got that back, I don't want you squeezing all the air out of me again.'

She pushed away from me. She raised herself and then, placing her arms under my armpits, she helped me up to sit on the edge of the bed. She then seated herself on my right side.

'What the fuck happened here?' she asked.

'Is it really necessary for you to use such trashy language?' I asked.

'Sorry, but you just fucking died on me.'

'What? Are you being serious?'

'Would I joke about something like that?'

'Well, you being a police inspector, I guess not.'

'It's gone three o'clock. I waited and waited but I heard nothing from you. I got no response when I banged on the door, so I broke in,' Judy explained.

'That's a criminal offence Inspector Marchant,' I replied with a wry smile.

'Can you contain that loathsome wit of yours for a while? This is serious.'

'Yes, I'm sorry, please carry on.'

'When I got here I found you prone on the bed. You had no heartbeat, so I did what I could to get you breathing. That's the first and last time I plan to do anything like that again. What happened to you?' Judy asked.

'I'm not too sure to be honest,' I replied, 'I remember laying down on the bed. Then it was like I had a really vivid dream. I went to a large palace, and it was like I was expected there. Some tall guy spoke to me. I was trapped inside a really small spaceship. Something was inside there with me. Then I guess you pushed my chest, which is pretty sore by the way, and I woke up. That's about it.'

'Do you remember St Mary's Hospital?' Judy asked.

'Yes, I'm going there for some therapy and tests.'

'Well, that's near enough right. But what about the reason why you volunteered for the tests?'

'So that I can trap and dispose of the rogue entity that is killing people,' I answered.

'Very well done. I want you to tell me more. Tell me about everything you remember.'

'Is this part of my therapy?' I asked, smirking.

'Just do it. Humour me, please. Don't forget it is not just you who is in the firing line here, I am involved too, and it is my life as well as yours that will be on the line.'

'A chance to die twice in a day. Wow!' I replied.

Judging by her frowned facial expression, that was not my best option to choose as an answer.

'Get on with it, we don't have much time,' she urged.

'Yes, I'm sorry. We first met six months ago when I believed a spiritual entity was responsible for the death of two local men. There was then a further death that I felt was linked. Originally, we got nowhere. But recently you and I agreed to share information on a number of further deaths that seemed to show the same type of MO, including the crash of a minibus carrying a netball squad that killed 12 schoolgirls. I was there, and you were driving.' I explained.

'Very good, that is an abbreviated form of what has happened up to now, but it'll have to do.'

'Also, we have no evidence that anything has happened at all,' I tapped my forefinger against my right temple, 'because it's all in here.'

'Well, that's not strictly true. The coroner, Dr Theodore Anstis is onside, of a sort. He has seen enough of our victims to realise there is something very strange happening. He had no choice but to record 'death by natural causes' on the records of all our victims, and it is unlikely, given his authority, that he will involve anyone else. We also have PC Stewart,' Judy said.

'Only under threat of his Friday night jaunts being exposed,' I replied.

'What?' she asked.

I tapped the end of my noise, 'I can say no more, suffice to say I think we can count on a bit of help from the constable should we need it,' I answered.

'Just one more thing I need to ask you. What is the most important thing about these deaths? Why are you and I involved?' Judy asked.

'Because there seems to be some kind of a link between this entity and me that we have not yet been able to establish,' I replied.

'That's good. Seems to me like you are pretty much up to speed.'

I looked into Judy's eyes, searching for a thought that lingered somewhere in my mind, but stayed just out of sight. I beckoned it forward, pleaded with it, and demanded it present itself for my conscious assessment and possible use.

'Wait a minute,' I continued, 'I went looking for this link. I felt I needed to know more of this connection before we took on this entity,' I finally recalled.

'Yes, you got it. That is exactly what is going on, except…'

'Except what?' I asked.

'We don't know much of what happened in your meditation, except that this entity may have the ability to kill you if you confront it.'

Chapter Three

'Are we ready to go?'

'What? Are you serious? Only a matter of seven minutes ago you were laying here on your bed, dead as a doornail. No breathing, no pulse, nothing.'

'But I'm not dead now,' I patted myself with both hands, 'at least it does not feel like I am dead.'

'Is it wise for us to rush you to the hospital? Is it OK now, for you to undergo any kind of tests or questioning? Do you think you are in any fit state to talk to anyone, let alone take on a spiritual entity whose power and potential you know nothing about? Come on, get real, you are in no fit state to do anything like that,' Judy pleaded.

'Judy, I feel fine. I am a bit tired, that's all. When we get there we can put off any tests until tomorrow and I can rest all day and all night. Get up fresh in the morning.'

'No, you cannot,' she insisted.

'Judy, we have a timetable, we have a plan. We might not get another opportunity. This thing is savaging people unabated. Judy, this journey we are on is immense beyond words. Not only is the spirit world in its entirety at risk, but so too is every single thing it is connected to, including the future of humankind. Now, if I am the only person in this world and in the next who can stop this entity from creating

Armageddon, then I think I have a duty to bloody well do my damnedest to restore some kind of order, don't you?'

'Well, if you put it like that,' she replied, visibly taken aback by the vigour with which I used my words.

*****

The journey to the hospital was quick, uneventful, and punctuated only by occasional comments that had no bearing on the issue at hand.

My thoughts at this time were scrambled. On the one hand I knew that I needed to focus on my reason for undertaking this journey and to be clear in my methods or run the very real risk of certain failure. On the other side of the equation, I was concerned about what I had been through in the last hour. And now, only a short time later, I was heading for a showdown with a killer entity.

The sum total of what I knew about this entity was very little. I knew about its ability to enter a human being and take a life leaving no physical evidence of its presence. My strongly held belief is that it resided in the spirit realm, and that it seemed to have unfettered access to our world. I also believed that the end goal of its actions had something to do with challenging the existing order of the spirit realm.

What I didn't know was why? I didn't know why God and the spiritual elders needed my help in fighting the challenge to their status, or in what way my help might be applied. I could not know, and had no way of anticipating, the outcome of any actions we might take in the hospital. I was ready to battle the rogue entity in an effort to protect God and Its cohorts, but what the outcome might be, and what impact any outcome might have on humanity, I had no idea.

'Not to put too fine a point on it, you look like shit,' Judy said as we exited the car.

'I would not expect anything else, having just died.'

I placed my right hand onto the front left wing of the car to steady myself for the short walk into the hospital entrance. I felt cold, even in the warm afternoon sun that bathed my head, arms and body. I shivered, hoping that Judy was too preoccupied to notice. She locked the car.

'Are you sure you can do this?' Judy asked as she rounded the front of the car to stand next to me, 'you look about ready to collapse.'

'I will be fine, promise. I might just need to gather myself a bit before we get inside,' I replied.

'OK, well let's go then. We are already nearly an hour behind schedule.'

'Spoken as a true stickler for procedure.'

'Is that what I am?' Judy asked.

'Of course, I might have been a bit nonplussed about you when we first met, but I know you now.'

'I'm that easy to read, huh?'

'Like a Year Three schoolbook,' I replied, trying my best to smile, but failing miserably.

I winced as I took a step forward.

*****

We registered my details and I was allotted a room. The room was small and pokey. A thin mattress covered with a sheet and thin cover lay atop a rack of creaky springs fixed all around a black metal-framed bed. The room had a small wash basin above which was fixed a grey metal shelf. Above the shelf was a mirror.

One look into the mirror was enough to confirm Judy's observation. My usually deep blue eyes had lost their sparkle, and my face looked pale and colourless. My hair, usually soft and shiny, now looked lank and listless. It was bunched atop my head and full of knots. The skin on each of my palms was dry. And when I tried to smile I could feel the skin of my lips crack under the strain.

'Now do you see what I mean? I will give you one last chance to open that door and leave. There is no absolute necessity for you to be here right at this moment as this is not, surely, a do or die moment. We can rearrange for another time. The DI is the head man, he supported your application and he will do it again. I know you don't place any emphasis on your own wellbeing, but please, even if it's just for my sake, let's pick up your bag and leave this place. As soon as you are fit enough to do this, we can come back again.'

Judy kept her fist clenched tightly around the handles of the sports bag that contained my belongings.

'No. The time is right now Judy. All the preparations have been made, everything is in place. I know you only want to protect me but who is to say exactly the same thing would not happen again? Only next time, it is unlikely you would be there to save me.'

'I did do pretty good, didn't I?'

'You did fantastic,' I agreed 'but now we have this thing cornered we have an opportunity to destroy it, and I will not let this chance slip through my hands. Not now, not again.'

Chapter Four

I had no energy to do anything but dump my belongings on the floor in front of the bed that was pushed against the wall. I leaned over the bed and rolled onto its unforgiving surface. The springs underneath creaked and then lay silent. I did not remove my shoes or clothing.

Judy had left the room to sit in a waiting area adjacent to the reception at the front of the building. My door remained unlocked so I would, at least in theory, be able to join her at any time. There was no secured gating to the entrance of the hospital. Those patients deemed a risk to other inmates, to staff or to the public, would most likely only be released from their room under strict supervision, their doors otherwise locked to outsiders. My guess was that a separate part of this complex held such people, far away from the relaxed atmosphere that seemed to pervade this space.

I laid on my back and looked up at the ceiling. It was clean and white with a small round shade covering a light bulb in the middle. My vision blurred at the corners. I had no reason to fight the tiredness that washed over me. The muscles in my legs, my arms, my stomach and my neck all loosened as I began drifting off into a deep sleep.

I was disturbed by three sharp knocks on the door. My body immediately tensed and my eyes opened wide. I turned to look over my left shoulder. There was no internal lock, just a grey metal handle that pulled down to open the door. The handle turned down, the door opened and the edge of a white coat moved into the doorway, quickly followed by a brown-trousered body topped by a pristinely white shirt. The white coat was unbuttoned. I looked up: a slightly puffy face with pinkened cheeks surrounded by curly black hair. Black rimmed glasses sat upon a slightly bulbous nose. A small mouth with thin lips greeted me once he had entered the room and shut the door behind him.

'Good afternoon, my name is Dr J J Allen, and I will be your psychologist during your stay here in St Mary's,' the man said as he pulled the chair towards the side of the bed and sat down.

I pulled myself up into a seated position, and looked at the man with tired eyes.

'I'm sorry, doctor…'

'Allen,' the man in the white coat helped me.

'I'm sorry Dr Allen, but in the last two weeks I have hardly slept a wink, too much going on in my mind, plus being a bit concerned about coming here, I guess.'

'And that is precisely why you were recommended to us at short notice. Your sponsors thought it necessary for us to carry out some evaluations of your situation as soon as possible. It was thought this might be a good start to unravelling all the strands and developing a plan of action.'

'So, doctor, what is our plan of action?'

'We will start tomorrow in the morning. We will not be barraging you with interviews and tests, you will have breaks in between. If you would like me to, I can print you out a draft schedule. The tests should be finished by early evening in two days. Then you can choose to leave immediately, or you could leave the next morning. But as for this evening, it looks like you could do with some rest.'

Dr Allen rose from the chair, placing it against the wall opposite the bed. I immediately resumed my prone position on the bed and prepared to rest, probably for the first time in a month. And as my eyes closed I heard the latch on the door click as it was pulled tightly into its wooden frame.

Chapter Five

I awoke, and immediately looked at the watch fastened to my left wrist. The time was just after 9am. If the watch was correct, I had been asleep for a little over 13 hours. I got off the bed and stood up. The last time I had been upright, I struggled even to stand on my own two feet. I moved over to the mirror on the wall above the sink. My reflection looked back at me. Though I now had a good colour in my cheeks, my hair was a mess so I used my right hand to pull my it across to the right and flatten it down. Better, but still rough. I went to the side of the bed, picked up my belongings and transferred them to the bed.

I reached into my trouser pockets searching for my front door keys and my mobile phone. I looked through the items on the bed and then those in the bag and the outside zippered pockets. Both were missing. I looked quickly under the bed, again drawing a blank.

I moved over to the door and reached out for the handle. The door opened easily. I looked briefly outside and then departed the room leaving the door open in my wake. I strode over to the reception desk and awaited eye contact with the person sat behind it. The 20-something brown-haired lady with plump midriff and steely dark brown eyes raised her head from the computer terminal that had held her attention.

'Good morning,' I said, 'erm, I seem to have slept for a very long time. Is it possible you could tell me when breakfast might be?' I asked.

'Good morning, sir, I am sorry but you missed breakfast. It is usually served between seven and eight o'clock. I could get you some cereal, orange juice and some coffee,' the lady offered.

'Oh thank you, I would really appreciate that.'

'We have rice crispies or cornflakes.'

'Rice crispies would be fine, thank you. I feel in the mood for a bit of a snap, crackle and a pop,' I replied, thankful that my sense of humour had not deserted me when my breath had the previous afternoon.

'Milk and sugar with your coffee?' the lady said without any flicker of a smile.

'That would be great, thanks very much.'

'And don't forget sir that you are meeting with Dr Allen in 30 minutes.'

'OK, thanks for reminding me,' I replied.

Yeah thanks, I thought, I had completely forgotten, that is if I ever knew before. I gripped the lip of the counter and went to turn away. Instead I turned back.

'The lady who accompanied my arrival yesterday, she wouldn't happen to be here this morning, would she?' I asked, a little too hopefully.

'Inspector Marchant stayed until 10pm last night. You did not stir, so she left. I don't know if she told the night staff of any further plans to visit. There is a policeman over there,' she said, nodding to the area across my right shoulder, 'he might be able to tell you some more.'

'OK, thank you very much.'

I walked the few steps to the waiting area on the opposite side of the entrance hall. I put my right hand at the entrance and peered inside. PC Ian Stewart was sat beside a small table, looking at a well-thumbed classic car magazine. He looked up.

'Sir, how are you feeling this morning?' he asked.

'A bit groggy, but I will be fine. They've taken my phone. Is there any way that I can get in touch with Judy Marchant?'

'I can get her in if you want me to,' he suggested.

'I would appreciate that. I need to meet the psycho doc in 20 minutes or so, but after that it would be a good idea for all of us to catch up,' I replied.

Chapter Six

Far from being boring, the consultation with Dr J J Allen was of interest, not least because I felt able to let out some suppressed childhood feelings about my mother and her ignorance of the needs of her three children.

It also gave me an opportunity to address my isolation as a teenager. I never had a large group of friends, always feeling I could not fit in with their ideas and even with their style of clothing. I should have learned way before now that it was more likely that my desire for isolation was far more to blame for the bullying I received than was my mother's insistence on dressing me like a clown. There was a strong possibility that psychologically I had closed down, withdrawn from life, preferring instead to sit and weep in the corner. It is true that a physical appearance can always be overcome with the right mental adaptations. What is also true is that I was afraid of adapting.

As I grew up I continued to withdraw and fight against this invisible, and now seemingly non-existent, ghost of suppression. I could see clearly, even as I spoke, the other side of the psychological coin. Alternative realities became easy to grasp, to understand, and to accept. Physical bullying, as frightening and as evil as it felt, was not the biggest threat to me. It was the emotional bullying that I forced upon myself that was my greatest enemy and my most fearsome slayer.

Feelings of degradation and worthlessness can never result from another's mouth or fists, they can only arrive from our reactions to such threats. It is the feelings we create to protect ourselves that cause all of the pain and suffering. If we are able to share these feelings with somebody we trust, it is not the other person who magically waves a wand and reduces these feelings, but it is our own realisation, through facing the truth in an observational capacity, that eventually serves to provide the armour and the bullets to fight back. Since the battle can only ever take place inside ourselves, if we are able to step back and look at our reactions to outside influences in a different light, the battle becomes much easier and there can only ever be one outcome: victory. As sure as the sun rises every morning, the delivery of nasty comments or the physical stiffening of a fist has the intention of causing pain, but the refusal to react in a way that will create suffering instantly makes any pain disappear.

The most important question for any psychologist must be *"have you ever tried to hurt yourself, or have you ever thought of ending your life?"* They will never use the word 'suicide' but this is what it amounts to. Suicide is giving in, an emotional collapse in the face of seemingly insurmountable problems or issues. But again, the perception of these issues differs from person to person. What might seem complete destruction to one person could be an opportunity to clear out and continue in a more positive mindset, to another. I have been asked this question so many times, and my answer is always the same. I never contemplated self-harm or suicide, but on many occasions I have wished wholeheartedly that God would remove me from this lifetime. At times it was disconcerting to wake up to another sunny morning. In hindsight, such periods of gloom and despair were always proven to have been opportunities to develop and grow.

I have ultimate faith in my belief that God would never let me live through anything that I was incapable of coming to terms with. It might be that consciously we have little or no idea of our emotional and spiritual strengths and weaknesses, or maybe it could be that we hide them away, but I have learned that anything I face in my lifetime arrives because it is the perfect opportunity for further learning from greater life experiences. There is nothing that we cannot come to terms with or overcome. All we need is to learn to step back, listen to the advice of those people closest to us, and to choose the better of the two options presented to us.

Dr Allen made copious amounts of notes on his A4 pad, all spaced far enough apart to not be lost in the totality of the whole.

'Thank you for opening up about many of the major events that happened in your life all of which, in one form or another, feed into your current situation. I have read the referral letters from your GP and from DI Menzies, they are interesting but lack detail. Since it was you who experienced the issues that led to these letters I would like to know from you what was the one major reason for your presence here today?' Dr Allen asked.

'Would you prefer the short or the long answer?' I asked.

'Whatever you feel is more suitable.'

'Well, to cut a long story short, I lost my mind.'

'Do you feel that this is true?' the doctor asked.

'No, actually it was the lyrics from a song from the 1980s but a very accurate description.'

'I only want to know what you think.'

'I am avoiding the question, aren't I.'

'It would appear so, yes,' Dr Allen replied.

'Well, the fact is that some of what I have recently experienced is not so easy to explain.'

'Can you at least try? You were very honest about your past experiences, so I would greatly appreciate it if you could treat what happened to you more recently with an equal reverence.'

'Yes, of course. You may, or you may not, be aware that I possess certain psychic abilities. I am also a qualified hypnotherapist, life coach and a healer. Suffice to say that I have an acute interest in all things spiritual. I cannot explain to you, or to anybody else, how these skills are visited upon me, except to say that I have the ability to know certain things about people of which others might be unaware. I feel I am not explaining things very well,' I admitted.

'I am following you so far, please do continue.'

'Through these psychic abilities I found out that a number of young people were dying of unknown causes. In a nutshell, it seems that a rogue spiritual entity is killing these people to challenge the position of God in the universal way of things.'

Dr Allen looked up from his notes and over the top of his glasses, his face was unflinching, not a twitch as he digested the information he had just been fed. I stared at him too, if he wanted me to retract the comment by looking away from his eyeline I refused to do that. It seemed like a very long time before he relented and returned to his notes, scribbling a short comment I could not see.

'What was the official reason behind these deaths?' the doctor asked.

'Natural causes,' I replied.

'And if they died of natural causes, what is it that makes you believe the cause of their deaths was something else?'

'The official cause of death was natural causes only because nothing else could be recorded. The coroner himself

31

knows these deaths did not arise from circumstance, and that they were caused by something otherworldly,' I replied.

'And who is this coroner? What is his name?'

'I cannot tell you. Don't you see? If the coroner admits that these deaths occurred by non-physical means, then how would that leave his career? This entity kills people in ways similar to those that might emerge from a failing of the human body, except the deaths are too clean to be from a natural source. The coroner is convinced these deaths were far from natural, but he has no way of recording that as a fact,' I continued.

'Well, it is certainly a bit of a leap from suggesting that a death is not from natural causes to blaming some otherworldly entity,' the doctor challenged.

'Yes, indeed it is. But I have other reasons to believe that this entity was responsible for these deaths.'

'And what might they be?' Dr Allen asked.

'I was told by my Guardian in the spirit world.'

The good doctor raised his head, his eyes piercing mine searching for the truth of that statement.

'And when do you believe you visited the spirit world?'

'I don't believe that I went there, I really did go,' I insisted.

'OK, my apologies. When did you go there?'

'I have been visiting the spirit world in meditation for many years, seeking guidance on issues of importance to me and looking for answers to the questions of our existence. But four weeks ago it was different. This is when I was asked by the higher elders in the spirit realm to take action to stop this entity. And this is when I found out that the rogue spirit's ultimate goal was to overthrow God.'

'And who told you this?' Dr Allen asked me.

'God did.'

Dr Allen lowered his chin and confronted me with his upturned eyes.

'Are you asking me to believe that God spoke directly to you?'

'You can believe what you like. I am just telling you what happened,' I replied.

'And what form does God take when you communicate?' the doctor asked, now scribbling furiously on the pad in his lap.

'God takes no form. It exists as an energy, just as we do.'

'So God might look like you or me, or anyone?'

'No. God takes no form. God is everywhere and nowhere. It exists as an elemental intelligent energy,' I explained further.

'So if you could not see God, how did you know He was talking to you?'

'God has no male or female traits. And It was not talking to me, It was conversing with me, I think you might agree there is a big difference between the two.'

'Quite.'

'I know it was God because that is what I called for, and that was how this communicating entity presented Itself to me.'

'I see.'

'To be honest with you Dr Allen, I really do not think that you do. You are a man of science. If it cannot be proven with some type of physical characteristics here on earth, then it cannot exist. Well, I have news for you. Most of what exists is outside of the range of your primitive scientific equipment. What you cannot prove does exist, and it does that beyond the recognition or your knowledge. It just happens that I am allowed, in this lifetime, to apply certain skills that allow me greater access to these unseen, unknown realities. They do exist, and it has been proven to me, at least so far as any proof of physically elusive realms can be.'

'And you said that you travel to the spirit world through meditation,' Dr Allen said, being very careful not to become too engaged in my theories and beliefs.

'Yes, I do.'

'But surely you are aware that meditation is simply a self-induced method of relaxation. The concentration of focus on one thing forces the human body and mind to slow its natural thought processes. The meditative experience can only be self-controlled, and as such it follows that whatever people might believe they experience in a meditative state must also be self-induced. There is no evidence whatsoever that a meditative experience involves any external entities whatsoever. Essentially, you, as the meditator, create your own experiences.'

'I don't agree with that,' I replied abruptly.

'Agree with it or not, that is entirely your choice.'

'Dr Allen, I respect your professional expertise, I really do, but sometimes the unexplainable is just as possible as the explainable. In my experience, in meditation we open ourselves to a connection with an existence that cannot be explained, and neither can it be scientifically dissected. There is no doubt that the vast majority of seven billion human inhabitants on earth believe in an extension of our existence beyond the physical life we are currently engaged in. Now, that belief is built on what? It is not there because science proves it, because it does not. And it cannot be there simply because people are told it is, I don't believe that the entire human race could be that gullible. I prefer to think that people believe in an afterlife because at some point in their lives they have a personal experience that proves, to their satisfaction, that their soul or their spirit will continue in a different form after they die. I will agree with you that suggestion might play a big part in their belief, but that cannot, of itself, justify the creation of a complete belief system with this one philosophy at its core,' I replied.

'That was very eloquently put. I think I have enough from this meeting to write up some detailed notes that will, no doubt, feed into our overall analysis of your stay here at St Mary's.' Dr Allen rose out of his seat.

I stood up from the bed to clasp his palm in a handshake, even though none was initially offered.

'Dr Allen. My background is real, my experiences are well documented and my reasons for being here are sound. I know what happened and I am as sure as I can be of what was the cause.'

Dr Allen forcibly released his hand from my grip, he opened the door and quietly left the room.

I had another meeting scheduled for early afternoon, and this would be with a Dr Sara Whyte, a psychiatric counsellor. That would be fun, if my meeting with Dr J J Allen was anything to go by.

I opened the door and walked into the waiting area to be met once again by PC Stewart.

'Did you finish any of those magazines yet?' I asked.

'I don't think I ever started them. I'm just looking at the pictures really.'

'Did you manage to get hold of Judy?'

'Ah, yes, she said she will get here at about five, she has a few things to clear up first,' PC Stewart replied.

'That will be great. It will give me another chance to play games with the docs here until she arrives.'

PC Ian Stewart leant in towards me.

'Can you tell me any more about what is going on here?' he asked in a hushed tone.

'Not yet. Maybe later. The most important thing is that you just watch out for me and Judy. Anything you think odd, or out of place, I expect you to come crashing through the door to my room,' I told him.

'Odd like what?' he asked.

'Odd like you don't hear anything from us for too long.'

'And how long is too long?'

'Use your judgment, PC Stewart. You ask a lot of questions.'

'Maybe there are a lot of strange things going on here. I have never heard of a DI supporting a self-referral to a looney bin, let alone a GP,' the policeman commented.

'The truth is sometimes stranger than fiction,' I replied.

'Umm!' It was a grunted reply that either meant the constable was bored, or that it was time to end this muted conversation anyway.

'I'm going to get a shower and freshen up before my next interrogation,' and with that I returned to my room.

*****

My meeting with Dr Sara Whyte was far more dull than the one with Dr Allen. I was left feeling that our discussion had been meaningless. I have no doubt that Dr Whyte got some good information. She was certainly scribbling away on her notepad, mixing that with sincere looks in my direction, compassion oozing from her dark eyes and her head slightly cocked to the side. Her training must have begun and ended with the practising and re-practising that look of empty compassion.

Life coaching always has an end result. A life coach dips into past events to develop a framework that will enable clients to adopt more positive attitudes in dealing with the issues of concern in their lives. Counselling, on the other hand, aims to delve as deeply as possible into old pains for the sole purpose of reliving those pains again, and again, and again. In my humble opinion, there can be little, or no, value in discussing issues in this way since a client might have already worked so hard in burying past hurts that to revive them again must surely only serve to undo the hard work already completed. I am sorry, but therapy is about building for the future, counselling can only be about digging up and reliving the past.

So for an hour or so, Dr Sara Whyte delved into my childhood, focusing on my relationship with my mother and father. There was little mention of my current situation, and nothing at all was mentioned about my struggles with the rogue entity.

When the session ended I sincerely hoped that was the last I would see of the psychiatric counsellor, but feared it was not.

*****

When I received my third visitor, some two hours later, I opened my eyes and lay still. In that time I had tried my best to relax my body and my mind. The handle turned and the door opened, quickly followed by the head of Judy Marchant. She slipped her body through the gap in the doorway and closed the door softly behind her. I turned my head but remained in my prone position on top of the bed cover.

'Hi there, how are you doing?' Judy asked as she pulled the chair beside the bed.

'I'm getting there,' I replied, 'it's good to see you.'

'I had to leave last night, I guess you got a good rest.'

'I was gone last night, but after what happened that might be expected,' I replied.

'Do you feel any fitter now?'

'I don't know about feeling fitter, but I certainly feel a lot better.'

'Sorry to cut short our polite chatter, but do you think this is going to work?' Judy Marchant asked.

'Coming to St Mary's Hospital?'

'Yes.'

'I don't know. I was OK talking with Dr Allen, but that woman Whyte was so boring that I could have spent my time better watching paint dry.'

'No, I meant do you think it will work coming here to challenge that entity?'

'I don't know, but I am starting to think that my near fatal collapse yesterday might just prove advantageous.'

'In what way?'

'Possibly the most important aspect of our plan is in our being able to cover, as best we can, what we aim to do and how we plan to do it. The fact that I am now needing to spend so much time recovering from my near miss yesterday plus the fact that I am undergoing extensive interrogation here must mean that any element of surprise we do have might be strengthened. So maybe we will be able to use the circumstances in our favour, and that could be vital.'

'Is that not the way God works?' Judy asked.

'What, in giving us a helping hand?'

'Yes.'

'Well, I can think of one or two ways that are far less dramatic and life threatening, can't you?'

'Yes of course, but maybe this was the best of the helpful options available at the time,' Judy Marchant replied.

'I guess It really does work in mysterious ways after all.'

'Indeed He does.'

'Let's get back to your original question. I have no idea whether or not my plan will work out. I have no idea what kind of armoury this entity has, and I do not know whether or not it can hurt us. We know what it has done to other people, so I guess it is fair to say that we might be at considerable risk of physical harm, and maybe even death. But I prefer to think more positively. I think there is a fair chance the entity needs me to move forward in its quest, that leaves me relatively unscathed. As for you, I doubt that it would put you in harm's way at the risk of losing my support. Unfortunately, the only things we do know about this entity are those ideas cast in my mind by the events leading up to today. Nobody, and no entity in the spirit realm, has declared or suggested outright that this is the case, it is purely based on my own presumptions. But I am going to go with my presumptions, because they make me feel better,' I explained.

'So let's assume that we are safe. In what ways might this entity be prepared to achieve its goals?' Judy asked.

'We don't know, and I don't think we know enough about its aims and objectives to take any wild guesses,' I replied.

'OK, we are safe and we have no idea what we might be up against.'

'That is about the long and the short of it, yes.'

'Let me get this right, just so I understand this plan properly. You are going to hypnotise me when we can be sure we have enough time to carry the procedure out without being disturbed.'

'Yes.'

'You will direct me to the spirit realm using suggestion and reinforcement. When there, you will direct me to a Recovery Area that you say is closed to any penetration by spiritual essences.'

'Yes. Generally speaking, in the spirit realm all thoughts can be known by any other spiritual entity should they wish to know what you are thinking. In the Recovery Area, there is a shield in place to ensure that recovering entities are protected from such intrusions, although thought reading is not seen as an intrusion in the spirit realm. But it is necessary, when recovering from traumatic or particularly disturbing events, that spirits be allowed unfettered peace to readjust to the spirit realms,' I explained.

'You said 'realms', do you mean there is more than one?'

'Yes, but let's stick to the plan, shall we?'

'OK. After I am safely delivered there you will join me through meditation.'

'Well, there is a little bit more to it than that.'

'As in a little bit more what?' Judy asked.

'Well, let's remember that the killer entity should still be locked inside my capsule. That being the case, it will need to be released. And the whole reason you are going to the spirit realm is so that you can act as bait,' I said.

'What? You never mentioned that to me,' Judy said, her shoulders tightening.

'Yes I did. In any case, since this entity cannot trace our presence when we are in the Recovery Area we need to let it know we are somewhere else. So, before going there we should, or rather you should, entice the entity to us.'

'And how am I supposed to do that?' Judy asked.

'I am hoping that once I am able to send out a message to the entity its curiosity will take over.'

'So you are not joking about me being bait. And you will not be there by my side at this time.'

'No. I will join you in the Recovery Area.'

'And who will release the entity?'

'I am hoping we will be able to rely on some support for that.'

'And how am I supposed to get from wherever I meet up with this entity to the Recovery Area?'

'You think yourself there, easy as that,' I answered.

'Listen, I have never been hypnotised before, I have never visited the spirit world before, and I sure as hell have never travelled using just my thoughts.'

'Don't worry, it will be easy. I will be guiding you every step of the way. In hypnosis you will do everything I tell you to do.'

'Kind of like you would like to do with me in life, right?' Judy asked with a wink.

'There should be nothing that can go wrong, so long as my assumption about this entity is correct, in that it will not harm us,' I replied, my reddened cheeks quickly returning to their normal pallor.

'So, if you are guiding me by hypnosis,' Judy pondered, 'then how are you going to join me? You cannot get there quickly enough by meditating, surely.'

'No, you are right, there will be a bit of lag until I can join with you, but you will be safely in the Recovery Area by then. My Spirit Guide will be there to help us out.'

'Hypnosis, the spirit realm, a crazy killer rogue entity, and now a Spirit Guide as an aide, what next?' Judy asked.

Chapter Seven

Judy Marchant left the hospital before my evening meal, which consisted of a reasonably tasty cheese-drizzled fettuccine with a salad side, followed by a crushed almond sprinkled rice pudding. By 9pm I was ready to settle down. I deliberately kept my discussion with Judy, and any thoughts I had about our plan, buried deep within the dark recesses of my mind. Breakfast was served at eight o'clock the next morning. I wolfed down my cereal, orange juice and coffee and settled back, waiting for the next set of tests and interviews.

I went through the tests, I answered my therapist's questions and I let them inspect me to their heart's content, but I played a sleeping part in all they levelled at me while at least half of my mind was somewhere else.

By four in the afternoon I was free. When the opportunity was offered for me to wander about the hospital grounds I chose to remain inside until the following morning. I now had a little more than two hours to fill before the evening meal trolley arrived.

I had already decided that I should extend my stay and leave the next morning.

I walked to the reception area and called my wife from a payphone on the front desk. She was not happy that my return would be delayed and neither was my son, but on the promise of a weekend away at a holiday park when I got out any potential problem was easily ironed out.

In the waiting area sat Judy Marchant.

'Are you set?' I asked.

'I guess I am as set as I will ever be,' Judy replied.

*****

I asked Judy Marchant to lay on the bed. I made sure that her arms were by her side with her palms down and that her legs were uncrossed. I pulled the single chair in the room to the side of the bed and sat down. The hypnotic process relies entirely upon a therapist's ability to slow down a client's thought patterns to such a degree that they become obedient to his, or her, directions. Having helped Judy enter the spirit world I would need to enter a deep state of meditation to join her there. This would be no mean feat. Judy's limbs, feet and hands relaxed, quickly followed by her muscles. Her neck and head were the last things to relax. Her head slid gently to the left side, facing me. When I was satisfied that she had passed into a sufficiently relaxed state, I started the process of introducing her to the spirit world.

'Good Judy, that is very good. You are now entering the spiritual realm. There are no cars, no planes and no pollutants of any kind in this beautiful place, there is nothing at all that might disturb your calm and peaceful state. Everything here is beautiful, clean and fresh. Fill your lungs with the crisp air that surrounds you here in this place, and as you do so you will become more and more relaxed.'

Judy's chest rose as she breathed in deeply.

'That is very good. You will find yourself sitting on a strong stone seat underneath a willow tree. The shade of the tree is very protective. You notice a man in a cloak approaching you. He will guide you on your journey through the spirit realm. He will look after you, he will protect you and he will keep you completely safe at all times. He will show you to the places you need to visit while you are here. When you do move around here it will be immediate, it will be instantaneous, but that is quite normal, and it is completely OK for you to travel in this way too. I would like you to introduce yourself to your guide, and listen as he introduces himself to you.'

Judy's head moved a little and her eyes shifted beneath her closed lids.

'That is very good. Your guide will now begin your tour of the spirit realm. In his presence you will feel completely free to ask any question at all, in the knowledge that he will always answer you. Remember that you are here to meet up with me, and to help me and your guide to entice the killer entity to a place where we can deal effectively and efficiently with it. Bare no heed to what this entity says or does when you meet up with it, because your guide will always be with you, helping you and keeping you in God's loving, protecting embrace. You are not here to confront this entity or to do battle with it. You are here for the sole purpose of delivering the entity to me under my instructions. You will inform me, in clear and concise terms, of everything that you see and everything that you feel needs reporting to me. Please lift the index finger of your right hand if you completely understand my instructions and the job that you are in this place to complete.'

Judy's right index finger raised.

*****

'*Good day Judy, I trust that you are aware of the reason why you are here?*'

My Guide communicated with Judy without words. Judy could not see his face, the grey hood of his robe shrouded all of his features in darkness except for his sharp nose. His voice was clear and calming, its transfer arrived in her mind full and well developed. She wondered whether she would be able to converse in the same manner. Her question was immediately answered.

'*Yes you can Judy. Telepathic messages are the only way of communicating here in the spirit realms. We have no need for many of the processes necessary on the earth plane, speaking and travel are two such examples. If you wish to travel somewhere you need only place that destination in your thoughts to travel there. It is very easy, and it will not take much getting used to.*'

'*Thank you, I am most grateful for your welcome,*' her guide bowed his head ever so gently, in response to Judy's reply.

'*You are here to meet up with the person who calls himself Len, but that will not happen.*'

'*What are you talking, erm thinking, about? I am here to meet with Len so we can destroy the entity that is killing people on earth. Is that not the mission that was set? Is that not what this is all about?*' Judy asked.

'*No, it is not,*' my guide calmly replied.

'*I am very confused now. My understanding is that this destructive entity found a way to subvert the normal way of things here, at least so far as the death experience is concerned, and it is manipulating the system for its own gain.*'

'*That is partly true, yes.*'

'*Well, I don't understand how my first point can be wrong and the second is at least partly correct. Don't these two options go hand in hand?*' Judy asked.

'Your first point cannot be true, it is an impossibility. As for your second point, it is true that the spiritual entity in question is using its energy to circumvent the natural regenerative process, the outcome of which is that certain human beings are being targeted for an early exit from their current lifetime. Though the possibility of these occurrences happening is measurable, the probability is not. So far as what happens to an individual trinity we cannot, at this moment, reach any conclusions. The reason as to why this entity might be acting in this way we can only speculate on. We in the spirit realm do not deal with speculation,' my guide explained.

'Hold on a minute. If I am here to help the good guys in any way...'

'As you are.'

'Then I need to get a better understanding of what is going on.'

'What would you like to know?' my spirit guide asked.

'Why would it be impossible to destroy this bad entity? What regenerative process? If you can tell that such events might happen how can you not know that they are probable, and to whom? What is the individual trinity? And does speculation not naturally precede decision and action?'

'I will try to answer each of your questions in a comprehensive manner. Firstly though, you should understand that our communication must be diluted so it can be effectively understood by you. The actions and processes within the spiritual realm are far more detailed and developed than it would be possible for you to understand. Should you be exposed to an absolute truth, it is likely that your head would explode, literally.'

'I am quite attached to my head, so let's try the beginners approach first.'

'This entity can never be destroyed because any form of energy continues ad infinitum, it can never finish. All it can do is vibrate at a different frequency so that it changes its form. If any energy should reach a barrier then it will adjust to a slower form the further it moves away from its source. This is the same for human beings as it is for all living organisms. This is why the vibrational frequency on Earth is heavier and far slower than in the spiritual realms. And the closer to the source the energy is, the faster it vibrates. It will appear to a human being that spiritual entities, and even God, are far more knowledgeable than they themselves are. This is true, since the higher the vibrational frequency of an entity the higher is its intellectual capability. Each living or intellectual being has, at its core, some form of energy. When energy is released from one form, as would happen if a human body died, it will simply occupy an alternative capsule in which it would continue to exist. The eternal journey, from source back to source, is the experience of all creation,' explained my guide.

'Okay, so far. I think.'

'Next, the regenerative process I mentioned is that which occurs with every organism, whether visible or not. Everything that is a part of the creative process passes through changes in its form when necessary. It is normal for everything that is a part of the creative process to be made up of three specific, but conjoined, parts. In the human being these parts are known as the mind, the spirit and the soul. None of these parts, of themselves, occupy a space. Each is an energy that exists as a non-defined mass. The mind and the soul exist in and around a human being, the spirit is that part of each person that permanently resides in the spiritual realm. These three parts of the trinity can act in unison, or they can act individually, so far as that action is agreed. This

agreement can be specified, or it can be presumed, from the actions of the individual parts of the trinity.'

'So let me make sure I understand this correctly. Our spiritual self resides closer to the source than do our mind and soul. When we go through the death experience we are somehow able to withdraw our mind and soul from our dead bodies to return closer to the source, and vibrate at a higher frequency.'

'That is correct, but it is not quite so simple as that. In the human body, your soul retains the same vibrational rate as is necessary in the spiritual realm, but it is your soul that communicates with your spiritual self while you are in your human experiential state. Your life experiences are fed by your mind to your soul. It is your soul that retains the memories of all your life experiences. It is not possible for your spiritual self to leave the spiritual realm during any lifetime, if this ever were to happen, which it cannot, then your energetic source would drift off into a void, forever. When your body dies, it is by the agreement of your mind, your soul and your spirit that this opportunity to move back to the spiritual realm is taken. Your physical body is then shut down. Since your own spirit cannot retrieve the other two parts of its trinity, it is likely that a spiritual entity with which you are familiar will guide you back to the spiritual realm,' my guide continued to explain.

'That is why we believe we see deceased family members when we die,' Judy reasoned.

'That is correct.'

'But, when they come for us, are they not in a spiritual form?'

'They are.'

'I thought you said, sorry, that a spirit could not leave the spirit realms?'

48

'The spiritual part of a trinity that is undertaking an experiential lifetime, that is correct.'

'But free of that bonding, any spirit could visit the earth at any time.'

'Oh yes, and they frequently do.'

'This is getting a lot more complicated, but I think I am hanging on in there.'

'Turning to your point about speculation. Now this really is a bit complicated and tricky, but I will do my best to explain it in a way you can understand.'

'That would be greatly appreciated. Thank you,' Judy acknowledged.

'When speculating about anything you are guessing an outcome. Sometimes you can speculate in a well-informed manner, and in that case speculation might well lead, eventually, to a decision and an end in action. But most times, speculation cannot possibly lead to decisions and action because the end results would also be speculative. In these instances speculation can never change into anything else, nor can it lead to anything else, because of its nature. It is the identification of options that inevitably leads to risk analysis, decision and then action. Before we can identify the available options we must be sure of the issues to be decided upon. This sounds like a very long process but it is not, it is a very quick and automatic process carried out many thousands of times each day on your planet by every earthbound individual. The situation is very different in the spirit realm, since the options do not need to be identified and analysed. Here, all the information needed to act is there, readily available, and open to all, so only the most beneficial outcome is guaranteed.'

'Wow, imagine how wonderful the human world would be if it were like that on Earth.'

'Actually, it would be an absolute disaster. If all decisions led to the most beneficial outcome for all people then there would be no need for human experiences, no need for emotions, no need to undergo learning experiences. The human existence would be obsolete, and there would be no need to live much beyond five minutes.'

'I had never seen it like that,' Judy admitted.

'Getting back to why you are here.'

'Yes, I think that would be a good idea,' Judy agreed.

'The two issues of meeting up with Len, and of the mission that he has taken on. Firstly, it is important that you gain insight to the workings of the spirit realm. This is because the only way that you can deal effectively with this rogue entity is for you and Len to work closely together, with a shared knowledge of the tasks that you face, and how various obstacles can be overcome.'

'I have to warn you that this is getting a bit beyond me now,' Judy admitted.

'OK, I will try to keep it as simple as I can without leaving out any crucial bits of information,' the guide replied.

'Thank you.'

'Despite what he might believe, Len was here during his meditation. In that time he met with, and confronted, the rogue entity. We have an area of pods where spiritual entities can connect with their human counterparts and engage in any sharing of information and future planning that might be necessary. To cut a very long story short, when Len died at 14, his original spiritual essence was removed from his trinity and replaced by another. This second spirit has worked with Len until now. When Len came here in meditation he demanded to confront the rogue entity. He did what he thought was right and joined with the rogue entity inside his pod.'

'He did what?' Judy asked.

'He joined with the rogue entity.'

'Why on earth, or in the spirit realm, would he ever think of doing that?'

'I do not believe that he ever intended doing that.'

'Would you mind explaining to me how the fuck Len could join with this killer spirit without intending to do it?' Judy asked.

'The white mark I gave him on a previous visit had the power to join Len's essence and that of the rogue entity. It was a concentrated form of the creative energy of life, it could do anything required by the holder of that energy. As for why Len might have chosen to join with this entity, it is a part of the creative blueprint that an original spiritual essence can rejoin its host trinity at any time, and this is what happened. The action of Len, in using the white mark as he did, essentially reinforced this joining process. It would have been an inevitable outcome anyway.'

'Yes, but inevitable is a bit different from a forced immediate action.'

'Nothing can ever be forced. Only choices can be made.'

'Wait a minute. I could give someone a drink and convince them it has no alcohol whatsoever in it, but in effect it does. That person takes the drink based on my assurance of what it contains,' Judy asserted.

'That is not the same.'

'Of course it is. Did you ever tell Len when giving him the white mark that it was, in fact, a tool to help him join the rogue entity to his trinity so it would become an integral part of him?' Judy asked.

'No.'

'Then how could he have been able to make a choice of how to use it? You gave him something that you said would help him with his struggle against this rogue entity. He trusted you, and he used the white mark trusting that it would be a strong and beneficial tool in his endeavour.'

'Yes, and it was.'

'It was? How? How can it have been beneficial for Len to be reconnected with an entity that seems to want to kill young people to fulfil its quest of dethroning God?'

'Is that what Len has told you?'

'It is what he believes, yes,'

'Then there is still much that needs to be done.'

'How?'

'It is absolutely necessary that any interactions between the spiritual and earthly realms are carefully managed and monitored. No human can ever come away from such interaction with a negative outcome, it just cannot happen. You will see just how important it is for Len to work with the spirit realm, based on the link between him and this entity. I understand your reticence to see how this can benefit him. But if we, and I mean all of us, are to effectively deal with the circumstances confronting us then it was necessary for Len to join once again with this entity. Since each part of a trinity cannot act without the approval of the other two parts there must be a majority decision on a course of action before anything can be done. If we are to effectively deal with this entity, then it makes sense for Len's mind, and his soul, to exercise their authority within the trinity to better be able to control any outcomes,' explained the guide.

'You set him up,' Judy thought.

'No, he made a choice.'

'He made a choice based on the absolute trust he had in you.'

'Yes, and that trust and the outcomes which result, will prove hugely beneficial not only to Len and to you, but to the whole of humanity, and to the stabilisation of the spiritual realms and beyond.'

'How can you be so sure of that?' Judy asked.

'If it had not happened, the consequences would have been incalculably negative,' my Guide explained.

'Possibly leading to the destruction of the current spiritual hierarchy,' Judy mused.

'Not just the hierarchy, but potentially the destruction of the spiritual realms themselves.'

'So what Len saw in Amy King's eyes could be true?'

'Yes. So hopefully, now you are better able to understand the gravity of this situation and of the need to carefully manage it.'

'OK, so where is this rogue entity now?' Judy asked.

'In one of the capsules that we spoke about earlier. We can go there if you wish.'

'Yes, please.' Judy confirmed.

*****

I knew that Judy was fully immersed in her hypnotic experience. Her eyes moved regularly beneath their lids. Her fingers twitched on occasion. Her heartbeat was regular and strong. She showed no sign of any distress.

I was confident that Judy would be looked after during her visit to the spirit world. It was not just a case of taking her there in hypnosis and leaving her to wander around aimlessly. Though I presumed that this was a place she had never knowingly visited before, she went there with a purpose, a desire and a goal. These things alone would help her to call whatever assistance might be necessary from the spiritual beings residing there. My instructions should also call the beings to her who would be of the greatest help during her visit.

I might have expected some kind of discussion from her, as to what she saw or experienced, but the fact that it did not come was of little concern. Once I felt sure that Judy was safely delivered to her destination, and that she was in the more than competent company of my Guide, it was time for me to join her. I relaxed my back into the chair and released all of the tension in my shoulders. My hands and fingers became light and comfortable on my thighs. I placed the soles of my feet flat on the floor and I closed my eyes.

*****

Immediately Judy found herself inside the room full of pods. She was aware of another entity inside the room besides my Guide, though she saw no-one.

'These capsules are individually linked to the spirits, souls and minds of those entities fulfilling a physical lifetime on Earth. Other types of capsules exist for human-like entities on planets other than Earth. The spiritual realms that deal with these other entities operate separately and distinctly from here. Should a spirit wish to interact with a human being they will enter their corresponding capsule, having first cleared their connection. The capsule will then be sealed for the duration of the time that they are linked with those trinity parts,' my guide explained.

Judy readily accepted the fact that life did exist on planets other than Earth, just as she accepted everything else in this place, without question.

'During his last meditation Len entered his capsule. His second spiritual form left the capsule and he was joined by his first, the rogue entity,' my Guide continued.

'Why did Len's second spirit leave if it knew he might be in danger by joining with the rogue entity?'

'Because that is the way the blueprint has it. An original spiritual essence will always have precedence over any secondary or replacement spirit. This is because the link

between original minds, souls and spirits is always much stronger. Even if they wanted to, the power of the connection between original trinity parts, will always deny any attempt by a replacement spirit to subjugate.'

'So why did the rogue entity leave Len?'

'You are aware that Len's heart stopped when he was 14.'

'Yes.'

'This was used as a perfect opportunity to action this switch. Following the growth of the trinity, of which Len is a part, it was clear that at some point the potential for the kind of issues that we face now to arise, grew too. Each trinity seeks, as its ultimate goal, oneness with the Creator. The journey of discovery and learning that allows a trinity to grow closer to the Creator is the essence of life itself. The truth is that each creation is a part of the Creator always, one that was spread amongst worlds and space to gather experience and feed it back to the Creator. The journey of every life force is to return to its original form.'

'That is quite a concept,' Judy suggested.

'It is not a concept, it is a reality.'

'OK, you say that it was clear that these issues were likely to arise. In that case, why could you not act to stop them? There must have been something you could have done.'

'It is not the way of the spiritual realms to interfere with the freedom of any entities to exercise their will. Freedom of choice and action are the core principles on which the blueprint of life was founded.'

'OK, at what time was it known that these problems might occur?' Judy asked.

'It was always known. The spirit world did not come first. The spirit world was created, just as was everything else.'

'Created by God?'

'No. Your God was created as a part of the control mechanism in the spirit world.'

'Our God? You make it sound like there are many.'

'There are many entities beyond God in the hierarchy of creation,' my Guide explained.

'I hear you, but it is very hard for me to comprehend anything beyond that of which I am aware. Sticking with the spirit realm, my belief has always been that of a heaven where all is love, peace and harmony, a place where there can be no room for any kind of anarchy or resistance.'

'Yes, and that is how it is.'

'Then how can one spirit create such turmoil that the outcome of its actions could result in the destruction of the spirit world?' Judy asked.

'Let me first make this clear, the rogue entity, of which you speak, cannot act alone, it is impossible. Should any one part of a trinity wish to act it would need the support of one of the other two parts of its core makeup.'

'So that means that this killer entity is not acting alone, despite the strong belief held by Len which was, seemingly, reinforced during his last visit to the spirit world,' Judy felt an anger return as she thought out loud.

'It is absolutely necessary that such a serious situation is handled in the best and most productive way possible while protecting the sanctity of each energy's entitlement to operate their own free will.'

'So Len is being used, as also might this rogue entity, if not to protect those entities that diligently study day in and day out both in the spiritual realm and on Earth, then for what?' Judy asked.

'The destruction of the spirit realms would automatically result in the destruction of all other planes of existence. Imagine the trinity of an individual creation, the mind, the

soul and the spirit. The spirit realms also exist as one part of a trinity. There can be no creative force, there can be no living entity, there can be no life without the existence of a trinity. There must exist agreement and co-operation of all the relevant parts of the whole, and this interaction cannot happen without the balance afforded by the three parts of the trinity.'

'So if the spirit realm was plunged into chaos, out of which it could not emerge unscathed, then all creation would be plunged into chaos too.'

'Yes. But also any interruptions, any kind of negative actions at all that are forced upon the spirit realms, would ripple out and affect all of creation too.'

'So Len is being used to restrain these potential negative outcomes, to minimise their effects on life as we know it?' Judy asked.

'What you might not realise is that before his birth Len volunteered for all of the potential outcomes that were possible in this lifetime. The situation we find ourselves in now results from all of the choices made at the mind, soul and spiritual levels. Len is being forced to do nothing.'

*****

I was unable to enter meditation.

I tried four times to relax, searching for a focus on the one issue or object that might reconnect me with the spirit world.

Everything failed.

I sat up straight in the chair and glanced over at Judy laying prone on the bed. Concern began to bubble up from the base of my mind. This situation is not right, for some unknown reason the plan could not be played out. Had it been hijacked? Was it possible that, despite all the precautions taken, the rogue entity became aware of our intentions and found a way to sabotage our actions?

This might have been the case, except that for all my searching I could find no sign of alarm either psychically or instinctually. Everything seemed calm and relaxed, and most importantly Judy showed no signs whatsoever of being in any distress or discomfort. It seemed more likely that any doubts I felt came from my being unable to fulfil my part of the plan. Nonetheless, even though I had some concern that the whole reason for Judy being in the spirit realm at all was so that we, together, could confront this rogue entity, I still found it impossible to feel that there was any need to feel concerned, and I trusted my Guide to be doing what was necessary to make sure she was safe.

I sat back into the chair and began humming, tunelessly.

*****

'So please tell me why it might be necessary for me to be allowed to communicate with you while Len is banned, on this occasion?' Judy asked.

'The reason is that it would prejudice Len and his life to an unacceptable degree, if he were to be aware of the information I have imparted to you,' my Guide answered.

'What is the difference, I could tell him on my return.'

'Yes you could, and you most likely will, but the exact detail of all we discuss will become a little bit foggy, a bit blurred.'

'But why? Why is that necessary? If we are still in battle with this killer entity then what sense in us both being unclear about what it is we face and how best to deal with it?' Judy asked.

'It is just the way it is. When you awake from a dream do you remember every single little detail, or do you remember the essence of the dream, which then allows you to work out its possible implications for your everyday life?'

'OK, so this will be like a dream?'

'Not exactly, but the outcome will be similar. In being here your energetic vibration will be raised significantly. You might even have realised that your understanding of what we discuss here is much clearer and more refined than if you were to discuss these issues in your everyday life.'

Judy thought for a moment. It was true. So much detail had been given to her that she was readily able to understand with minimal follow-up quantification.

'And when you return to the Earth plane your vibration will slow again, to reflect the lower energies of that realm. When your energetic vibrations slow it is inevitable that some of the information you have gathered will be squeezed out, so that you can only retain that which you have room to accommodate.'

'Len is expecting to meet up with me here through meditation, so why would it prejudice his life to be here with us now?' Judy asked.

'There is a difficult balance that must be met in all interactions between the spiritual and the Earth planes. No matter how much a person or a spirit might request a greater level of interaction, the fact is that if such enhancement were deemed to be likely to cause any problems or negative outcomes, then the defences inherent in all our blueprints would be triggered. It is a necessary safety system to ensure our full potentials can be realised.'

'It is better, and more beneficial, to learn by our mistakes than to have our hands held in guidance.'

'Yes, always and in all ways.'

'So can you tell me if meditation is made up from the desire of the individual? In other words, is it a purely self-engineered journey?' Judy asked.

'That depends on the clarity and the sincerity of any request that is made. It is the same with prayer. If the desire is true and the enquiry will result in positive outcomes, and it is not just a wish, then of course a meditation or a prayer can be answered in a positive way. It happens very often, in fact, that a meditative experience or a prayer can take people to many unexpected and exciting places.'

'Why not a wish?' Judy asked.

'A wish is a desired outcome, but it is not the desire itself. A desire must be something that reaches deep into the core of mind and soul. If someone holds a true enough desire for anything then the mind can request access to the spirit realm through the soul. And when all trinity parts agree the potential benefits of a desired request, then that request is granted. It is the same in prayer.'

'So what now?'

'The entity responsible for the early deaths of people on Earth is contained within the capsule before you. The capsule is sealed, and will remain so until the direct link with its trinity is terminated.'

'So it can be destroyed.'

'No. The termination of the trinity link simply leads to the disconnecting of its component parts, until the next time such a link is established.'

'So, all the time that this entity remains inside this box it is linked with Len?'

'And with the soul of the trinity.'

'How long until it is removed?'

'That can only be a matter for the trinity parts to decide.'

'What? Len could remain linked with this killer thing for the rest of his life?' Judy asked.

'That is possible, but improbable. Each part of the trinity acts only for the most beneficial outcomes of each part, and of the whole. It is most likely that a request will be made that the spirit part of the trinity be removed.'

'So what is the task that has been set for Len, if not to destroy this entity?'

'There was never to be any attempt to destroy the entity, as I explained before, that would be impossible. One of the options made available to Len before he began his current lifetime was that, should such issues arise as they did, he would have an opportunity to contain his original spirit self, and thereby isolating it and drastically reducing its effect on Earth and in the spirit realms. When Len was offered this opportunity he accepted. The outcome is as you see before you.'

Judy moved forward and looked inside the capsule. It was not easy to see anything beyond the smoked glass of the sealed lid. Judy did notice, however, that the more she stared at the lid the clearer became a picture in her mind of what was contained within. When she could clearly make out the figure inside the pod she stumbled backwards.

'But. It's, it's Len inside there. He looks like he is sleeping,' she muttered.

'When a spirit entity links with their soul and human mind counterparts they must lower their vibrational field. Most spirits find this easier to achieve if they assume the bodily appearance of their host. If the spirit body is identical in every way to the human body with whom they connect, then the link is made stronger, and communication will be clearer,' my Guide explained.

'For a situation with such potentially disastrous outcomes for my planet, and for the spirit realm, this all seems a bit farcical. Len is expected to control this entity until such a time as it can be dispelled from his trinity, for a

second time. In the meantime you, his other Guardians, God and whoever, will just sit back, relax and wait for a human being with mental difficulties and certain physical inadequacies to battle this thing while it remains inside him, maybe planning, manipulating, conniving its way through his life?' Judy asked, incredulous.

'I fully understand how you feel. Yes, the potential outcomes of this situation are very serious indeed. There is no question of Len needing to control this entity, but his awareness of it should lead to a greater degree of authority being exerted. Len's Guardians, and all the spiritual entities who have power to exert an influence in his life, are ready to help and assist him at any time. And it is precisely because of Len's mental difficulties and physical inadequacies, as you call them, that he is ideally placed to be at the centre of this concerted action. It is why he was born, it is why he has lived the lifetimes he has lived. This is the very reason Len was created. And I can assure you that he is ready for what is to come.'

Chapter Eight

Judy's index finger fluttered and then stood upright before dropping again to the surface of the bed. She then made the same movement again. I took this as a sign that she was ready to come out of trance.

'OK Judy, you are ready to return to an awakened state.'

I went through the awakening procedures and Judy followed my instructions impeccably. She opened her eyes, turned her head and stared at me for a few seconds.

'Wow! That was amazing. How long was I out?' Judy asked.

'About 25 minutes,' I replied.

'Is that all? It felt like forever.'

'Sorry I was not able to join you, I just could not connect to the spirit world.'

'Yes, I know,' Judy replied.

'Well, I'm sorry if I scuppered the plan, I guess we need to develop an alternative approach. This situation will not just go away.'

'It's already done.'

'What?'

'Your job was never to destroy the entity,' Judy explained.

'But I don't understand.'

'You were supposed to contain it, in order to reduce its effect on Earth and in the spirit realm.'

'And how come I don't know anything about this?' I asked.

Judy explained, in as much detail as she was able to, what happened during her hypnosis session. She explained how the rogue spirit could not be destroyed. She explained how the plan I had developed became defunct when I trapped the entity inside my pod. She told me also the reasons why she was chosen to visit my Guide, and why I was unable to accompany her. She told me that my Guide was insistent that this was the only way that the threat posed by the entity could be dealt with.

'If this rogue entity is trapped inside my sealed pod when will it be released?' I asked.

Judy sat up straight in the bed and looked down at her feet as she answered.

'Maybe never.'

'What? I am expected to carry this thing on my shoulders for the rest of my life, and then through my afterlives too?' I asked, shocked.

'I don't know, I can only report back what I learned, and some of that is none too clear. I can only tell you what I remember of the things I was allowed to know. And I can't even be sure that all of what I am telling you is the absolute truth.'

'I'm sorry, I know none of this is your fault. But if this is my burden now, I guess I have no choice but to accept it,' I replied.

'There is one ray of hope.'

'And what is that?' I asked.

Judy lifted her head. Since she had returned to wakefulness, she had a vibrancy in her eyes that I had never before noticed.

'You have a responsibility to deal with this issue now, but you are stronger. You have the full weight of your Guardians and the spirit world supporting and helping you,' she said, 'and you also have me.'

*****

PC Ian Stewart read the notebook nestled in his lap. He looked at one page, flipped forward two pages, back one, then again forwards. He was searching desperately for a clue to solve a riddle that had circled his mind unabated for the past week.

I was reported as having been at the crash site just before the accident, which was true enough, but Ian Stewart found it increasingly hard to separate my appearance at the minibus crash, his later discussion with Judy and I in the police station, and his being sat for hours in the waiting area of a psychiatric hospital while Judy and I attempted to summon some killer ghost also linked to the minibus crash. Or something like that.

His notes gave little away. It was more the feeling he had as he listened to my story that disturbed him. One of his suspicions was confirmed by Judy when she admitted that she had been driving my car and I had, as was reported by two independent witnesses, been leaning out of the passenger window desperately signalling to the minibus driver immediately before the crash.

But things were just too blurred around the edges for his liking. Ian Stewart was clear in his mind that I had demonstrated some kind of knowledge that could not be easily explained away. So some type of psychic ability must be a reality. Palmistry, tarot cards, horoscopes, goddamned mind reading, it all might be true. And if that is the case, then so might this rogue killer entity bullshit. And this was why he sat flicking forward and backwards repeatedly while his mind jostled with one absent disjointed thought after another.

Chapter Nine

I resigned myself to a sleepless night, and that was what I got.

How many times in my life had I come up against a brick wall? No going over, no digging under, no going around. It seemed to me that life was full of dead ends; we think we are doing alright until something, so startlingly and obviously clear, shows us that we are not. Thanks to God for the opportunity to have got so far trusting, as faithfully as I could, my psychic senses and my intuition. Thanks too for these abilities, so rare as to be on people's wish lists of most treasured things they would like to have. And thanks for Judy's visit to the spirit world. No, scrub that one. Most definitely, no thanks for the insight provided to Judy Marchant but denied to me.

That is just the way it is. That is the process. That is the blueprint. Well, fuck you God.

And so I decided to hide myself away and write a book based on my experiences with this killer entity. The bits in the book about my life and upbringing were entirely true, seen, as they must be, through my perspective of what went on and what scars were left on my persona. I changed some of the names of the individuals involved, and I needed to write and rewrite the manuscript to keep the narrative as true an account of the facts as possible. I labelled the book as fiction, since any tale that is based on true events without being, or pretending to be, a verbatim record of them must be so described.

Chapter Ten

I called the book *RIP – Synergy*, I don't know why but the title just seemed to fit the story. I used a pen name that was pseudo linked to my own surname. I found an agent and I was lucky enough to sign a contract with a publisher. From an early age, I had always wanted to publish a book, though I could not have envisaged accomplishing this feat in such surreal circumstances.

It seemed to me that some of the stark realities of life, and death, were too often glossed over by writers more inclined to spell out their beliefs as the one truth. I preferred to use my own experiences in a way that might allow my readers to make up their own minds about how the processes of life affect them in their everyday lives and, more importantly, to promote the idea that individuals can make positive decisions that really can lead to greater harmony and achievement. The darker side of life also cannot be ignored, and I hoped also to portray the dangers of the many potholes we dig for ourselves and those that appear as a result of our actions, or inaction.

Once it was clear that a large number of people wanted to read *RIP – Synergy* I had a few problems convincing my agent, and the publisher, that I wished to avoid too much publicity. I turned down radio shows, national television interviews and anything else that sought to glorify or embellish the events portrayed in my book. My ethos had always been that the facts, the ideas and the philosophy of the book, were its main selling points, not the person typing them into an Asus laptop.

RIP – Synergy was particularly successful in America and Australia. I did some television interviews and radio shows overseas. I found it much easier to do the tours, meet the people, and to promote the book in countries other than where I lived.

There was some talk of a movie, but this more likely stemmed from loose lips rather than any major studios. The lack of a movie outcome was not such a bad thing. It seems that a movie has a much greater impact on people's minds, as if spoken words and action speak louder than print. I can understand that, but it is common for a movie to fail in too many ways to portray the issues in a story and to turn the tale into something far less meaningful and dramatic, particularly if insufficient attention is paid to its meaning in favour of deeper characterisations of the individuals within the plot.

I took every opportunity to sell the message that the words in the book should not be read as the truth, and that each reader should use them in whatever way worked best for them as an individual.

*****

Pretty soon, it was obvious that my privacy was far from guaranteed in using a pseudonym.

'Hey man, you're the guy who wrote that RIP book, ain't ya.'

The boy wore white untied sneakers, baggy jogging pants and a loose sleeveless black tee shirt with an unreadable emblem on the front. His baseball cap sat propped on his head to the right side. His shoulder was pushed against the cold glass of a shop front, his feet crossed in front.

'The book was called *RIP – Synergy*,' I replied cautiously.

'Yeah, that's the one. You know, I always wondered what it might be like to kill someone from the inside, leave no marks, like that spirit dude. He was cool,' the boy said.

'Is that cool?' I asked him.

'Sure it is, wouldn't you do something if you knew you could get away with it? And the best thing about it is that you say God will forgive me. I can do anything I want. Do you know how great that feels?' the boy asked me.

'If I could do anything and get away with it, with no need for redemption, no, I can't say I would kill someone, something called morals might get in the way. I think I would always try to make the best choice and to my mind, killing someone is unlikely to ever be the best choice,' I replied.

'But in that book you say you don't judge.'

'I try my best not to,' I replied.

'But what if your kids were at risk man, surely you would kill to protect them.'

And this is the dilemma. If you state that you would not kill anyone, ever, then what if it was a choice between a potential perpetrator or your kids? And that is another issue with God; It knows all. Be very careful of what you state out loud because it is more than likely that at some time in the future your statement will be tested.

'That is an entirely different issue. Are we then talking about murder or are we discussing the saving of a life?'

'And God don't judge anyway is what you said.'

'I guess you really did read the book.'

'No man, I caught it on the radio, I was flicking through, started listening right from the second time it was on, followed it all the way to the last episode. It was radical, man. That dead dude was awesome.'

'Well, thank you, I appreciate it.'

'Just shows that God ain't got it all. He ain't got it all, man.'

'I really appreciate your interest, thank you for following the story,' I said as I turned to move away.

'But that's right ain't it, God doesn't have it all.'

'No. God does not have it all, you do,' I said as I left the boy grinning outside the store.

The most difficult thing to adjust to were the stares, the looks that stated *"I know that guy, but where from?"*. I don't know what my expectations might have been, maybe I had none. But I was now all too aware of the consciousness of people when they looked in my direction. And my first television interview in Chicago lifted me into a stratosphere I was not inclined to inhabit for any length of time.

*****

'I would now like to introduce you to the guy who talked to God, the guy who faced up to his worst nightmares and walked away unscathed. The guy who has entered so many American lives, and who now refuses to go away.'

Three spotlights opened up and shone in my face immediately after my skittish introduction. I shifted nervously in my seat as the small studio audience disappeared behind the glare assaulting my eyes. The guys pointing and flipping pages over clipboards busied themselves, I could hear them, but the glare of the spotlights obliterated my view. The only person I could see was Bob Thornton, anchor-man for *Chicago Downtown Lowdown.*

Greasy, dark coiffure-haired Bob. The guy in the navy suit and crisp white shirt, the man with the cement-fixed, laser-toothed, grin. A polite ripple of applause spread through the audience, which consisted mostly of the broadcast company stooges employed to sit in otherwise vacant seats for the live broadcast.

'Good evening Bob, how are you today?' I asked in reply.

'Well Len, you being the psychic, I was hoping you might be able to tell me.'

Muffled giggles from the audience accompanied my wry smile. Bob Thornton propped a copy of my book on the desk in front of him, as he continued.

'This book, *RIP – Synergy*, seems to have created a bit of a stir. Would you put that down to your advocacy of a life after life, or to the absolute terror created in the minds of the public due to the violent nature of this invisible, undetectable, rogue entity that you say might attack and kill anyone it comes into contact with?' he asked with overt aggressiveness.

Bob Thornton, for all his smiles and attempts at gratuitous self-effacement, had launched straight into confrontation mode. This was not the line of questioning I was led to believe I would face.

'Well Bob, I believe the issues in the book are a little bit more extensive than that. First of all, whether or not a spiritual realm exists remains open to debate, it is only my perception that it does. Second, introducing the public to a rogue spiritual entity is simply personal conjecture,' I countered.

'But you say in the Forward, do you not, that this book is based on true events? So should the American public be fearful that their lives might be cut short because of some sort of psycho ghost that lives in a place no-one can prove even exists?' Bob Thornton asked.

'The book is based on true events, that, at least, I can guarantee. There are issues that have occurred in my life that are faithfully reported as they happened. These events were used to build a story around them. I would have thought that this was made perfectly clear in the text of the book.'

'You have not answered my question, Len.'

'I thought, Bob, that I answered your question quite adequately. The fact is that we will all die one day, but who or what is it that might determine when that happens? My book is far more about how the spiritual realm might interact with us in our lifetime, about the potential consequences of the choices we make, about how we can make positive change by simply being aware of the choices available to us in every moment of every day. My book, hopefully, leaves the door open to allow people to better explore their own spirituality in the hope that they will allow themselves to adopt any, and every, attitude to their everyday lives, without even thinking of needing to follow teachings that might otherwise serve to sever their ability to think about themselves in any way they choose. God is not, and can never be, the same God to me as It is to you, or to anyone else.'

'Once again Len, it seems you have failed to address the issue. But we will move on anyway. You say in your book that you regularly talk with God. Do you always adopt such a confrontational attitude towards the Big Guy? Some of the language you use, and I think you know what I am talking about, could easily be described as blasphemous. How would you answer your critics in this respect?'

'I have a relationship with God that does not preclude honesty nor the use of any kind of language I choose. Surely by restricting my feelings or dampening down my rhetoric I would run the risk of missing the point of any communication. Surely there can be no reason to evade issues or step around your feelings, particularly in things that are so important to so many people,' I replied.

'Listen, Len, I can accept that, and I think most of my viewers can accept that too. But is it not true that in being so blunt and forceful you have created a storm about your book that, rather than promote all of the very worthy and seemingly useful information contained inside, acted to detonate your philosophies not with a long acting fuse but with a nuclear bomb.'

I was taken aback by the ferocity of the points being made, valid though some of them were.

'Have you read my book, Bob?' I asked.

'I have skipped through it, yes,' cue a slight wink by Bob at the nearest camera accompanied by a less than confident chuckle.

'With all due respect Bob, any book that is skipped through will remain unread. Some of the philosophies and ideas inside the book were undoubtedly passed to me by an intelligence existing in a place other than here. The complex simplicity of the messages cannot have come from anywhere else. In my opinion you cannot be blunt or forceful in a dishonest way. I will admit that I used everyday language in my discussions with God. If there is any useful information to be gained from my experiences then I see no point embellishing it with phrases or innuendo that detract from the core meaning. I believe there is only one purpose in our lives, and that is what we choose to do with the experiences we have and how we choose to interpret and use any information that comes our way. That is what the book is about. And if you have not read it yet, Bob, then I suggest that you do,' I countered.

Rather surprisingly my words were met with wild approval from the studio audience. I had no idea how many of these clapping, whooping people had read my book, or even how many were aware of it. Bob Thornton just took it all in his stride, the consummate, if not sweaty-browed, professional.

'Now Len, being busy with all the tours and talks, book signings and all, are you still in touch with Inspector Marchant? And are the dangers, clearly highlighted in *RIP – Synergy*, still very real? Should we still be afraid?'

'I have spoken to Judy Marchant on several occasions. I wouldn't say we are in regular contact, but we do communicate. I think we have both been very busy so any opportunities for us to meet up and chat have been extremely rare just lately. Is there any danger from an entity that was effectively trapped in a sealed container at the end of my book? I think that might be like asking if Bob Thornton is in line for an Oscar?'

*****

When you have the desire, and you have enough time to set aside from the thoughts and rigours of everyday life, know that then, in that quietness, in that stillness, you can communicate with God. In fact, I would go so far as to say that everybody has an absolute right to communicate with God.

We all do it in prayer. But remember that prayer can only ever be a one-way process. In prayer we give out a list of wishes. We plead, we beg for assistance for ourselves and for other people. If we are not asking for direct help then we are praising God and Its actions in our lives, and in the lives of billions of other people. But it is the knowing that God can communicate with us through words, through scenes, or through the next thing you see, hear, or do. That is the key. Then comes the realisation that God is always there waiting to communicate with us.

And why the need for a second book? Was it not the case that all that we needed to know about our life and interaction with spiritual entities, everything about the rogue entity, its plans and its demise, was not all we needed to know about God covered in *RIP – Synergy*?

Well, actually, the answers are no, no and no. Nothing is ever as it seems. Always try to remember that. And what was recorded in the first of the RIP series of books was based on my perception. But this can never tell the whole story. It can only, and it is right that it should only, be the rising curtain in a play, a means of outlining the main issues in the plot. Part one enables us to get our bums comfy on our seats, to place our coke and popcorn in a convenient and safe berth, to maybe release our shoes from our feet, to stretch our legs and to relax into our seat.

Now it is the time for lights, camera, action.

So sit back and enjoy the main part of the feature.

Part Two

The Time Before the Time After

Chapter Eleven

Judy Marchant was asleep, she knew that, but the party seemed like fun anyway. She sat on a long, deep, black leather sofa. She pressed her hand against the cool surface of the machined cowhide. It certainly felt real enough.

Judy's outfit was full of colour: red and indigo with yellow slashes, deep and vibrant, and wide in size, topped by yellow, orange and red flowers with petals spread wide and rigid. She loved the dress, it felt comfortable and fitted her in easily with the glitziness of the party. The only issue of concern was that the hem of the dress rode up above her knicker line at the front and the back. If she tried to rise it would be more than likely that her hips and below would be totally exposed. She had no idea whether she was wearing knickers or not.

She was aware of people around her, male and female, all similarly brightly dressed. She knew they were talking, laughing and dancing, but she heard no sound at all. The seat she was sitting on faced a white wall with an open fireplace that had a large picture above. She could not make out what the picture showed. Its centre seemed black. The edges of the picture were browned, like an aged photograph. Judy knew the picture had a clarity within it, but she was unable to make out what the image might be.

Occasionally party members drifted into her peripheral vision, but none seemed so brazenly uncovered as was she. Judy watched the people gyrate rhythmically, she saw their mouths move in conversation, she watched the muscles of their faces contort and stretch as they laughed. But still, the room remained silent.

Though not conversing with anyone, Judy was still aware of a buoyancy and a joy that pervaded the room. She even felt the top half of her body move gently to the sways of the other participants' dance movements. She gripped a glass tumbler in the palm of her right hand. The fingers of her left hand rested gently on the opposite side of the container. The glass was half full of well-shaped cubic ice. At the bottom of the glass lay an amber liquid. It looked like it could be whisky, Judy's alcoholic tipple of choice. She raised the glass to her mouth, but she had no memory of tasting or swallowing any of the liquid inside.

Three more gyrating, chatting, laughing people came into view to Judy's left side. A man in bright, stripy shorts, a girl in loose dungarees, and another man in a brown shirt and drainpipe black trousers. All three looked like they were having a good time.

As she turned back to face the wall once again Judy noticed that an old man was seated on the sofa with her. He was maybe two metres away. The man wore a grey cap squarely on his head, a grey suit of jacket, trousers and waistcoat, he also wore a smooth yellow scarf with red speckles modelled into a cravat. His head was turned towards her. Their eyes locked.

'Nice party.'

The old man mouthed the words before Judy heard any sound. By the time his lips began closing in finishing the first word of speech, the start of the sound, muffled and quiet, reached her ears. These were the first sounds she had heard and, no matter how disconnected, she welcomed the old man's voice.

She did not recognise the man, and neither did she know his voice. Though he seemed very out of place in the atmosphere and tempo of the party, Judy realised that inside her dream state anything could happen. Up to this point there seemed little to be gained from her experience, except for the shy embarrassment of maybe being caught out with a group of people with no knickers and an exceedingly short dress.

'Yes,' Judy replied, 'but I don't really know what is going on.'

When the sound of her voice did eventually arrive, Judy could feel each syllable, each separate tone, as if the words formed lumps of physical matter as they travelled up her throat and out of her mouth. She was so intensely aware of her words that she swore she could taste them too.

The man to her right grinned widely, exposing only four teeth that could be seen inside his mouth. Spittle crusted the top edges of his thin, colourless gums. As he closed his mouth the spittle spread along his lips and dribbled slightly from each crease, where his top lip met the bottom one.

'Do I know you?' Judy asked.

'Well, it would be truthful to say that you do not know me, because we have never met, not in a physical sense anyway. But it would also be true that you will know of me,' the old man replied.

'I am confused. Are you here because you are part of my dream? In which case, what is it that you are here for?' Judy asked.

'Yes, I am a reason for this scenario to be taking place, though it would not be my choice to meet with you in such a gaudy environment. I am here for the same reason as are all these other people, the people in the room that you see dancing to the music.'

'But I don't hear any music,' Judy replied.

'You don't?'

'No. All I can hear are your words, and they are very confusingly delayed,' Judy explained.

'Oh, that is odd.'

'Yes, it is very odd indeed.'

'No. I mean it is odd that you don't hear any music, but everybody else seems to. Why else would they dance?'

'Do you hear the music?' Judy asked the man.

'Yes of course. It is awful. Too loud, too raucous, too unnecessary.'

'You said that you are here for the same reason as all the other people in this room,' Judy reminded him.

'Oh yes, I am sorry, I should correct myself. What I meant to say was that I am here for the same reason as the people here that you can see. The people that you are directly, and consciously, aware of.'

'Again, I am getting confused. Surely, either they are here or they are not?'

'Well, let me put it this way. The room to you, and this whole party, may seem to be packed out,' the old man started to explain.

'That is because there are a lot of people here,' Judy said.

'Actually yes, in one way that is true. But what you need to try to understand is that the feeling you have of this place being packed out with people is rather an expectation than an actual fact. At a party you would expect a lot of people, so your perception is that this place is full of people chatting, drinking, laughing and dancing.'

'And doing all those things silently,' Judy added, in delayed fashion.

'Well, yes.'

'And for what reason would you, and these people I am consciously aware of, be here?' Judy asked.

'Well. As is the case with me, you do not know these people, but you do know of them.'

'Back to square one with the confusedness,' Judy exclaimed.

'I should have introduced myself a long time ago,' the old man said, 'I am your great granddad, on your mother's side.'

'Then you were right when you said I did not know you,' Judy said.

'I died in an accident when I was 51. That was a little more than 30 years before you were born.'

'So that would make you more than 120 years old.'

'There is no such thing as time when you are dead.'

'But, and I am not meaning to be rude in any way here, you look a lot older than 51.'

'I can appear to you as would best suit your perception of me. It would not be suitable for me to appear before you at an age similar to your own, your conscious and subconscious minds won't accept it. There is a natural age progression that can be applied in situations like this, conversely there is also a process for age regression,' the old man explained.

'So you are here presumably to give me some kind of a message, or guidance?'

'And the other people that you are aware of, should you wish to focus on them, are either other members of your family that are deceased, they are your spiritual helpers, or they are interested onlookers.' The old man seemed to ignore Judy's question.

'Onlookers?'

'Yes. Individual spiritual entities can observe any living person or situation if it is felt they might gain insight, knowledge or better understanding by doing so.'

'In dreams, right?'

'Not just in dreams, but in times of wakefulness too.'

'So it is likely that when I am moving around doing my everyday things, having everyday conversations, thinking everyday thoughts, that I am being watched?' Judy asked.

'It is not just likely, it is probable.'

'That is a bit disconcerting. But if the people I notice here are deceased family members, or if they are spiritual helpers, how is it that I recognise no-one? Why do they appear as strangers? Would it not be better for them to come over and introduce themselves?' Judy asked.

The old man laughed.

'You are in a dream scenario. There is only so much you can remember of a dream when you wake up. Yes, there is some value in you storing some information in your subconscious mind, but if all of what happens is remembered it could never be brought forward into your conscious awareness. The scenario playing out before you can only have one meaning. It can only have one purpose. I know that, and every entity inside this room knows it too. And it is only that one meaning that can be stored, and recalled.'

'Excuse me, but you are here, inside my dream, to deliver a message to a person you never met, a person who has heard nothing about you. Why is this message not best left to somebody I have a greater connection with?'

'Nothing?'

'I'm sorry, what?'

'You said you know nothing about me.'

Judy shook her head.

'Oh, that is a little bit disappointing.'

'I'm sorry.'

Judy reached out for the old man's arm. She knew she touched his jacket but she felt nothing.

'You expressed your surprise that this message was not delivered by somebody you knew better. Such as?'

'Such as my brother. He died 10 years ago in a motorbike accident. You know that, all of my dead relatives know that, hell, even my neighbours know that. So would it not have been better for my brother to deliver this message? I have missed him so much, but not one time has Steven ever visited my dreams, never once have I felt him even close to me. Why was he not here to give me this message?' Judy asked.

'Because your focus would not be on the message, your focus would be only on your brother. The effectiveness of this communication would be entirely lost. Equally, at the other end of the spectrum, if it was someone you had no ties with at all, it is unlikely that the clarity of the message would remain with you. Again, the purpose of all of this would be lost,' the old man explained.

'So this party, these entities, this dream, has not been concocted by my sleeping self?'

'Not entirely, no. In fact, it is a very seldom occurrence that any dream is constructed by a human mind, whether consciously or subconsciously. You will be aware how, in a dream state, your situations, where you are, what you are doing, how you are doing it, can change quite dramatically. This is because at these times your mind is seeking dominance over the spirit communication. But the spiritual message will always prevail, in one form or another.'

'And the purpose of this party is what exactly?' Judy asked.

'It is an attempt to keep my visit away from prying eyes and ears,' her great granddad replied.

'That is all a bit cloak and dagger, isn't it? Sure, I am in the police force, but I hardly think that makes me a target for any anti-establishment operatives out there.' Judy tried to reason.

'This is nothing to do with your career. This is about the situation you are involved in with Len, and that is the central issue in your life right now. Your career must take a backseat, at least while a threat exists.'

'A threat? This is getting spooky, and you are seeming rather creepy. I think it must be time for me to wake up now, excuse me.'

Judy prepared to rise from the sofa, pulling desperately at the front hem of the ridiculously short dress she wore. As she began to rise to a standing position her great grandfather grabbed her right forearm. He was amazingly quick and his grip was surprisingly forceful. His old eyes glared into hers, sparkling like crystals. So clear, so bright.

'I am here to offer you a warning, Judy. You must be very careful where you tread. Be aware, and I mean be completely aware, of your surroundings at each and every moment. Watch, listen, and take notice. It is imperative that you pay attention to every detail,' her great grandfather warned sternly.

'Or?'

'Or your life could be in jeopardy.'

*****

Dr Theodore Anstis sat at the table holding a small plastic cup of what was described on the dispenser as white coffee. The contents of the cup were lukewarm, but somehow the act of holding the brown plastic container helped him focus his mind on the issues drawing his attention at this time.

'Donald, can I ask you something?' Dr Anstis asked as he stared straight ahead at a message-laden pinboard.

The man to his left looked up from a well-thumbed newspaper. Dr Walsch was large framed, or so he preferred to think of himself. The fact was that, though he seemed to carry excess weight he was not, and never had been, a fat person, but he buttons of his heavy white coat always stretched and strained to accommodate his bulky circumference. His charcoal trousers were always pulled unnecessarily high and his black socks only ever seemed to meet the hem of his trouser leg when he walked.

'Go ahead,' the big man answered.

'I heard a rather strange story, oh, about eight months ago. I got approached by Inspector Judy Marchant. Do you know her?' Dr Anstis asked.

'I don't know her personally, but I do know of her, yes,' the bulky man answered.

'She came to me with a strange tale linked to local deaths that happened at the time. All of these deaths were people under 32 years of age, and they all occurred within a three-week period. That in itself is not too strange, and usually we can determine a death with pretty clear internal and external causes. From that we can make a good, solid guesstimate, of what might have happened. Do we agree on that?'

'Yes, of course, please go on,' the bigger man requested as he folded the newspaper and placed it on the table before him.

'In these cases I could identify a cause, every time, but these people appeared to have died from injuries sustained in a way that I could not fathom. For a start, in every case there were no external injuries, and, from what Inspector Marchant told me, there were no indications of any other person being involved, or even being in the vicinity of each victim when they had died,' Dr Anstis said, slowly, 'I know this sounds crazy, but the marks and abrasions I saw, the signs of some kind of attack that clearly led to these people's demise, seemed very clearly to have originated from inside their bodies.'

'Internal injuries?' asked the big man.

'Not as we might know them, no. I mean cuts, but cleaner than I have ever seen before. Pressure applied to heart and windpipe that clearly showed the imprint of fingers and, in one case, a palm.'

'From the inside?'

'Yes.'

'Well, how the devil would you classify that?'

'Natural causes,' Dr Anstis replied.

'I would suggest those deaths were far from natural,' Dr Walsch replied.

'What else? There was nothing else I could report.'

'And why didn't you follow accepted protocol and ask the pathologist to carry out a post mortem examination, if the cause of death seemed unknown? You must know surely that this is the first move?'

'Yes, but the nature of the deaths and the approach I had from Inspector Marchant meant that it would seem counterproductive to get anyone else involved. Ms Marchant knew something strange was going on. That's why she approached me in the first place,' Dr Anstis said.

'That is more than wacky Theo. If anybody other than you was telling me this I would have them sectioned. This is crazy stuff.'

'Yes, and now you see why I kept quiet, until now,' Dr Anstis replied.

'But what did you do? What will you do? Has this stuff ended now?' Dr Walsch asked.

'It has certainly quietened down these last few months, and I have heard no more from Judy Marchant.'

'But do you think it could start up again?'

'I don't know, Donald, I just don't know,' Dr Anstis replied before gulping down the last of his drink.

'I never knew him, but from what I heard he was not well regarded.'

'Why not?'

'Because he spent no time with his family. He had six children, but he was never home. He worked hard, but then he preferred the company of his workmates than that of his wife and children.'

'So why did my great grandma put up with him?'

'I guess she loved him. You have to understand that things were different in those days.'

'I understand that, but if he worked long hours was he not entitled to have some relaxation time?'

'Yes, of course, but I heard that he beat his wife and his kids. Sometimes your great grandma hid inside the house because he marked her. That is what I heard.'

'So why don't I know any of this? Why is my family such a mystery to me?' Judy asked.

'When you got through school you always knew what you wanted to do for a job. You were focused on your studies and on planning your future. I don't remember you asking anything about your extended family. It was never a case of anything being hidden from you, it was just that kind of discussion never took place.'

'Well, I am asking now.'

'Your great granddad had four sons and two daughters. His eldest son had already been working in the same mine as his dad for some years when he died, and his second son had recently joined the workforce there. The mine closed a few years later and the family moved to this area to support themselves. Two of your grandad's brothers committed suicide. I know nothing of the circumstances. In those days it was simply accepted that they died, and no attention was paid to what happened or why. I am given to understand that his two sisters were suspected of working on the streets, but that is just hearsay. Again, these kind of things tended to go on in the background. And you know the more recent history of the family,' Judy's mum explained.

'That is pretty dark.'

'Everybody has some skeletons in the closet.'

'And what about you and dad? You have never really sat down and discussed anything with me.'

'I think that is a private matter,' Judy's mum said sternly.

Judy lifted both her hands in an exasperated manner,

'I just thought that anything you might want to get off your chest is best laid out, here and now.'

'And what did your great granddad tell you in this dream of yours?' Judy's mum asked, ignorant of her daughter's gesture.

'Not very much actually. We were at a party but I could not hear anything except what my great granddad was saying,' Judy replied.

'His name was James Prudhoe. How did you know it was a party if you could hear no music?'

'There were people who seemed to be dancing, but they kind of flitted in and out of my vision.'

'Did you know any of these people?'

'That was another funny thing. Great Granddad James told me that I did not know the people there but that I knew of them. And that is exactly the same way that he introduced himself to me.'

'How can you know of someone but not know them?' Judy's mum asked.

'Great Grandad James told me that they were deceased members of my family. At least that was how he described the people I could see.'

'So how did you know that any other people were there, if you could not see or hear them?'

'I don't know. It was a dream, Mum, and sometimes strange things happen in dreams. What I do know is that I did communicate with Great Granddad James.'

'It's a load of poppycock, Judy. Once you die that's it, that is the end of you. It was probably just your imagination running wild,' Judy's mother stated.

'Why do you have to be so stubborn, Mum? You always insisted you were right just because you said so. Me and Jake were grown up long enough to have our own thoughts and opinions. I love you Mum, I just wish that you would open your mind a bit more to what goes on around you,' Judy replied, exasperated.

'Yeah well, there is no proof of anything else, so I'm sticking to my view,' her mum said, determined to have the last word.

'And there was never any proof the world was round, until there was.'

'Hmm,' and so, the older lady did have the last word.

Chapter Twelve

I awoke from a particularly vivid dream. It was not that the details of the dream were so clear and concise, it was the feelings, the experience and the emotions generated within the dream that seemed more raw than might have been expected.

I felt drained and my mind was not able to compute even the simplest of things, like how to open my eyes. I lay there unmoving for what seemed like an eternity. Rather than think about the emotions I was feeling I used most of my energy in banishing them just so that I could get up from the bed.

I moved my right leg, and then my right arm. The movement seemed to shift me into becoming more aware of my physical surroundings. I moved my body over to the right side and opened my eyes. I blinked several times. It was not that the room was bright, but my eyes seemed acutely sensitive to any light. I looked around the room but whatever I saw quivered, settled and then quivered again. I managed to raise myself into a seated position, and slumped my head forward onto my chest.

I placed both feet on the floor and gently rose into a standing position, using my hands and the strength in my biceps and shoulders to help me. Every object in the room seemed to be moving.

My wife would surely notice the dire change in me had she been in the house, but she had got my son ready and taken him to school before leaving for work. I tried to read the time on the oversized wristwatch that adorned my son's bedroom wall. It was no use, the hands on the watch face danced and leapt around while the numbers blurred beyond recognition.

I reached for the stair rail and gripped it on the second attempt. I pushed my opposite shoulder against the wall and began stepping down one stair at a time, pushing my shoulder into the wall with my other arm. I made it to the bottom and slowly swung myself around. I closed my eyelids, leaving only a thin slit through which to see. I made my way carefully across the room to the battered black sofa, sat down, and gingerly placed my head in my hands.

I became aware of a very high-pitched buzz that seemed to come from the back of my neck. There was no pain, just this annoying internal screech. I was not dizzy, although the fact that my eyes were ultra-sensitive to light seemed significant.

I moved to the kitchen. Pulling the cup towards me, I placed some coffee inside and flicked on the electric kettle. The quivering of the charcoal-coloured worktop seemed worse up close. When I looked at the cup, I saw one central vessel flanked on either side by two opaque, moving ones. I managed to shuffle some coffee granules inside and aimed the sweetener dispenser at the central and most solid cup. The kettle clicked off and I hesitantly lifted it up. I splashed hot water into the cup. Drops of water fell onto my hand, and I sharply withdrew it from the cup. I grabbed at the plastic carton of milk and splashed some towards the worktop, aiming as well as I could at the middle cup.

I did not care too much for the taste of the coffee. As the steaming, dark liquid slid down my throat, I was hoping for some interaction between the coffee and my ailing sight. I stepped carefully to the sofa. I closed my eyes and waited. My recall of the dream was. non-existent. All I retained were the strong emotions connected to these unknown elements. A feeling of loneliness, of anger, betrayal, and a sense of loss.

*****

'Hey, hey you!'

The tone of the approach was hostile, and the straightened finger jabbed into the back of my ribs was too sharp to be unintentional. I sucked deeply again on my cigarette, before releasing blue smoke into the air and turning to the right in one smooth motion. I was met by another smoker, a late twenties lady. Slim, with tight jeans torn at the knee and a thick brown bomber jacket zipped to the top.

'Are you speaking to me?' I asked politely.

'Of course I am, who else would deserve my attention?' she replied.

I lifted my shoulders in an exaggerated shrug, taking a further puff of my cigarette as I did so. The end glowed, and an extended length of burnt and disintegrating ash fell to the moist ground. 'What gives you the right to claim to be God's equal?' the lady asked sternly.

'I beg your pardon?' is all I could think to say in reply.

'You said that God and you are equal. You said you were personally asked by God to assist the spirit world in ridding itself of the threat posed by this rogue entity. You stated that everybody has the same power as you, but that most don't know how, or don't care, to use it.'

'I'm not sure that is exactly what I said,' I replied.

I spoke because I felt I had to, and not because I wanted to take part in the conversation.

'It is, near enough. What gives you the right to suggest that you can communicate with God directly? Who are you to suggest that you are better than anyone else on this planet? And what right do you have to suggest anything about what other people can, or cannot, achieve? What about people with mental or physical disabilities, where do they fit into your best mate's plans? You claim to not be from a privileged background, you claim you had a tough childhood, you claim your mum neglected you emotionally. But do you really know how people suffer in this world?' my inquisitor asked.

My cigarette burned to the end and I stubbed it out on the ground in front of me.

'I'm really sorry if you took offence to anything that was in my book, but that was not my intention. It just so happens that, by my own personal circumstances, I was lucky enough to write a book that got published and was read by many more people than I might have believed possible. The views expressed in that book are partly mine, coming from my own perception of life, and partly they are a work of fiction. The parts of the book that are fictional can only be fed by my experience. I don't believe that any writer can conjure up a book without feeding their character, or other characters they might have come across, into the storyline somewhere. The same can be said about places they might have visited and situations they might have been made aware of,' I replied.

'So all that stuff about talking with God was bollocks, it was made up, is that what you are saying?' the lady asked.

'The actual conversations will have a good chunk of fictional elements added, yes. But the practicality of my being able to converse with God is not. Anyone can talk with God, and almost everybody does.'

'I don't, since there is no such thing as God.'

'So why object to the fact that somebody else perceives that a conversation with something you do not believe in, can actually happen?'

'It is not that I do not believe in God, it is just that I believe no proof can ever be found that such a thing exists,' she answered.

'And that is a very good point. The word God is simply humanity's explanation of the unexplainable energy that exists in an invisible and undetectable way. You might have noticed that I refer mostly to that force as 'It', and that is because what It is will most likely always remain indefinable,' I tried to explain.

'So you don't believe in God?'

'I believe that there are a number of creative forces in the universe that, at least by conventional means, remain undetectable. But that does not mean that such forces are beyond our reach. In a deeply relaxed state who knows whether we are able to truly connect with these energies, or if we are able to contact our inner selves that, in themselves for most of the time, remain hidden. Whatever the case might be, millions of people have gained personal insight, achieved emotional strength and spiritual growth, by going to these places and by bringing something positive back with them,' I explained.

The lady lit up another cigarette, I did the same.

'So did you really communicate with God?' she asked.

'Yes, I did.'

'So how was it?'

'It was exhilarating.'

'No, I mean, what did you see, what did God look like, what feelings did you have?' she prompted.

'How did it feel physically you mean?' I asked back.

'Yes.'

'Well, first of all I was in meditation, so any feelings I had at the time would be created purely from my own perception of the situation. The creative force, that many would call God, did not take the shape or form of a physical being. I did not feel intimidated or under any pressure at all. I conversed as I would normally, I asked questions, and they were all answered with an honesty that was refreshing. I was there to ask questions and God was there to answer anything that I was able to comprehend. There are not many words I can use to describe how I felt, what I was thinking, or how I was reacting to the situation, it just happened as it happened,' I replied.

'But what if it was just a case of your own relaxed inner self coming to the fore and communicating with your conscious mind?'

'What if it was? It doesn't really matter. What feeds all of us during our lifetimes are our perception of events that take place involving us, and those involving other people, and not the events themselves,' I answered.

'What is it like being psychic?' she asked.

'That is the hardest question you have asked me.'

'It just seems a bit wacky, that's all.'

'It is wacky, I guess. But what is even wackier is that I don't know the answer to your question. I don't like to call my psychic tendencies 'abilities' because they are not. It is not something I have learned or trained for, it is just something that is there. I will say though, that I might well have had these tendencies since birth, but I was not aware of them until I started exploring my life, and the unknown forces most people might call spiritual. I started meditating, quietening the constant buffeting of the physical world. I guess that I also became more aware of my thought processes and I gained a measure of control over my reaction to different influences in my life. I was able to get in touch with my inner self, and after this time it became easier for me to draw in the energies of other people and the circumstances in their lives. I don't hear spirit voices. I don't see apparitions. Any information that I do pick up is just there in the energetic makeup of the person. So far as healing goes, that is even harder to explain. I just focus on calling light from the universe to the place inside a person that might need cleansing, or purifying. Sometimes I see myself cleaning a particular part of their body, stretching and manipulating internal muscles or organs, or purifying their blood. It does seem to work,' I explained.

The lady stubbed out her cigarette. I took one last deep drag on mine, and then did the same.

'And is it true that you came face to face with a rogue entity that wanted to destroy God and take over control of the spirit world?' she asked.

'I cannot possibly comment on that, it is a matter entirely for my readers,' I replied, straight-faced.

'It has been interesting talking to you, but I have to get going now,' the lady said as she hoisted her small rucksack onto her right shoulder, turned quickly, and melded into the travelling throng of people moving towards destinations unknown.

My eight-year-old son tells me that God makes all of us from a computer, so what do I know anyway.

Chapter Thirteen

Judy Marchant stood barefoot at the picture window that faced the sports field at the back of her friend's fourth floor flat. The street lamps in the distant road shimmered as they lit the sodden pathways and tarmac beneath them. Over the wall that surrounded the sports field Judy could see several rows of similar flats, with two factory chimneys beyond.

Judy had never favoured the suburbs, she preferred the quietness of the countryside to the rambunctious nature of an urban sprawl. Here, there never seemed any time or inclination to wonder how or why things were done, it was more a case of just getting up and doing it. But in the country life seemed slower, more ordered and less chaotic. In her job Judy needed to be ordered and precise, but it seemed that as soon as she left work she inevitably got dragged into the hustle and bustle of the concrete life she inhabited.

Judy had always enjoyed seeing tasks through to the end and her mind operated in the same way. To Judy there should always be a beginning, a middle and an end, to everything. Even if she was unable to find a solution, so long as her progress could be measured against this solidly defined criteria, then Judy could rest easy at night. The same approach pervaded every area of Judy's life. Her food, clothes, accessories, her hair, her car, almost everything followed the same pre-set sequence. She even prepared to pay her household bills in the same methodical way, she knew exactly when each was due, and she ensured sufficient funds were available when necessary. Judy had never used a credit card. If she did not have the money available to make a purchase then the item would just have to remain a glittering dream in a shop window.

Judy felt no real jubilation from her successful transition to an officer of the public protectorate, mostly because it was expected. If you follow the rules and question when you need to gain greater understanding of an issue, then success is almost guaranteed. The only other aptitude that should be applied is willpower, and Judy had that in abundance.

Being the youngest of two children and being a girl, Judy Marchant learned early on that her willpower was a gift, but also a necessity. Jake always combed his hair to the correct side, he always obeyed commands, and his doggedness was eventually rewarded with academic achievement. He did have a period of mixing with the wrong crowd, but that did not last long. Jake ended up being a desk clerk in an insurance company. A steady and settled job that pleased both parents. It was a safe career choice, it was stable, and it created a male mirror image of his staid and colourless parents.

She put so much into her career that Judy was aware her personal life had taken a back seat. She had a number of relationships but none that she considered worth pursuing on a long-term basis. Her child-rearing days had disappeared into the dust of a desert not well travelled. She had few regrets about not experiencing motherhood. Her drive to prove a success at everything she undertook was far too dominant a personality trait.

'Hey, don't you ever quit being on the lookout for crime?'

Her friend Nadia entered the living area with two steaming hot mugs of coffee.

'What?'

Judy turned her head slowly.

'You have been there for ages, surely the playing fields can't be that interesting?' Nadia asked.

'Oh, no, I guess I was just lost in thought, that's all.'

'Would you mind coming over here and sharing your thoughts? I have nothing else planned for the next five weeks. Part of being a recently separated spinster means the gaps in relationships last longer.'

Judy walked over to the sofa and sat beside Nadia.

'What happens when you think you are involved in something really big, something massive, and then it just disappears, as if it had never happened?' Judy asked.

'This sounds like a guy thing.' Nadia replied.

'No, it's not. Well, in a way it is, but it's not.'

Nadia leaned her head sideways quizzically.

'It is not so straightforward as that, it is much deeper and more meaningful,' Judy continued.

'Go ahead, I am all ears.'

'I got involved in this situation. Some crazy things happened. Then it stopped, just like that. And, to be honest with you, it was so surreal that I am questioning myself as to if any of it really happened at all?' Judy tried, unsuccessfully, to explain.

'Judy, I have known you a long time. You always use the right words, and your ability to explain something is certainly something I wished I had.'

'I have never said anything to anyone about this. It's too fresh, too raw,' Judy said, cautiously.

'But troubling enough that you didn't even mention my slippers as soon as you walked in the door,' Nadia said wiggling her toes inside a lifted bright orange bulbous slipper with the head of a clown on top. The clown had a brightly painted face and big googly eyes that rolled around inside their clear plastic casing as the slipper moved. Two oversized white-gloved hands bouncing on coiled springs above its head.

'That is disturbing, Nadia. Are you sure you had no seriously bad childhood experiences?' Judy asked, a smile pervading her lips for the first time this visit.

'So, just tell me what it is, I promise I won't laugh,' Nadia said.

'It's no laughing matter, I can assure you of that.' Judy then went on to outline the deaths of young people and how even the coroner could not adequately explain what might have happened to them.

'And what about the perpetrator? You said all these deaths were down to one person, but how is that possible? A total of 16 deaths in only four weeks, that is four every week,' Nadia said.

'Well, there was a multiple incident in Essex, on a motorway.'

'The kids in the minibus?' Nadia asked.

'The kids in the minibus, yes.'

'That doesn't seem to add up. Why would a killer change from killing one person at a time, to taking out a minibus full of schoolkids? Where is the connection?' Nadia asked.

'Trust me, I know it sounds crazy,' Judy Marchant looked up at the ceiling, as she spoke softly, 'Nadia, this must not go beyond these four walls. Can you promise me you will keep shtum?' Judy quickly jerked her head down again and stared intently into her friend's eyes.

Nadia visibly jumped a little in her seat. She looked away, feeling uncomfortable at the sudden shift in the conversation, before slowly looking back at Judy.

'OK,' she affirmed.

'OK is not good enough,' Judy said sharply, 'you must promise me.'

'OK, I promise.'

Judy swallowed hard before continuing with her revelations.

'I was there at the time of the accident, Nadia. I saw it all.'

*****

I guess that during the course of the next few days, I allowed myself to drift effortlessly away from all transient thought. It felt good to be free of the pressures of the mind. For most of the time I sat, zombie like, on the living room couch, staring blankly at the lightly patterned cream-coloured wall before me. My reactions were not by chance, they were deliberate.

In the spiritual realms time does not exist. It then stands to reason that the past, present and future exist all at the same time. And if this is accepted to be the case then why can the same not apply to life on this planet? Hypnosis must hold the key. The only issue that might get in the way of recalling any information under hypnosis would be the degree to which a client can accept spiritual possibilities. The more closed a client is to the concept of life after life, the less likely they are to uncover any proof of such a personal experience. But on one occasion one of my clients wholly accepted the concept of a timeless existence on earth, and was able to recall a future lifetime yet to be lived.

So time does not exist but the soul does, somewhere. And what of our spirit? What of the essence that makes up the holy trinity that is us? Well, as discussed at some length in my previous book *RIP – Synergy*, it is my belief that the spiritual essence of every person resides in the spiritual realms. It is our link with our creative home. And it is the rudder that steers our ships on a course of spiritual enlightenment through physical experiences.

It is my firm belief that we can create anything at all in our existence, so long as our focus and belief is strong enough and unwavering. And that in using such belief, it must also be possible to undo, or negate, what we have created. And this is exactly what I did in the days that followed my dream. I sat still, for as long as was physically and emotionally possible. I emptied my mind, I emptied my awareness of all things physical, I felt like I was emptying my very soul. And that proved to be a big mistake.

*****

'That is crazy. How? Why? What the…' Nadia stuttered.

'That's not the creepiest thing about it. I was involved in this, I was at the blunt end, and I witnessed what happened to a lot of them. Nadia, this was not some serial killer. All of this was done by something not of this Earth,' Judy Marchant continued.

Nadia laughed. 'I'm sorry, I'm really sorry,' she said quickly, 'I know I promised I wouldn't laugh, but you are telling me that an alien or a ghost killed 18 people,' Nadia shifted in her seat, propping herself into a more upright position. 'Say you are not being serious, tell me Jude that you are just winding me up, right?'

Judy Marchant slowly shook her head.

'It all happened, Nadia, exactly as I described. I can't explain any of it because, at least to me, none of it makes any sense. Maybe I should not have said anything. But Nadia, we have known each other for more than 10 years. If anyone knows me enough to tell that I am not full of cock and bull, then it would be you.'

Nadia shrugged her shoulders, 'and what about the guy? Is he anything to do with this?' Nadia asked.

'What guy? I don't think I mentioned any guy,' Judy replied, perplexed.

'When I suggested that maybe this was a guy thing, before you went doolally on me with your hocus-pocus, you know, when all of this was making a bit of sense at least, you hesitated, but you did not deny that a guy was involved,' Nadia explained.

'OK. This guy, Len. He is a psychic of some local renown. He is the one who reported the first two deaths. I got involved, and it ended up costing me my reputation and very nearly my job. People under 30 do not usually die of natural causes, not unless they have some serious ailment and neither of these guys, at least so far as could be established, had any such problems. So I, rather foolishly in hindsight, took up the case. I got nowhere, and worse, I felt obliged to divulge details of my informant, or at least his occupation, to my immediate boss. Big mistake. So anyway, six months later this guy comes in again claiming to know about a further death, same *modus operandi*, same age, and same circumstances. And, to cut a long story short, I wound up chasing some ghost, demented spirit, call it what you will, until we ended up at St Mary's Hospital,' Judy explained.

'The looney bin?' Nadia asked.

'It is a hospital that specialises in psychological therapies and community mental health care,' Judy replied.

'That's what I said, the looney bin.'

Judy Marchant ignored the comment and went on to explain how she was introduced to the spirit realm through hypnosis and how, after meeting up with a guide, she felt drawn to following through with the situation to the end. She also explained that she was the one who saved my life when my heart stopped in meditation at my apartment.

'That is some story. Were you told that you have a part to play in all of this? I mean, from what you are saying, it seems to me that you might have been just in the wrong place at the right time,' Nadia said.

'I don't know, Nadia. The rational side of my mind, which I used to use twenty-four-seven, gives a great deal of credence to the fact that the only reason I became involved was by coincidence, and that it could not possibly be any part of a bigger plan. But there is a nagging doubt that seems to grow day by day.'

'How come?' asked Nadia of her friend.

'For all his obvious faults, what Len told me about this entity, and how and why it picks its targets, together with his obvious conviction in the story, has a great deal of rationality behind it. By all accounts, this man is well respected and very successful in his chosen fields. His past is blemish free. He drinks no alcohol. He also has no history of psychological issues. So what is there that could possibly make his story, in the kind of detail he provides, poppycock?' Judy asked.

'Maybe he does have mental health issues. Maybe he does hear voices in his head. Could he not have been affected mentally when his heart stopped?'

'Well, I guess that might be a possibility, I cannot be sure how much time had passed before I was able to revive him in his apartment this time…'

'Whoa, whoa, whoa, Jude. This time? That was not the first time his heart had stopped?'

'No. It also happened when he was 14, due to some allergic reaction,' Judy Marchant explained.

'Well, there you go, right there is your answer. A bit of this guy's brain was fried when his heart stopped, not once, but twice. That fact alone waves a big red flag right in my eyes.'

'Yes, I can understand you saying that. Except for the fact that he lived the past 38 years with no indications of any serious mental health issues. He held steady jobs from the age of 16 until 10 years ago. And in the last four years he has been a very successful alternative therapist.'

'You know that means diddly squat to me Jude. I have never believed in ghosts. I doubt I would believe even if one crept up behind me and bit me on the bum. You know me Jude, what you see is what you get. If I can't see, taste, or feel it, then it doesn't exist.'

'Len wrote a successful book based on his experiences with this rogue spirit. From what I understand, he even toured America promoting it,' Judy explained.

'What is it called? Are you in it? Do I have a celebrity as a best buddy?' Nadia asked excitedly.

Judy Marchant smirked. 'No, nothing like that. The book was called **RIP – Synergy**. There is a character in it that loosely resembles me. In any case, the story is based on what took place, but it is not a verbatim record of the true events.'

'In all honesty, Jude, it just doesn't mean very much to me. I know I am an outsider in all of this, and it seems to me that, despite your reservations, you seem to firmly believe that something is going on. But with all due respect to you and to this Len character, I can't help feeling his screws might need a little bit of tightening up,' Nadia suggested.

Judy Marchant took a sip of her tepid drink. She purposefully diverted her gaze from her friend, while searching for a good reason to accept what she was being told, to drop this issue once and for all, and to get on with her life. But she couldn't. No matter how hard she tried to convince herself that the whole situation was hogwash, no matter how hard she tried to believe that her recent experiences with me were somehow created by some invisible hypnotic or post suggestive manipulation, there remained within her a greater desire to uncover more, to seek to answer her own questions about what had happened. She found herself being drawn ever deeper into the greatest detective mystery she had ever come across. One that she was determined to solve.

Chapter Fourteen

I leapt up from my prone position. I looked at the bedside clock through bleary, half-opened eyes. Ten minutes past three in the morning. I felt shattered and knew I had managed only two hours' sleep. The sheets beneath me were damp with the residue of my sweat.

I sat up and jumped out of bed in one sweeping movement. My underpants were wet too, the thin fabric clinging tightly to my otherwise bare skin. I ran my right hand over my forehead, across my brow, and then up and over my head. As I pulled my hand away each finger was moist.

I walked around the end of the dishevelled bed and flicked at the light switch. The room was swathed in brightness. I moved over to stand in front of the small pine surround mirror that hung on the far wall opposite the bed.

My face, scalp and neck slid into view in the mirror's reflective surface. I stood still for more than a few moments, my eyes fixed firmly on those of the stranger that stared back at me. My pupils seemed shallow, their surface almost milked over, their natural sparkle seeming faded and worn. My eyebrows reached over sunken eye sockets, as if to devour them completely. Beads of sweat trickled down my forehead and onto a face that was ashen and dark. I ran my right hand over my face to check if the image I saw before me was real.

I turned away from the mirror and glanced over the items in the room. Everything seemed to be in order, occupying the places they should, and yet, I sensed that something was different.

*****

Judy Marchant left Nadia's place in a sombre mood. What was supposed to have been a light-hearted meet-up with an old pal had turned into a rather deep and unsettling exploration of Judy's recent history. She carried this low mood home with her, trying her best to bury it in the cacophony of music that blasted from her in-car radio.

On her arrival home her low mood continued unabated. She tried listening to more music, she tried watching a movie, she tried reading a book, she even tried logging into one of her many online shopping accounts. Nothing could shift her feeling of morose solemnity. During this time she was mostly aware of a heaviness that caressed her shoulders and pressed down hard on her spine. She was not aware of when she finally drifted off to sleep, but it had taken a long time for her to settle, and for her eyelids to eventually close.

The next morning brought with it some relief from her dark feelings. The necessity of her focusing on the jobs at hand in her workplace slowly served to dissipate these feelings, but it was not until lunch time that she felt able to function anywhere near effectively. No matter what she did, however, Judy Marchant was aware of a presence at the back of her mind that waited to pounce at any sign of weakness or vulnerability.

The day came and went, as did the next and the next, and it was with a great deal of relief that on the fourth day she awoke with a more positive attitude and a more strident step. She at last felt released from whatever had gripped her. She looked forward to her work, as last week's Judy Marchant would, and she could not wait to right the wrongs that society delivered onto her desk.

*****

My agent, Frank Lebusso, called saying that he wanted me to attend a book signing. Standard enough stuff, he said Sit down, sign books, and be genial and polite at every given opportunity. He reminded me that I should remember not to smile too much, since the subject matter of the book called for a face of 'intellect, compassion and understanding.' These were his words, not mine.

The book signing was the next day. I got myself a rail ticket and prepared an overnight bag. These events could be draining, the need to be attentive and alert at all times and the need to try to answer every question thrown at me would tax even the most patient of people, and I was not a patient person. Inevitably, the vast majority of questions would relate to the spirit world, what it was like, who or what frequented the place and how. Occasionally people might ask, rather nonchalantly, for a psychic reading or for insight as to how their Aunt Bessie or other family member were adjusting to life on the other side. I always made a point of avoiding all questions that were not related to the book, pointing out my website address should anyone wish to make an appointment for any in-depth personal information. Frank met me at the mainline station. I arrived an hour before the book signing so that I could drop off my overnight bag and get acquainted with my overnight home. Frank always drove to such events, no matter how far away. And he always arrived first. He spent some time going over the same old drivel about how to present myself, what to do and what not to do, and to ensure I had my directions to the destination on-point.

My room was about as comfortable and inviting as an old aunt's fart. The curtains across the windows were faded orange with brown stripes, and no thicker than a paper towel. The net curtains in front of them were yellowed from age. The furniture was old and fragile, and consisted of one open single-shelved bedside stand and a slightly slanting double-doored wardrobe. There were no drawers inside the room. The walls were a cream colour, and were OK apart from one or two places where the wallpaper joins had risen. On the low bed the mattress was thin, forgiving, and covered with a single cream sheet and a mustard-coloured throw over blanket. A single thin pillow sat on top of the cover.

I crouched onto the bed and drifted off to sleep.

I was awoken by the trilling sound of my phone. My eyes flicked open with a start. I reached for the phone and answered the call. It was Frank, urging me to get a move on, or be late for our appointment at the book store.

I slid across the covers to the edge of the bed and stood up. I looked in my bag and pulled out a black pair of trousers, a clean shirt, and a loose necked jumper. Not city smart, but good enough for the occasion. Within two minutes I had dropped the room key at reception, and was stood outside the front entrance of the hovel. Sorry, the hotel. I made my way by gravelled footpath to the right side of the building where Frank was standing beside a car urgently checking his watch. I jumped into the back seat of the car and Frank slid in after me. He gave directions to the driver and we moved off smoothly.

'Late again, Len, when on earth are you ever going to show up to an event on time?' Frank asked as he looked at his watch face again.

'It's only a couple of minutes, Frank. Everything is going to be fine, don't worry,' I said, looking out of the car window

*****

'Inspector Marchant,' the tall figure of PC Ian Stewart stood at the door to Judy's office, 'I thought you ought to know that PCs Redfeld and Williams have just returned from a crime scene. I think you should see them, ma'am.'

'OK, send them in. Thank you.'

The two constables emerged from behind PC Stewart and entered the doorway. Both removed their caps as they stood at attention in front of Judy's desk. PC Redfeld spoke first.

'James Fortnum was 30 years of age. We were called to the scene by a neighbour who lives opposite, a Miss Donna Elliot, who began noticing a smell coming from Mr Fortnum's apartment. She says the smell got much worse yesterday. When we arrived the odour was pungent. We found the deceased in his bedroom under the bedclothes. From our initial inspection it seems he died maybe two or three days ago. We checked around the apartment and found no signs of a disturbance. Our first impression is that Mr Fortnum probably died in his sleep. We sealed the front door of the apartment, and his body was removed to the morgue. Dr Theodore Anstis has the body now. The scenes of crime team sent Dr Ainsworth and Mr Carrion over. From their initial reports it would seem that this is not the scene of a crime,' he said.

'Have you informed any next of kin?' Judy asked.

'No children, ma'am. Mother, father, one brother and one sister. The mother and father have been informed.' This time, PC Williams responded.

'OK, thank you for the update. It seems there is not much more we can do but await the coroner's report.'

The two reporting officers left the room as quietly as they had entered. Judy Marchant put her pen on the desk and looked to her left, to the window that overlooked the suburban sprawl at a second-floor level. The report of the death of James Fortnum seemed mundane but something struck a chord with her much deeper inside. Quite what, she was not sure.

*****

We arrived at the back of the bookstore. Frank got out of the car first and I followed swiftly after. A lady in a smart purple suit of loose fitting jacket and knee-length tailored skirt waited to greet us. She glanced at the clipboard she held to check the names of her visitors before introducing herself as Katie something or other. She led us through a small warehouse bay stacked with row upon row of sturdy cardboard boxes and to a small room curtained away from the corridor leading from the bay area. The room was constructed of plasterboard with a none too impressive thin cover of lilac-coloured paint. Two metal-legged orange plastic chairs sat opposite the purple drape that covered the entrance. In front of the chairs was a heavily marked square wooden table with two plastic beakers of water and a glass water jug adjacent. She pointed to a pair of metal coat hooks fixed to the plasterboard wall beside and above the table, and asked that we make ourselves comfortable while she prepared our stage in the main part of the store beyond.

Frank removed his overcoat. He clapped and then rubbed his hands together briskly.

'You ready then, champ?' he asked.

'Ready as I will ever be. And before you say it, I will not give too much of the story away, I will keep any personal historical information to the barest minimum, I will steer clear of answering directly any questions about the degree to which the book is based on actual events, I will keep direct eye contact to a minimum at all times, I will refrain from inserting any finger into either nostril, and I will write only what is absolutely necessary to get through the signature phase as quickly and efficiently as possible,' I answered in one delivery.

Frank immediately stopped rubbing his hands together and shifted his neck slightly inside the collar of his shirt.

'Spoken like a true pro,' Frank replied, 'it seems you can read me like a book.'

My agent continued to adjust his clothing, brushing cloth, pulling his trouser waistline first up and then left and right across his stomach. Not a large man, but not small either, Frank was in his early sixties. He liked to portray himself as a bit of a city gent. Frank had a quick wit that got him invites to the most unlikely of bashes. For Frank, being in the limelight was a necessity for his job even though he represented only four reasonably well known, but by no means famous, authors and one bit-part actor.

'Frank, why is it that when we travel I always end up somewhere only barely habitable?' I asked.

'Maybe that's because, darling, our bookings are usually in some of the less salubrious areas of this great nation of ours. It is important that any overnight stay is within five to 10 minutes of our destination. Time is of the essence in our business, and besides that, you are hardly yet Nobel Prize material. This is your first book and gratitude must be given to the great Lord above that He sees fit to rain any success our way. You happen to have hit a rich vein in your subject matter, but let us not forget that the vast majority of first-time writers will be in the same valley as you but they will never find that elusive stream of success that you did. You are still a relatively unknown artist, and it is only when you are truly established that the finer trimmings of life might just become available. Until then it is necessary that we follow the trail of denarii that has so generously been laid out before us,' Frank explained in his inimitable way.

'Yeah, I guess you are right. You usually are,' I replied.

Frank tapped a forefinger on his nose as Katie what's-her-name returned.

'Are you ready?' our hostess asked, holding open the drape to hasten our exit from the waiting area.

I was scheduled to talk for five minutes. Frank introduced me to our audience, with little unnecessary blurb. Most of the small gathering formed two lines for a signature and a quick chat with me, the people arranged perfectly by our host Katie. The finer detail of this event is not important. For the purposes of this journal it is what happened right at the end of my visit that is deserving of your attention.

Chapter Fifteen

'Joe, can I get a second opinion on this please?' Dr Anstis called to his assistant, Joe Walker.

Joe approached the bench where Dr Anstis was peering intently into the opened throat of James Fortnum, he picked a mirrored magnifying monocle from the work space to the left of the bench and attached it to his head using the Velcro and elastic band that sat above his brow. He pulled the monocle down in front of his naked right eye and leaned a little towards the area of Dr Anstis' immediate interest.

'What are we looking at Dr A?' he asked.

'Do you see here?' Dr Anstis pointed a thin metal spatula towards the tracheal tube of the dead man before him. He gently used the spatula to clear away a paper-thin layer of sticky mucus that lay across the outer surface of the passageway.

'I'm sorry Dr Anstis but I am not sure what you are calling my attention to?' Joe said as he leaned a little closer to the prone body stretched out beneath him.

'Just here Joe,' Dr Anstis said, resting the spatula immediately below the three marks he had noticed earlier, 'what do you make of it?' he asked.

'Well, I can see there might be a slightly more pronounced discolouration than might normally be expected post mortem, in the area that you are indicating, but I don't see anything that might be too untoward,' Joe said.

'Now look again Joe, do you notice the small scratches?' Dr Anstis asked.

Joe Walker leaned closer.

'Can I have that?' Joe asked without rising from the body.

Dr Anstis handed him the metal spatula without speaking. Joe pushed very lightly against the tough cartilage under the lowest mark. The cartilage gave way slightly, a small slit occurred as one side slid a little away from the other. He pushed the spatula a couple of millimetres into the gap and opened it up. He moved up to the second slit and did the same thing, then the third. He jerked his head up.

'Dr Anstis, what on earth happened here?'

It was just then that Judy Marchant made her appearance in the room.

'Ah, Inspector Marchant,' Dr Anstis said without looking up from the carcass in front of him, 'I guess you might be wondering why I called you in.'

'Please call me Judy, no need for formalities here. Wondering why you called? No. I'm more interested in the details of what you might have found,' Judy Marchant replied.

'Yes, quite, quite. Come over here, and I will show you.'

The plastic apron hugging Judy's bosom crinkled and creaked as she walked towards the coroner. It was clear to Judy that the body on the metal slab was in the early stages of putrefaction. The bottom of the man's legs, ankles and feet were bloated and ashen following the release of hydrogen sulphide and methane from those areas. From the knee upwards the body looked in remarkably better shape, caused mostly by Dr Anstis' opening of the chest cavity, neck and down to the man's limp grey genitals. The odour given off by the body was none too bad, due to the diligence shown by the surgeon and his assistant in keeping as much of the body in good condition as was possible, in order to carry out their examination.

Judy stepped beside Dr Anstis. The coroner rose from his crouched position and lowered his mask.

'So what do we have?' Judy Marchant asked.

'James Fortnum, 30 years of age. Judging by the level of decay in the body it is likely that he died around three days ago. There appears to be no sign of any struggle. From his medical records it seems that Mr Fortnum contracted type 2 diabetes at 18, and this was controlled by metformin-based tablets. His heart and lungs look in OK shape and there are some signs of poor dietary balance in the food he ate, though he was too young for this to have had any significant effect on his health. His brain function would seem to have been OK. After more than 48 hours it can be a little difficult to spot any obvious discrepancies, but there are really no signs of any distress to internal organs or blood vessels, except...'

'Except what?' Judy asked.

'Well, this is why I called you Ms Marchant. Can you come a little bit closer?' Dr Anstis shuffled to his right allowing Judy a better view. 'You might need to use a magnifying glass.

Judy took the headband offered by Joe Walker and quickly attached it to her head.

Here,' Dr Anstis pointed with the spatula, 'on the trachea just by the bronchi. The normal layout here is that the cartilage you see runs all the way down here in concentric circles that lay across the trachea, at roughly a 90-degree angle. But look here, do you see the three scratches? Hardly noticeable this long after the event but they are there.'

Judy leaned in again towards the corpse. The three scratches varied in length with the middle one being perceptibly smaller than the other two. Judy pulled on the monocle attached to her headband and squinted into it. 'I see them, but they are almost imperceptible,' Judy replied.

'Yes, and that is the problem.'

'How do you mean?'

Dr Anstis pushed lightly at the middle of the scratches and one side slid away from the other.

'But these are cuts, not scratches,' Judy said.

'Yes, they are. Any kind of pressure trauma might cause a collapse, but there is no sign of that happening here. Without bruising or any abnormal discolouration, I mean beyond that shown in the surrounding areas, it appears as if these three cuts were most likely to have been the cause of death,' the coroner explained.

'Could they not just be a birth defect or some kind of pre-mortis injury?' Judy asked.

'That would be impossible. Any such imperfections in the trachea would prove fatal since the victim would be unable to breathe in any sustainable fashion. Any birth defect such as this would exterminate life within a couple of minutes. Also the tracheal pipe is surrounded by cartilage for protection because of its importance in sustaining life,' Dr Anstis replied.

'You said that these three cuts are the most likely cause of death...'

'Ms Marchant, it seems to me that we have here another one of those cases where I know the cause of death, at least with a 99 per cent certainty, but I am unable to report my findings. The death of Mr James Fortnum will, of necessity, be ruled to have occurred as an unfortunate incident which, although very rare in people of such a young age, will have natural origins. I can do nothing else. But it appears, once again, that what we actually have here is another cause of death that has no natural, or forced, entry point. The injuries leading to this man's death could only have been inflicted from the inside,' the coroner went on.

'But that must be impossible,' Judy exclaimed.

'The injuries I showed you, impossible or not, would undoubtedly have caused a very swift shutdown of the brain followed by the failure of all other life sustaining organs.'

Dr Anstis straightened and removed the elasticated monocle magnifier from his head. He walked around the dead man and moved serenely towards the exit doors. He beckoned to Judy. She followed him through the double doors. In the adjacent scrubbing room they both removed their plastic gloves and aprons and deposited them into a large disposal bin. Dr Anstis turned to Judy Marchant.

'You, young lady, have some explaining to do,' he said simply.

Dr Anstis promptly turned around and exited to the corridor outside. Judy Marchant followed. Judy inhaled deeply and then ran through everything she felt Dr Theodore Anstis should know. She told him how I had approached her, about how each murder was investigated, about the circumstances of the minibus crash and how she happened to be there. She told him about being with Amy when she struggled to survive an attack by the rogue spirit but stopping shy of telling him about her trip to the spirit world while under hypnosis.

'And that,' Judy said with a large intake of breath, 'is about it.'

'Though naturally inquisitive I must, nevertheless, always maintain a scientific stance. You do realise there can be no scientific backup whatsoever to support your story,' the coroner commented.

'Except that which you witnessed yourself,' Judy replied.

'Well, even then every death you say is connected to this rogue spirit must arise from the everyday course of life experiences.'

'But Dr Anstis, you yourself commented on the seeming impossibility of some of the wounds you attribute to causing death in these people,' Judy pushed.

'While that is true, each death must be recorded as having happened by natural causes.'

'But surely you can join the dots so that your experiences can be seen to add at least some degree of validity to the events I described to you,' Judy suggested.

'Oh, I cannot possibly deny that fact.'

'And now, it seems, whatever we thought we had achieved last time out, seems to have had little or no impact on the ability of the rogue spirit to kill people as it chooses,' Judy Marchant continued.

'I cannot make any comment on your suggestion. All I can say is that yes, it does seem quite possible that the cause, if in fact it can be allocated to one individual being in whatever shape or form, might quite possibly be picking up where it left off before.'

'I will take that, Dr Anstis, as a yes then.'

*****

The end of the line approached. I had signed in excess of 50 copies of my book, personalising each with a light greeting and daubed signature on the front of the title page. A swift vocal greeting and thanks for their attendance preceded each signature. It was very likely that most people in the queue had already digested the book cover to cover from internet downloads. I had some comments and questions along the way but nothing too taxing. The very last person in the queue was an old man of a fairly rough appearance. His shirt was untucked at his waistline and the bottom of it looked creased. His tan-coloured trousers hid legs of little substance. This man was thin and his jumper was at least a couple of sizes too big for his frame. The white hair on his head was dishevelled. The most marked thing about this man was that he did not appear to be holding a copy of the book.

The old man leaned across the desk that separated us. He smelled of a mixture of almonds and cheap aftershave. His eyes were a very pale blue, almost grey, in colour, and they appeared to be a little misty around his pupils. I could clearly see several strong white hairs protruding from each nostril and ear. He reached out his right hand and I responded immediately by doing likewise. His grip was almost painfully strong. He pulled me towards him as he stared into my eyes.

I was aware of some movement behind me. It seemed that Frank Lebusso and Katie Whatsername had both taken steps towards me as the old man had grabbed my hand in his steely grip. I quickly raised my left hand above my head to signal them to stay where they were. If this man had an opinion, after waiting so patiently for at least an hour, then it was only right that I should hear him out. The man finally spoke in a low, whispered tone. His gravelly voice was stark against the silence in the room.

'You think you have won, but you have not,' the old man said.

'Well sir, I can assure you that...' I did not get to finish what I was saying before the old man cut in, this time speaking more fervently than before.

'What happened before was just the start. You cannot fight what you do not understand. He gets stronger every day. What you know is just the tip of the iceberg, and the girl knows that. You are the one who must accept the responsibility for all that happens, you are the one who welcomed him in, and it is only you who can rid the world of this menace. Do you honestly think that waking the world up to the danger through your book is going to change anything? You think that you have asserted yourself over him, you think you have gained at least some degree of control, but let me tell you that you have achieved nothing. All you have done is to place yourself right where he wants you. He is the one who is in control now. You think you are the only one who has faced this demon, you are not. His army grows. You must find the key to unlock the doors to free all those poor souls that have been forced to work for him. Only you can do that. Only you can ensure the continued sanctity of the Holy Kingdom, and may God have mercy on your soul.'

The old man slowly released my hand. He took a step backwards, his eyes remaining firmly fixed on mine. He turned and then walked down the nearest aisle towards the exit from the store.

I sat frozen in the seat. I was dumbstruck by what the old man had said. I turned my hand slowly over so my palm faced upwards. I noticed that where the white mark remained, the one given to me as a weapon by the spirit world all those months ago, that now was overlaid at the right edge by a dark grey mark of similar size.

Chapter Sixteen

Judy Marchant picked up the phone and looked at her call history. She pressed at the name that had refused to answer the last seven times she had called. She refused to leave any messages, sure that the other person would call her back. But he did not. The ringing tone drifted into her right ear once again, and this time, at the third dial tone, her call was answered.

'Who is it?' the recipient asked.

'I know it's been some time but surely you haven't forgotten my number already?' she asked.

'Judy?'

'Yes, of course it is Judy.'

'What do you want?' the person asked.

'I've been trying to call you for ages. Where have you been?'

'Had my phone on silent. I was at a book signing.'

'Ahh yes, of course.'

'Anyway, what can I do for you?'

'Hello, might be nice. How are you?'

'I'm getting along OK, I guess.'

'You don't sound so sure.'

'What do you want? It's early and I have things to do.'

'Well, excuse me for your grumpiness,' Judy replied sharply.

'After so long, I'm guessing you wouldn't just call to ask how I am doing. It is much more likely you might want to stay as far away from me as you can, seeing as how each time we get together people either get killed, or we end up messing each other's lives up.'

'Speak for yourself, I would like to think that I enrich people's lives, help them to find closure,' Judy said. 'I certainly have never thought of myself as having anything to do with messing people's lives up.'

'I was speaking for myself. So far as your life path is concerned, that can only be a matter of speculation.'

'Anyway, I do have something I want to run past you,' Judy admitted.

'And there is the clincher,' was the grumpy reply.

'I became aware of two recent deaths and I wondered if you might have any info for me?' Judy asked.

'And what makes you think that I might be able to help?'

'The deaths were of natural causes, once again. One guy and one girl, both under 30,' Judy explained.

'And? What makes you think I have anything to share with you?'

'Don't you think it's suspicious?' Judy asked.

'Not really. It is a sad fact of life but people die all the time, young and old, it is a part of the natural scheme of things.'

'I'm not convinced. There is something inside of me that doesn't feel right,' Judy said, 'and I thought that, with what happened before, there might be a connection. In fact, I am feeling more and more sure that there is a connection,' Judy insisted.

'Look, whatever happened with us is in the past, it's been and it's gone, it's finished. We did what we had to do at the time, that's all. Maybe we achieved something and maybe we didn't, I don't know. But I'm not about to go opening up a whole new can of worms because of two deaths that I know nothing of,' I replied, well aware that a small amount of frustration and possibly even anger, bubbled beneath my words.

'It seems to me you are avoiding the issue here,' Judy issued a direct challenge.

'And what issue might that be? What exactly is your well trained investigative brain focusing on here Judy?'

'You didn't get any of your weird reactions recently?'

'Weird reactions? Judy, what on earth are you talking about?' I asked.

'You know how you felt before when a spate of young people died, you know what you saw and felt, you can't deny that,' Judy insisted.

'I am not denying anything, Judy. All I am saying is that I have felt no weird feelings whatsoever and I don't see how any of this can have anything to do with me.'

'Well, maybe not now. I was touring with my novel about a rogue spiritual entity that killed otherwise healthy, young people, and that used me as a vessel to engage its victims. And then there was God, the essence that seems to exert control over all life, except I was to learn that in fact, it did not. And to the use that God's kingdom put me in challenging and overcoming this rogue spirit, doing its dirty work, maybe because something all-loving and all-knowing could not bring itself to challenge one of its adoringly created conceptions in such a way. Yes, I was well aware of all of this, it was all in the book. Who was it who coined the phrase that "truth is stranger than fiction?" Whoever it was, they were a much greater and more insightful person than I.' Judy tried hard, but did little to impress with her interpretation of me.

'I am presuming you have no evidence of a perpetrator?' I asked.

'None,' was Judy's simple reply.

'I suggest then that maybe these are just two unfortunate incidences in the process that we call life. People live, people die. If there are no discernible signs of a perpetrator, then why your interest Judy. Don't you only deal with crime?' I asked.

'OK, OK. It is a feeling I have in my gut, and that is not caused by any spicy food, let me assure you. I just thought you might tell me of anything you experienced recently that might be tied to these two young people.'

'No, I haven't. But if I do feel anything you can rest assured that you will be the first, and probably the only, person I will contact.'

'OK, I get it, you are washing your hands of this. How come you were so focused before, so convinced of what was going on and now you seem so blasé about it? What does all this have to do with me? Are you sure you know nothing whatsoever about this? It fits almost exactly into the pattern we picked up before,' Judy asserted.

'Judy, I went with what my gut told me. I picked up things intuitively, just as you seem to be doing now. As to what this all has to do with you, do you not recall that in hypnosis you received specific instructions on your role, and how the situation might develop? Then maybe this is something that you can pursue. If you feel something deep down all I can suggest, with my psychic hat on, is that you follow that wherever it might take you,' I replied.

'Ahh. It all makes sense now. Maybe you are upset or even angry that I was approached by your Guide to help rid the world of this rogue entity. And maybe you don't like that,' Judy suggested.

'That is ridiculous. I spent my whole life offering guidance to people so why would you suggest that I am, in some way, choosing to turn my back on you because of some churlish, primal aggression?'

'You have your instincts but I have mine too,' Judy replied.

'Judy, I don't really understand why you are getting so excited about this?'

'And I cannot believe that you are not,' she countered.

'Look, we did what we had to do. It was invigorating, it was scary, but the danger is past now. Isn't it time to move on?' I asked.

'Those young people did not get a chance to move on, they are dead,' Judy replied.

'Now look, none of us can take any blame for that. If they really did die because some entity is convinced that it can challenge God, that is happening there, Judy, and not here,' I responded.

'But it is happening here, can't you see that? It is happening to you, to me. For God's sake, Len, why can't you see it is happening to all of us in one way or another?' Judy countered.

'What are you talking about Judy?'

'This is just an idea Len, but what if we have the timescale of this thing all wrong?'

'How do you mean?' I asked.

'What if this is not the start of a challenge to God? What if that challenge is already happening? Len, this situation could have been going on for centuries for all we know. And look at the state of the world around us, the connectedness of our existence should show you that something is going on up there,' Judy answered.

'All I can see Judy, at least so far as the heavenly instructions passed to me are concerned, is that we did what we were asked to do, period.'

'I can't believe you can't see what I am seeing. And I am supposed to be the sceptical one,' Judy said indignantly. 'I cannot believe that you are not feeling the same as I do about this. I saw Dr Anstis. He opened up a 30-year-old guy who had three perfectly symmetrical cuts in his windpipe that could only have been created from the inside. Does that not mean anything to you?' Judy challenged me.

'I don't see that it should,' I replied.

'You are unbelievable. You know you are the focus of this whole thing, and even you cannot deny that. For fuck's sake, Len, it was you who were guided about where to go, who was affected, and what you would find, and it was you who the spirit world chose to combat this thing. Len, you even know that this rogue spiritual entity has some kind of a link with you. You know all of this and yet now you decide that you no longer wish to be involved. What happened to the fearless, intrepid, courageous, even stupid, psychic pioneer I once knew?' Judy asked desperately.

'I guess he died, for the second time,' I replied.

'Is that it then?'

'What else can I say Judy? We did what we did, I did what I was instructed to do and, so far as I am concerned, the threat was cleared. And that is the end of the story,' I explained, again.

'Something must have happened to you, it just has to have done. You are just too tied to what is going on for you not to have reacted in some way. What about when you are sleeping. Had any vivid dreams lately?' Judy asked.

'No,' I replied after a lengthy pause.

'And now you are outright lying to me.'

Judy Marchant clasped her hands tightly together to her chest. She looked up at the ceiling.

'Please dear God, if ever I needed you before, I sure as hell need your guidance and assistance now,' she unclasped and then immediately clasped her hands together again, 'sorry for the H reference.'

Chapter Seventeen

It must have been about one o'clock in the morning and Judy Marchant felt restless. She would ordinarily have been in bed and fast asleep at least an hour before, but on this occasion she tried all manner of things but nothing served to relax her. She sunk into her sofa and flicked at the power button on the remote controller to bring the TV screen to life. She chose the first channel, and then flicked her way through each one in ascending order.

Judy was looking for any news bulletin, current affairs programme or interview that might catch her attention, at least enough to take her focus and allow her to wind down in preparation for a deep and meaningful sleep. She eventually settled on a story about a lady who felt her home had been invaded by a ghostly apparition. The woman was in her fifties now, but the story was set some 28 years earlier when she and her husband had purchased their first home. She seemed calm as she told her tale but it was clear that the trauma she suffered at that time was too readily brought to the forefront of her mind, as if it had happened that very day. As Judy watched the screen she became aware of something else.

Each time the camera switched to the woman Judy could just make out the shape of another figure. It was almost as if the lady's features were superimposed over this other face.

The features of the alternate face were indistinguishable. Judy rubbed her eyes and then returned her focus to the television screen. The background image remained. Judy scooped up the remote control for the recorder in one hand, while switching the input signal to the channel carrying the recorder. As quickly as she could she set the channel to the same as that of the television and pressed the instant record button.

Judy got up from the sofa and moved closer to the screen. She raised her right hand to gently touch the warm image. She traced her index finger over the outside of the woman's profile, as if in doing so she could better define the image laying beneath. Judy creased her eyes up as she followed the outline of the image on the screen.

The picture changed to show the outside of a motel room at night, rain sheeting down across an orange lamp that overlooked a car parking area. The commentary on the programme continued. Judy pressed a button on the remote control to stop the recording.

Judy played the recording five times without gaining any greater insight to the overlaid image which could only just be made out with considerable concentration.

Judy released the screen back to the recorded programme list. She was on the point of abandoning her quest for greater clarity, and also of finally admitting to herself that she had imagined seeing anything other than that intended by the programme makers, when she picked up the TV remote. She returned to the sofa and pressed the menu button and was shown a scrolling list of possible options. She chose the picture settings and looked through the additional list supplied. Judy played the recording again. This time, as it was running, she made adjustments to the richness of the colour, contrast, brightness, the warmth of the display and to the depth of the picture.

Judy paused the picture at the point where she felt the background image was at its most prominent. As the picture dimmed in intensity Judy increased its depth and decreased the richness of colour. As the focus of the woman faded the image beneath her became clearer. Judy realised now that the superimposed image was not, in fact, behind the woman but it seemed to sit in front of her. She made further changes, bit by bit, until finally, the underlying image she had searched so intensely for, became clearer still. It was made fuzzier still by the paused activity of the recorder, but as she stared at the picture she could make out very subtle features of the secondary image. The longer she stared at this image the clearer its features became.

'Oh my God,' Judy exclaimed as she dropped both remote controls to the floor and sank to her knees.

Chapter Eighteen

PC Ian Stewart was at the front desk sorting through some case papers when PCs Franklin and Isiah entered the reception from the rear of the building.

'Can I get one of those summary papers from you Ian?' PC Isiah asked, as he leaned nonchalantly on the wooden surface of the front desk. PC Franklin held his notepad and stood propping open the door to the right.

There was little discussion between Franklin and Isiah. It could, therefore, be safely assumed that whatever incident they returned from had an air of routine surrounding it. Whatever the issue, it was necessary that details be recorded on their return before the next stage, or otherwise, of their investigation could be considered. PC Isiah brought the report back to the desk and handed it to Ian Stewart. PC Stewart waited until the other two constables had started back towards their patrol car before he looked at the report card. It seems that they had attended a property rented by a 30-year-old male called Ian Robusch. Mr Robusch had been found in the hallway of his dwelling. He was laid face down, his left arm under his chest and his right arm extended above his head. PC Franklin had checked the man's neck for a pulse, but found none. It seemed to the two officers that his death would most likely have occurred sometime between six and eight hours before they arrived. The two constables had attended the scene following a call from Mr Robusch's fiancée, who stated that he had been due at her home at one o'clock in the morning, to travel with her to her mother's house in preparation, later that day, for the christening of their one-year-old son, Elijah. It was only at his fiancée's insistence that the two constables attended and found him prone on the floor, dead.

The summary report contained no reference to any signs of a disturbance inside the residence, and there were no signs of any forced entry to the property. The report was, therefore, due to be run past Inspector Marchant before the body could be handed over to the appropriate authorities, which would most likely be Dr Theobald Anstis.

PC Stewart tapped the sealed spine of the report against the surface of the desk. He turned to address the two clerks behind him.

'Hold here for me a couple of minutes, I need to see the Inspector,' he said as he turned to leave the reception hall.

*****

Ian Stewart knocked twice on the frosted glass window.

'Enter,' came the muffled female response from inside the room.

'Ma'am,' he said simply as he strode towards the front of Judy Marchant's desk.

'PC Stewart,' Judy said as she looked up from a pile of papers.

'Ma'am, PCs Franklin and Isiah wish to submit this report.' He placed the report on the desk. 'It concerns a body they found this morning, that of a Mr Ian Robusch.'

'So why are you delivering this report to me, why are they not doing that?' Judy asked, picking up the report and opening it.

'Ma'am, I would like to respectfully request that I be allowed to attend the scene before Mr Robusch is handed over to the coroner,' he replied.

'And for what reason? The scene has been attended and there seems little in this report to suggest that a second visit would be necessary. This is clearly not a crime scene PC Stewart,' Judy Marchant answered.

'I realise that, ma'am. However, I have good reason to suspect that Mr Robusch's death might be linked to that of James Fortnum.'

'And that reason would be?' Judy Marchant looked up at the young constable.

'Well ma'am, I am not quite sure how I should put this, but ma'am...'

'Come on, PC Stewart, cough it up, we both must have other things to do that are equally pressing, I know I have,' Judy interrupted.

'Ma'am, I am well aware that on both occasions there has been no indication of anyone else being present before, during, or after each death. What is also very clear to me is that it is possible that the causes of death of both Mr Robusch and Mr Fortnum might prove similar enough to suggest that the same fate, whatever that might be, may have befallen them both,' PC Stewart explained.

'Well surely that would be a matter for Dr Anstis to deliberate upon. I am not convinced, PC Stewart, that we need become any more involved in this matter than we already are, at least not now.'

'I would just like to add, ma'am, that it also seems clear to me that we might even be facing another spate of deaths similar to those that occurred six months ago and, although I was not involved in any great detail in those events, I know that you were. This is why I thought it might prove prudent for me to visit the scene, and at least see if this connection might be confirmed or denied from what I find there. Without wishing to sound too dramatic, ma'am, I should also like to suggest that you might consider visiting the scene too. I am eager to make myself available to you ma'am, should you need any further assistance in this matter.'

Judy read the report as she dismissed PC Stewart from the room with a flick of her right wrist. A short while later she marched briskly towards the reception area. Without breaking stride she called PC Stewart over and continued walking down the short flight of stairs towards the exit.

PC Stewart called out to one of the other on duty constables to take over his post and attempted, unsuccessfully, to catch up with his boss. He eased the external rear door open and exited the building, just as Judy Marchant was stepping into her car. Ian Stewart rushed over to the parked car and entered on the passenger side. The car was already being reversed by its driver before he had time to put on his seatbelt. Neither of the car's occupants spoke until the car had nosed out into the side road leading to the main highway that crossed the front of the police station.

'I would like it, ma'am, if you could consider my tagging along should you choose to take up any kind of investigation into these recent deaths. I will admit that I have thought a lot about what might have happened to you and Mr Hooke, and it seems to me, even based on what little I know, that there is something that would warrant further investigation. Even if I could adopt a supportive role to you both, I would appreciate that,' Ian Stewart said without taking his eyes from the road in front.

'Thank you, PC Stewart, I appreciate your offer. But if I am being entirely honest with you, as I feel I should, then I am not so sure that I can count on the support or guidance from our psychic friend if I should take this any further,'

Judy replied, 'it seems that Mr Hooke might have other more pressing issues to deal with.'

'Are you being serious, ma'am?' Ian Stewart asked.

'I am being quite serious. Since the death of Mr James Fortnum I tried to speak with Mr Hooke, and he seemed most keen on avoiding any discussion either about what happened before, or about Mr Fortnum,' Judy Marchant explained.

'But it was him who brought this whole issue to your attention and, at least from where I am sitting, it does seem to be him who is the focal point of everything.'

'Nevertheless, I guess that Mr Hooke has his reasons, and who am I to try to persuade him otherwise?' Judy Marchant replied.

'Ma'am, if I might say so, would it not be nigh on impossible to resolve anything without Mr Hooke's involvement?' PC Stewart asked, thinking it to himself rather than expecting an answer from the senior officer sat next to him.

'Let's just see what we might find, if anything, at Mr Robusch's home shall we?'

*****

With a combination of Judy's dexterity and her skeleton key the door opened easily. It was clear on entry that the flesh of Mr Robusch's face had started to degrade. Judy Marchant entered the apartment first. She beckoned Ian Stewart inside and quickly set about closing the door.

The body lay in the same position as was reported. Ian Stewart stepped across it to the far side while Judy stayed on the near side. Ian Stewart lowered to a crouching position and ran his fingers over the side of the dead man's face. The skin was cold to the touch, and it felt slightly leathery. PC

Stewart withdrew his fingers and rose back up to a standing position. There appeared to be no pool or spatter of blood around the body.

Judy removed her bag and pulled her right arm through the shoulder strap. Cupping the bottom of the small bag in her left hand she opened the top zip and fumbled around its base. She soon found her silver ballpoint pen and lifted it from the bag. Placing the pen between her teeth she zipped up the bag and placed the strap over her right shoulder again.

'What is it?' PC Stewart asked, craning his neck across the dead man but seeing nothing.

Without replying Judy Marchant lowered herself so that her legs bent at the knee and she was seated upon her raised ankles. She moved over the man's body and probed with her pen into the small gap between his neck and the carpet of the hallway. She pushed the end of the pen into the gap, and pressed down on the very corner of the almost wholly hidden item underneath. The sheet of glossy paper was very gently, and very carefully, extracted, millimetre by millimetre. Gradually Judy Marchant was able to expose enough of the paper to reach down and lift the dead man's left shoulder sufficient to fully remove the crumpled paper. She stood up and smoothed out the printed side of the sheet.

The type was set against the watermarked image of a temple. A lit lantern hung from a crooked tree in the foreground, and the address and contact number of the advertiser was set out clearly across the base of the flyer.

"TO THE RULER, THE PEOPLE ARE HEAVEN; TO THE PEOPLE, FOOD IS HEAVEN"
LIMITED AVAILABILITY, REDUCED PRICES THIS WEEK ONLY.

'What is that?' Ian Stewart asked.

'It is an advertising flyer from a Chinese restaurant,' Judy Marchant replied, as she opened her shoulder bag and secreted the flyer inside.

'Does it have any evidential value?'

'I doubt it,' Judy replied curtly.

The remainder of the apartment yielded very little to indicate how Mr Robusch might have died or why. Within minutes the two police officers had removed themselves from the apartment and were returning to Judy's waiting vehicle. Nothing more was said until Judy Marchant stood poised, with her hand on the handle of the door to her office. She turned to face Ian Stewart as he followed her up the small stairway.

'Be sure to release the scene to the coroner's office. We will speak on how best to move this matter forward later,' she said.

She unzipped the bag, reached in and pulled out the recovered flyer. *'What does this mean?'* she thought as she stretched the flyer tightly between her fingers.

Part Three

Crimson

Chapter Nineteen

'PC Stewart, can you come with me please?'

Ian Stewart rose from his seated position and tapped on the right shoulder of the officer seated behind him. Without speaking he released the catch on the swing door that allowed him access to the reception area. He stepped out of the building just as Judy reached her car. He saw the car door open and her head duck inside the vehicle before he had taken the 15 steps to arrive at the passenger side. He opened the door, slid into the car and strapped himself in.

'May I ask where we are going, ma'am?' he asked.

'Dr Anstis called me and suggested I attend his office. He is completing his investigation of Mr Robusch and it seems he has something he wishes to discuss,' Judy Marchant replied.

'And I am here because?' Ian Stewart enquired.

'Because you made it clear that you wished to become involved in this case.' Judy turned to face her junior colleague, 'so now is your chance.'

'Thank you ma'am, I appreciate that.'

'Have you ever attended an autopsy before?'

'No, I have not, ma'am.'

'Ahh, in that case, you are in for a treat, just don't breathe in through your nose too deeply. That would be my advice.'

'Is that what Dr Anstis wants to see us for?' Ian Stewart asked.

'I believe that is what he wants to show us, yes,' Judy replied.

'Show, ma'am?'

'Yes, show. Dr Anstis has called me to his office on four separate occasions, and each time it was so that he could show me the body of a person who was supposedly killed by Mr Hooke's spiritual entity,' Judy explained.

'So what was the cause of death in each case, if you don't mind me asking, ma'am?'

'Unnaturally natural,' Judy replied.

'I am not following you, ma'am.'

'Each death was listed by Dr Anstis as being, though unusual, a result of natural causes,' Judy replied, 'at least that is what his official reports say.'

'So am I right in thinking that Dr Anstis himself believes that something non-human might have caused these deaths?' Ian Stewart asked.

'I would not go that far,' Judy replied.

'Well, what then?'

'Let me put it this way, a death by natural causes can only be applied where there is no other definitive explanation as to what caused the cessation of life. But in these cases, no alternative explanation can only be applied because the cause of death is a mystery and, since it is Dr Anstis' job to determine the cause of death, then the only logical explanation could be death by natural causes,' Judy explained, 'although the evidence would seem to indicate otherwise.'

'So what caused these deaths, if indeed they are all linked, and what indications do we have as to who or what the perpetrator might be?' Ian Stewart asked.

'The answer to both of those questions is unknown.'

'Can I ask what you believe, ma'am?'

'You could ask, but I am not sure that I could offer you an answer. Let me just say that, having seen the evidence for myself, I have more of an open mind about who or what might be responsible than I would have before Len E Hooke walked into my office that first time.'

Coroner's Office procedures were known by Judy Marchant, but for Ian Stewart it was a new experience. On arrival in the preparation room Judy and her accomplice needed to wash and dry their hands. Then open a sealed plastic packet and don the enclosed coveralls to enter the autopsy chamber. First Judy, and then Ian Stewart, removed the ankle-long cape, and tied it around their waists. Finally, they used a mask over their noses and mouths that slipped easily around the back of their ears.

'Are you sure you are ready for this?' Judy asked.

'Ready as I will ever be,' Ian Stewart replied.

With that, Judy Marchant moved to the door connecting the two rooms, peered in through the clear glass inset, and pressed the small red button to the right of the door. The lock released with a loud clunk and Judy passed through the doorway, closely followed by her colleague.

'Ahh, come in, come in please,' Dr Anstis said without rising from the task in which he was involved.

'Dr Anstis, you wanted to see me,' Judy Marchant said.

'I will be with you in just one minute,' Dr Anstis replied, and within that time he had completed the task he was engaged in, 'there, all done. Joe, can you please finish up here and sew this poor unfortunate woman back up again? Neatly as you can, thanks.'

Dr Anstis raised to a standing position and placed the spatula he was holding onto a cloth that lay on top of a small square metal trolley. He beckoned Judy and Ian Stewart towards an examination table next to the one he had been working at.

A prone body covered by two linen sheets lay on the table. There were blood traces where the sheets overlapped, and these travelled up the deceased person's torso. It was clear that this body had not yet been sutured, suggesting that the examination remained incomplete. Dr Anstis moved to the head of the table and beckoned his visitors into a position on either side. The coroner removed the cover from the top of the body.

'It is not so much that I wanted to see you Inspector Marchant, as I wanted to show you this,' Dr Anstis said.

The coroner inserted a spatula into a cut in the man's forehead. Here it was clear that earlier work had been done to create, what looked like, two windows with three deep cuts top, bottom and through the middle. The cuts had been made with precision, each line ruler straight. Dr Anstis lifted the right square of tissue and pulled it back gingerly with his fingers, he reached to his side and lifted a shiny metal clip and clamped it to the flap of tissue. He did the same on the other side, until both flaps exposed the dead man's skull. Judy could see a line that traced the outside of the skin window, into which Dr Anstis inserted his spatula. The front part of the skull came away easily. The coroner moved his spatula a little to remove some of the greyish jelly-like substance from the recent wound, exposing the front of the man's brain. Judy glanced over at Ian Stewart who had started to look decidedly pale.

'Could you both grab a magnifier from the desk behind me please?' Dr Anstis asked, 'now, this is a little bit delicate, and it did take me some time to find it,' the coroner said.

'And what is it that we are supposed to be looking for?' Ian Stewart asked.

'You will see, all in good time,' the coroner replied.

Dr Anstis gently opened up a small slit in front of the brain and twisted the spatula so that the slit opened into a small gap. Inside the gap a tiny blackened object could be seen.

'What is that?' Judy asked.

'If I am not very much mistaken,' the coroner replied, 'that is a dried garden pea. In fact, I found two of them secreted inside this man's brain.'

'What? How could that be? Is somebody having a laugh with us here? Is it the first of April come late?' Judy asked, incredulous as to what was being said.

'Pea brain,' Ian Stewart said simply.

Judy Marchant looked over at him with a look of disdain on her face.

'More than that,' Dr Anstis continued, 'I found these two objects secreted in between the two frontal lobes. The frontal lobes of the human brain are considered to be our emotional control centres, and home to our personalities. They are not the unique controllers of, but they are involved in, motor function, problem solving, spontaneity, memory, language, initiation, judgment, impulse control, and social and sexual behaviour.'

'Dr Anstis, just let me get this right. When you say these two dried peas were secreted there, that is different from inserted right? Am I correct in thinking that it was you who cut open this man's skull?' Judy asked.

'That would be correct.'

'So that must mean that there were no sign of any wounds or scarring before you opened him up in this way.'

'That would also be correct,' Dr Anstis confirmed.

'Are they really two dried pes?' Ian Stewart asked.

'Looking at their composition, I would hazard a guess that this is what they are, yes,' the coroner replied.

'That would have to be impossible. How on earth could two dried peas show up inside a man's brain unless they were put there after he died?' Judy asked.

'Before today I would have agreed with you, it would be impossible. But I can assure you categorically that this man's head was never opened up while he was in life, and the only person to have done anything with his body post mortem would have been me,' the coroner explained.

'So is that what killed him?' Judy Marchant asked.

'Oh no. No, no, no. Mr Robusch's brain stem was severed,' Dr Anstis replied.

'Could that happen naturally?' she asked.

Dr Anstis shook his head vigorously. 'Absolutely not, the vital organs are very well protected, none more so than the brain. The brain stem is key to the operation of everything within the human body, it is the channel of communication through which every part of the body interacts with every other part,' he explained.

'So this is another situation where an internal death blow has been dealt with no external sign whatsoever that any such injury had been inflicted,' Judy suggested.

'Precisely,' Dr Anstis acknowledged.

'Would he have died instantly?' Judy asked of the coroner.

'That depends on whether his brain stem was severed in one blow, or whether it was cut through. The wound looks completely clean, though I would have no way of knowing how long the injury might have taken to inflict,' Dr Anstis replied.

'Can you guess how long he might have survived the injury?' Judy continued.

'If it was a clean severing of the stem, the brain could have survived up to three to four minutes, but messages from the brain to bodily organs would stop immediately, so it is unlikely the heart could continue to function beyond 20 seconds or so. But if the brain stem was severed more slowly, these messages would continue to be delivered and received, until such a time as the cut severed the communicating channels completely. In this case I could not possibly hazard a guess as to how long Mr Robusch might have survived after the first incision,' Dr Anstis replied.

'Would Mr Robusch have known what was going on? And would he be aware it was life-threatening?' Ian Stewart asked.

'Oh, undoubtedly. The human body has a great many protective systems that operate on a subconscious level. Though science cannot prove this fact, there is sufficient intelligence out there to suggest that we can tell the difference between life-threatening, and non-life-threatening, situations and injuries,' Dr Anstis explained.

'So there is a possibility that Mr Robusch could have known that he was dying,' Judy said.

'Oh yes, but only if the brain stem was not severed instantaneously,' Dr Anstis replied.

'Pea brain,' Ian Stewart repeated.

Chapter Twenty

Judy Marchant switched on the small camera pointed to the front and fixed to the windscreen immediately below her rear view mirror.

'I told you that you would be in for a treat,' Judy said to her passenger.

'And in that you were not wrong, ma'am,' Ian Stewart replied.

'I would hope PC Stewart that being a senior officer in the force might mean I get very little wrong, apart from my wardrobe, of course.'

Ian Stewart smiled, but did not reply.

'So tell me what you made of it?' she continued.

'It was weird, to say the least,' Ian Stewart replied. 'I don't understand how anything could kill a man from the inside while leaving no marks. Even when someone dies from internal injuries there are always tell-tale marks on the outside of the body. But the weirdest thing was those two peas inside his brain. What on earth could that possibly mean?' he asked.

'Your guess is as good as mine, but after meeting up with Mr Hooke plenty of weird things have happened, and I can personally vouch for that. But it seems to me it was more of a personal message than anything else.' Judy replied.

'A personal message for who?' Ian Stewart asked.

'Either to the person who discovered them,' Judy turned sharply to avoid another vehicle, 'or to me.'

'Seems a bit too random for that,' Ian Stewart said.

'Maybe not. Don't forget this has been going on for some time now, but the murders seem to be a lot more expressive than they were before. So maybe this thing is taunting us as a further expression of itself, or to prove a point.'

'And what point might that be?'

'The fact that it can do what it likes, when it likes, and there is not a damned thing we can do about it,' Judy suggested.

'So if Mr Hooke himself is not the perpetrator, and I think we can agree on that, could he not in some way be the instigator?' PC Stewart asked.

'If he is, then I don't see how. I cannot deny that there does seem to be a link between these deaths and our psychic friend, but as each day passes that link does seem to be growing more and more tenuous.'

'In what way?' Ian Stewart asked.

'Well, for starters Mr Hooke has made it perfectly clear to me that he wants nothing more to do with this case, and yet since then Mr Fortnum and Mr Robusch have died in strikingly similar circumstances,' Judy replied.

'So why then did both you and Dr Anstis refer to a perpetrator directly being involved? And if that is true, then should not some specific forensic analysis of both scenes be carried out?' Ian Stewart asked.

'Well, this is where the weirdness ratchets up a notch. It is true that in each case the official cause of death reported by Dr Anstis was natural, in other words the involvement of a perpetrator was ruled out. However, the suggestion of Dr Anstis, and I would entirely agree with him, is that some kind of a perpetrator must have been involved based on what he found inside each victim. It stands to reason then, at least officially, that every death scene cannot be deemed as a scene of crime, and therefore need not be subject to any forensic investigation or analysis,' Judy explained.

'And unofficially?' Ian Stewart asked.

'That is a different matter entirely,' was Judy's short reply, 'and one on which I could not possibly speculate.'

'But you do have a theory, right?' Ian Stewart persisted.

'If this was 20 questions, PC Stewart, you would only have two left,' Judy Marchant replied.

'Have you been counting? How very astute of you, ma'am.'

'That was number 19, to which the answer to both your question and follow-up point is why I am a police officer, because of my astute demeanour,' Judy replied.

'Last question,' PC Stewart began.

'Fire away,' Judy replied.

'I have asked this one before, but after seeing Mr Robusch and his injuries I will ask you again, ma'am. Who or what do you believe might be responsible for all of these deaths?'

'If you are asking for an emphatic answer to your question, then I don't have one. But if you would be interested in what I think, then I can give you an answer. What I think is that Mr Hooke might well be right in his argument that there is some kind of an energy that we cannot see, that we cannot sense, that we cannot track, behind these deaths. And the reason I think this is because I can find no better explanation. There are too many similar incidents happening to think they might be coincidental. And I have witnessed things that are beyond my comprehension. You saw the injuries suffered by Mr Robusch. Can you find any rational explanation for them?' Judy asked.

'No, I cannot,' Ian Stewart answered.

'And neither can I. And if Dr Anstis had any way of determining a more logical answer than that suggested by Mr Hooke, then I feel sure he would have given it a long time ago. He has no need to call me in to witness anything other than that which he himself cannot explain. And I can assure you that if there was any professional person who could explode the myth of this rogue entity travelling around killing people as it wished, then Dr Anstis would be that person. There is too much at stake for him not to do that. But he has not, and so, no matter how irrational or implausible the idea might be, it is all I have to go on and I have no choice but to work with it,' Judy explained.

'Is Len E Hooke this guy's real name?' Ian Stewart asked.

'I think you already ran out of questions,' Judy said, 'but no, I do not believe it is.'

Chapter Twenty-One

Judy Marchant took the rest of the day off work.

She could normally be depended on to stay in her office until well after 8 o'clock in the evening. It was not that her job demanded such extended periods of work – on the odd occasion she was required to put in an extra shift – but usually her working hours were contracted just as much as were her colleagues'. But Judy liked to stay until her work was complete.

Not yet a member of the OCD club, Judy did, nonetheless, insist on dotting as many i's and crossing as many t's as she could. Neatness and a sharp attention to detail were her thing at home, and she saw no reason for it not to be so at work too. If she had any children she might be considered a bit of a fussing mother, but those days of trying to procreate to develop new life had not even crossed her mind, and now it was too late, or so she had convinced herself.

Judy liked to have complete control in her life, she liked her personal space too much to share it with anybody. She had been in love before, on a number of occasions, but what seemed like love at the time can so easily be dismissed as having been something different in hindsight. Judy Marchant had never married. How on earth would such a monumental change allow her sense of tidiness and completeness to remain intact? The answer was clearly that it would not, so why even consider marriage?

Judy made an explicit rule that work stays in the workplace. Each time she left the building she left her work behind. She had no problems adhering to her rule but the issues concerning Len E Hooke had refused to budge, ever since her interest had been peaked on her first interaction with Dr Anstis. The questions that were left unanswered by this visit plagued her. Judy insisted on finding answers to every situation that she encountered, and usually she found them, except for this time. It was the evidence she saw for herself, plus the respect she held for Dr Anstis, that kept her interest and determination alive.

*****

Theodore Anstis suddenly turned to his wife, which caused her to drop the TV guide in startled response. He reduced the sound on the television set before speaking.

'Georgie, what if something happens that you just cannot explain, no matter how hard you try? And what if this event defies all possible logical or rational explanation? What if there are no answers, and all you find when looking for an explanation are more questions? How do you think you might react?' he asked.

'Theo, you startled me,' his wife replied.

'Sorry, but this thing is really bugging me.'

'Is this to do with your work?' Georgina asked.

'Well, yes and no, I guess,' Theo replied.

'I thought we agreed that you would not bring your work home with you, and besides, you know I cannot help in any of your scientific investigations, there is nothing I could possibly add which you would not already have explored yourself,' Georgina Anstis replied.

'But this is not a scientific issue, not really, although I guess it is to some degree. Georgie, this is more about how we process things, it is more about a state of mind, about thinking outside of the box, it is a psychological rather than a physical thing.'

'Those are big words, Theo,' she turned to her husband, 'Of course, with any kind of important issue it would be best for me to look at what I can do immediately, then I might look at what might be possible, and finally, if I could do nothing else, I would need to let it rest until it might be possible to do something at another time,' Georgina replied.

'But what if no matter what angle you looked at something, it just did not make any sense?' Dr Anstis asked.

'Well, in that case, and if the situation still bugs you, I guess the only route to go is to look at those answers that might be nonsensical,' his wife replied.

'Yes, that is what I thought you might say, and you are right,' Theodore Anstis said, 'as always. The problem is that I was trained to think in a scientific way, and there is no space for the irrational in science. Either something is, or it is not, there can be no in-between.'

'Well, I guess that this is an in-between moment, and surely that must call for some in-between thinking.'

'You are right again, and that is the problem I face at the moment,' Dr Anstis explained.

'Is it this situation that has been bothering you for the past 10 days? And, if I might say, you seem to have acted similarly six months ago. You got over it then, you must have found some answers that time, so don't the same answers apply this time?' Georgina Anstis asked.

'The situation went away last time. It bothered me for a while and I guess the problem never left my mind, though it was just pushed back while I got on with other things.'

'And now the same situation has come back?' Georgina asked.

'Yes, but maybe because of what happened before it seems to be bothering me more this time around.'

'Don't worry,' Georgina said as she slid across the surface of the sofa. She put her arms around her husband and laid her head gently on his chest, 'you always sort out everything. And I have every confidence that you will do so again.'

'I hope you are right,' Theodore Anstis said unconvincingly, 'I really do.'

*****

Whenever something did not add up, Judy Marchant recalculated time and time again until it did. And so Judy spent the whole of the evening thinking and rethinking every event, every discussion, and every piece of body language she observed that related to the incidents involving this rogue spirit. The evening turned into the early hours of the morning. Judy had decided to review the notes she had taken with a fresh mind the next day, the problem was that each time she resolved to do this so new pieces of information flooded her mind. Judy eventually fell asleep on her sofa with a pen still gripped between her fingers. On waking in the morning she continued to jot things down into her notebook.

'Okay, what am I missing, what is it that I am missing here?' she thought as she sat at her desk that morning. A small pile of papers sat at the right corner of her desk which would need to be reviewed and actioned later. At the moment though, she had no mind to do anything but pursue her current train of thoughts to their natural conclusion.

She decided that a break was as good as a rest. Judy leaned forward, switched on her computer and the machine whirred into life. She waited for the opening screens to pass before she was able to enter a password and get into her documents. Judy took the memory card from her bag and uploaded the images of her most recent car journeys into the computer. On the documents screen she saved the images to a designated file and opened it up. She took a blank sheet of paper from the bottom plastic tray of three that were stacked to the left front of her desk. She placed the paper in front of her and, after a moment's pause, she began writing on the white sheet, frantically scribbling word after word as the computer screen footage flickered in the background.

*****

I pressed the cigarette out into the small blue ashtray that had been emptied that morning. I remained in my seat, took another cigarette from the pack and lit the end of it. If my mind was not settled from one cigarette, I invariably lit another.

Although the plan agreed with Judy was not played out in full, we did manage to trap the spirit inside the pod designated to me in the spirit realm. This was clearly the action required of me by my Guide and, so it seemed, by the Elders that sit at the right hand of God. But recent events introduced doubts that this action was enough to achieve our desired goal.

Judy Marchant was clearly of the opinion that the events of six months ago were repeating themselves, and I had no good reason to doubt her. Ever thoughtful, detailed and voracious in her appetite to draw the final curtain on events, I doubted that Judy would use her valuable time and energy chasing any leads that would not, ultimately, prove fruitful.

So if it was the case that this rogue entity was killing again, to what purpose was the spiritual realm using us to carry out the actions that we successfully did? Could it be that their goals were different to ours and, if so, what were their goals? And why did our spiritual leaders send us on such an ineffective course of action, instead of offering a simple blueprint of how we might finish this entity off, once and for all?

These questions spiralled around and around in my mind. There were many other questions that I had not even contemplated. Questions like, how could a spirit being, supposedly made up of exactly the same essence as every other spiritual entity turn against the realm in which it was created, in such a dramatic way? And, how could our originators create such a wonderfully complex and complete commodity as life, in all its glorious forms, and forget to build in some kind of defence against potentially mutinous acts? Is it simply the fact that they became complacent in assuming that all spiritual entities would toe the official line while carrying out their inevitable duty of existing? And the most basic and simple of all questions, what possible reason could there be for expecting a simple mortal such as me to take up the challenge and defeat such a formidable foe? Why couldn't they clean up their own little mess on their own, being gods and such?

The cigarette ended and I lit yet another. I got up from the chair, put out my cigarette and ran my right hand over the coarse stubble covering my chin.

*****

'Got another one just come in Ian,' PC Redfeld said as he placed a sheet of paper onto the reception desk. 'Ian, another one,' he said again, louder and more insistent this time.

'Oh, right, sorry I was on something else,' PC Stewart replied.

'That's what your wife told me too,' PC Redfeld said, winking as he moved back from the desk.

'That's not funny shit-for-brains,' Ian Stewart replied.

'Whatever. Anyway, I thought you ought to know, just in case you and ma'am are looking for another opportunity to rendezvous.'

'Redfeld, enough is enough. You don't know what you are talking about, so button it, please.' Ian Stewart replied all too aware that he could feel his cheeks starting to flush as he spoke, 'and what's the address, I wanna take a look myself before anyone else nonces up the scene.'

PC Redfeld moved back in towards the sheet on the desk and pointed at it, before smirking at his colleague, and retreating towards the hall that led to the investigation rooms. Ian Stewart plucked a notebook from his top jacket pocket and picked up the piece of paper. After jotting down the address he replaced his notebook and made his way through the barrier and out towards the exit.

*****

Judy Marchant pushed herself away from the desk and looked at her monitor. She saw a clip of the rear of a bus moving ahead as she stopped at a red traffic light. As the bus pulled away she paused the clip and then rewound it. She played it again. On either side of the back of the bus, and below the rear window was an advertising plaque. Each one advertised the book by Len Hooke, *RIP – Synergy*.

She paused the video at the point where the advertising plaques were most visible through the camera lens. She shuffled her feet and moved her chair closer to the desk. She leaned over and peered at the image. She looked away from the bus and at the rest of the screen shot. A small number of people were gathered at the traffic light to the right of where the bus was starting to turn the corner. Other people could be seen mid-walk on the pavement behind the small crowd waiting to cross the road. Towards the front of the screen the number of people thinned out. Further back still she noticed a man in a grey hoodie and blue jeans leaning against the window of a shop. The man's body was at an angle to the camera but his face was looking towards it. At this distance she could make out little of the man's features.

She sped the recording up until it ran to the end. She then played the file all the way through, and nothing out of the ordinary drew her attention. She came out of that file and went into an earlier entry, again nothing of interest. She continued onto her third from last journey, and as she scanned through it she noticed the man with the hoodie again looking towards the camera, this time he was one man in a crowd of people walking towards the car on the passenger side. Only his shoulders and head were visible but, once again, his features were cloaked by the grey hoodie.

Judy went through nine of these files showing the last 22 car journeys., In five of the last 12 journeys she saw the same man in the grey hoodie and blue jeans. In every shot he was facing the camera. At times he was closer to the car than at others, but each time he wore the same clothes and his face was partly obscured. The journeys she covered included an area of some six square miles. She looked again for recognisable scenes, trying to pinpoint exactly where the man had been in shot, then she marked each area in a street index. The places he had been suggested a local man, but little more could be gained. She picked up her phone and keyed in a number.

It was a number she knew well.

Chapter Twenty-Two

'Hello?'

'Len, I will keep this as brief as I can, but I need your help,' Judy said.

'If you want me to get into this case with you the answer remains no, I cannot do it, not just yet anyway,' I replied.

'Well, at least that is slightly more encouraging than the last time we spoke. But that is not why I am calling, not really, at least I don't think it is. I need you to help me find out if someone is following me.'

'I don't deal with stalkers, you do,' I replied.

'Well, this is not a stalking case, at least I do not think so.'

'Judy, why are you so puzzled? You are asking me to help you on something and it seems you have little or no idea what it is about?'

'That is just about spot on,' Judy replied.

'And that is why I am a professional psychic, or at least I was.'

'Was? Have you given that stuff up now?' Judy asked.

'Since the book was published I have been a bit snowed under with appearances, book signings, interviews, it has gone a bit crazy lately.'

'Yeah, the book,' Judy said lazily, 'anyway, there are some crazy things that I am looking into and that is why I need your help.'

'Judy, I really do not have any time to help you on this case, I cannot afford to get involved, and I have already explained my reasoning for that,' I repeated.

'Look, Len, I know what you said, but if I did not feel this was vital I would not ask anything of you. I am not asking you to get involved, I am simply asking for some of your expertise in puzzling something out that, without your help, I will never be able to solve. But it is that important to me Len, please help me,' she pleaded.

'I don't do private sessions now, and I haven't done any for more than three months, I might be very out of practice so our likelihood of success will be greatly reduced,' I explained.

'OK, OK, I accept that, but I can pay you for your time,' Judy said.

'It is not about the money, Judy.'

'I can pay you £100, £200, £300. I don't care how much, but this is so important to me that I must give it a shot. Come on Len, please, you are the only person I can trust,' she begged again.

'When?'

'So you will do it? You don't know how much this means to me, you are a lifesaver Len, and so much more besides,' she replied in a much happier tone.

'I did not say I would do it, I would need to know a lot more about what you want first. I just asked you when?'

'Tomorrow,' Judy replied.

*****

Ian Stewart entered through the front door of the property The first thing he noticed was the smell of room fragrance. The woman who lived here had died in the kitchen, so this was where he headed to first. The room looked neat and tidy. The ambulance crew would have removed the body soon after his two colleagues had vacated the property. From what he knew the deceased woman was 28 and a single mother of a five-year-old child.

A lack of any disturbance inside the house suggested the woman had died alone. Looking around the kitchen Ian Stewart noticed a mobile phone on the worktop. He picked up the phone and pressed the button on the back, but the screen remained blank. Ian Stewart looked quickly across the kitchen worktops for a charging lead. He found one in a small ceramic dish on top of a pine bread bin. He put the thin end into the base of the phone and plugged the lead into a vacant mains socket. He turned away from the charging phone and left the kitchen.

He moved into the lounge. The room opened into a small dining area with patio doors that looked out onto a small lawned area at the back. He moved through the dining area and glanced out onto the garden. Again, there were no signs of any disturbance. He reached for the handle; the door was locked. He moved back into the lounge and again the strong smell of fragrance filled the air. If either of the two sofas in this room had been used, it was obvious that the cushions on them had been placed neatly against the back of the chairs afterwards. Everything in this house seemed neat and tidy, immaculate even.

He returned to the kitchen. The mobile phone showed a five per cent charge, enough to power it up. The menu screen showed seven unopened text messages and three missed calls. Looking at the phone's call listing it showed that the missed calls had all come from the same number, the last call being made four minutes before he had arrived. The unopened text messages were all received within the past two hours, suggesting that the woman had died shortly before this time. It seemed that all the text messages were from the same number as the missed calls.

He opened the messages and scrolled down to the last outgoing one. 'HELP ME' in capital letters was all it said. All the follow-up messages enquired, in one way or another, about what was going on? It was interesting that she should choose to send a text message and not make a call, which might also explain why the emergency services were called after the event and by someone other than the dead woman. While suicide could not be ruled out the evidence seemed to suggest it unlikely. The deceased woman must have been taken by surprise, having had little time to raise an alarm.

Ian Stewart had seen enough. He powered the phone off and placed it with the charging lead on the worktop. He took one last look around the immediate area before striding out through the front door.

*****

Judy Marchant stood in the cold, dim hallway to the front of my apartment. She rubbed her palms and clasped her fingers together as she waited for an answer. 'You look like shit,' was the first thing Judy said to me when I opened the door.

'It is nice to see you too, it's been a long time,' I replied, 'please come in and make yourself comfortable.' I stood back and beckoned Judy inside the apartment.

I knew what Judy was here for and I agreed to help only on the basis that this was a one-time occasion. Judy rested on the sofa and I pulled up a swivel chair, so that I was over Judy's right shoulder and slightly above her head. As I had

167

done before, I prepared Judy for the hypnosis session. It took a little longer this time for Judy to enter a trance state.

When I felt sure that she was sufficiently relaxed, I instructed Judy to imagine she was looking at the image on her desktop computer that most clearly showed this mysterious man she sought to identify. I asked her to make his image bigger, bolder and brighter. I did not ask Judy to involve me in anything she saw, and when I felt sure that Judy was ready, I helped her to zero in on the man's features. I instructed her to peel away any layers of shade or other obstacles to their identity. Judy's eyebrows moved closer together and her forehead creased, and as the skin folded up on itself she peered hypnotically at the image before her, just as if she were looking at a photograph that was none too clear.

Judy's eyebrows raised and pulled her eye sockets open, the two flaps of skin around her pupils pulling tight to remain shut. She opened her eyes suddenly and sat bolt upright on the sofa. She shook her head, pulled her legs to the floor and made a grab for her shoulder bag that sat upon the coffee table in front of her. She stood for a moment in between the sofa and the table.

'Can I get you some water or a coffee maybe?' I asked, as I got up from my seat and moved swiftly to cup her elbow in my hand.

'No, no, thank you, I have to go,' Judy replied abruptly.

'Judy, it is not usual to come out of trance so suddenly, and certainly without the assistance of your therapist. I would prefer that you sit and gather yourself for at least three or four minutes before you can think of leaving,' I said, as she forcibly removed herself from my supporting hand.

'I think it would be much better if I go, but thank you for your help, and I trust that we will talk again sometime soon.'

These words were spoken as Judy turned, removed herself from the lounge area and strode briskly towards the front door. As she opened the latch on the door it was obvious that she was struggling to stand erect. Judy Marchant turned and paced swiftly towards the concrete steps that led to the building exit.

The one image that etched itself into my mind was of how much fear and surprise could be seen in the pupils of her eyes just before she left.

Chapter Twenty-Three

It could be that the killer had tried to mask his deeds so that it might appear that the victim had committed suicide, but their efforts had been poor. For a start the cut on the inside of each forearm would not be so deep or lengthy. Second, the killer must have known that even had the victim been able to apply such a cut to one arm, they would have bled out and died before having a chance to make an identical cut on their other one. Another telling point was that each cut was so precise as to follow exactly the course of the radial artery from wrist to elbow, even where it overlapped the median cubital vein, so that vessel remained undisturbed.

It was the precision of the death-dealing cuts that awakened Dr Anstis' interest more than anything else. And why would a killer take so long making such precise cuts especially when the victim's blood would inevitably be covering them from head to foot. The initial analysis, carried out by the Scenes of Crime Officers, showed blood spatter across a wide area in the bedroom at the point where the victim was slain. Other than that, there were no signs to suggest the presence of another person.

Linsey Baird-Waugh had been 21 at the time of her death. She was single and worked as an air hostess for a well-known UK-based airline. The early indications were that Linsey led a happy and fulfilling life. There was little in her past that might raise concern, no indications of any family trauma, no financial or relationship issues. There seemed little point in the death of a happy, pretty, stable young lady in such a way. Miss Baird-Waugh was delivered to Dr Anstis on the same day that Katie Morgan, a 28-year-old mother of one, had been brought in. Ms Morgan's body was laid out and being prepared by Joe Walker when Miss Baird-Waugh's body had arrived. Looking more closely at the cuts to Miss Baird-Waugh's arms it was impossible for Dr Anstis to determine which was made first.

Since taking up his office it had been Dr Anstis' job to inform the relevant authorities of the cause of death on all of the bodies that passed before him. Only recently had he found that he was not, at least to his own satisfaction, able to do that. The internal injuries he had witnessed on some bodies were just too implausible to have been caused by any natural chain of events, so, could that possibly mean that they were made by supernatural means?

This was an issue so far wide of Dr Anstis' remit that he simply could not report what he had found in any of these cases. And even if supernatural causes were in play, how could a human body be entered with no physical signs or symptoms on the outside? The human body contains a complex system of defence and attack against any intruder, so even if a force or foreign object were able to enter, how could these natural security systems be bypassed?

Miss Baird-Waugh had presented a different challenge. It would be impossible to write off her death as being by natural causes. The authorities would no doubt be looking for a killer even one that might have tried to make it look like a suicide. Dr Anstis alone would know, from the precise and calculated fatal cuts that Miss Bair-Waugh had fallen victim to the same unknown assailant as all those other young people who had passed through his workplace in the recent past.

The question now had to be why this entity would create such a mess? What could its motive be? It had shown before how subtle and calculated it could be, so there seemed little sense in creating such a bloodbath at the scene. Unless, of course, this was done with good reason. And why the gap between the first spate of deaths and now? These were matters for Inspector Judy Marchant and not for Dr Anstis, though this did not stop it weighing heavily on his mind.

This time Dr Anstis did not need to open up Miss Baird-Waugh to determine the cause of death. *Precise incisions in the radial artery in both arms* was listed as the cause of death. It was up to SOCOs to reach their own conclusions based on what they might, or most likely would not, find at the crime scene. Dr Anstis would fill out his report with other observations, but none as telling as this one. He asked Joe Walker to clean up the cadaver as much as possible, and moved over to the next lifeless body.

Dr Anstis lifted the light blue cover from the face and, noting immediately the young age of the victim, he glanced up again at the bloodied cover over Miss Baird-Waugh.

'Here we go again.'

*****

Ian Stewart spent four nights looking for unexplained deaths on the internet, and he found very little. There was plenty of historical data but nothing that might help him answer the many questions he had about recent events. The deaths of Ian Robusch and James Fortnum seemed to fit the pattern of those followed by Judy Marchant six months earlier and, though he had no solid proof in the case of the young lady's apartment he just visited, he was of the opinion that she lost her life in a similar fashion.

Judy Marchant had told him some of the background to these cases but he was finding it hard to fill in the gaps. Whether she deliberately kept information from him or not was irrelevant, what mattered to him was doing his best to get a clearer picture in his mind that he could work with. Six months ago it seemed that all these deaths were linked to the psychic, Len E Hooke, but now things were different. According to Judy Marchant Mr Hooke had refused to become involved this time around, and it seemed that she might prefer it that way too. So why the change? Why now did these three deaths appear, at least at first glance, to be unconnected to the psychic? Mr Hooke readily admitted that he had known, or had come into direct contact with, some of the earlier victims, but not this time around. A criminal psychologist will tell you that the MO of a serial killer is unlikely to change to any great degree from their first murder to the last, so could the answer lie in the fact that this killer really was not of human origin?

*****

Judy Marchant returned home tired and weary. The last two weeks had passed in a whirlwind of unexplained events and dramatic revelations. She strode quickly into the kitchen and popped two pain relief tablets into her hand, she half-fill a tumbler with water and swallowed the tablets in one gulp. Judy was unaccustomed to the pain that throbbed in her forehead. She sat eyes closed and motionless on the sofa in her lounge, waiting for the medication to take full effect.

Eventually Judy released the loafers from her feet and attempted to stand up, but was gripped with the pain once again as she rose from a seated position. She bent down, picked up her shoulder bag and placed it on the coffee table. The pocket fell open as the bag material settled onto the hard surface. She selected the Chinese restaurant flyer from the bag and pulled the edges tight to smooth out its creased surface.

Judy heard her letterbox lid shut with a sharp metallic clang. She rose and walked to the hallway to retrieve whatever it was that had been posted through the front door. No letters, but two flyers, one for a local estate agent and one for a local spiritualist church advertising a service that evening. Something in the flyer caught her attention, and one question flew into her mind. Why would they send out flyers for a service on the same day it happened? She held the flyer between her hands before folding it neatly in half.

On returning to the lounge she placed the flyer carefully into her shoulder bag, picked the bag up, slipped on her shoes, and headed for the front door.

*****

Theodore Anstis sat for some time in the driver's seat before he started the engine of his car. In the relative quiet of the walled car park he contemplated the validity, or otherwise, of his recently drawn assumptions. There really was nothing else he could do. Not much was making any sense to him at the moment and yet, somewhere, on a deeper physiological level, it did, perfectly.

Dr Anstis earned his money by telling the truth, this was something that was sacrosanct in his profession. But recently he had found it necessary to hide certain crucial facts in the reports he had made, and that did not sit comfortably in his mind. The necessity of his lies could not be doubted, but that did not make accepting them any easier. But the issues clouding his mind were more to do with the causes of these bodies turning up on his slabs than any outcome in his findings.

Having two lifeless bodies on his slabs at the same time was not unusual, especially in cases of road traffic accidents. When exiting the examination theatre this evening the two bodies he left behind were different in crucial ways, not in who they had been in life, but in the injuries each had sustained. One body had seemingly been attacked internally with no external clues as to the death-dealing blows' origins, while on the second body the killing force was clear for all to see. These bodies arrived within two hours of each other.

At first glance, the differences in injuries and causes of death would appear disparate, but Dr Anstis' recent experiences had taught him that these two bodies were linked, at least so far as the protagonist was concerned. In the case of the first body it was perfectly clear, a killing with no traceable external injury, it had to be him, or more precisely it. But it was equally clear that the exactitude of the injuries, and with the improbability of their being self-inflicted on the second body, must mean that the same entity was responsible for both.

*****

Judy Marchant stood at the entrance to her neighbour's flat. Donna Elliot came to the door in a navy blue dressing gown and matching slippers. She pulled the top of the gown together as she opened the door.

'Oh, Judy, you would be the last person I might expect to see on my doorstep,' she said.

'Yeh, I know, it has been a while,' Judy replied.

'So to what do I owe this unexpected pleasure?' Donna asked.

'It's OK, I don't need to come in or anything,' Judy said as she reached into her shoulder bag, 'it's just that this flyer was put through my door about five minutes ago, and I wondered if you knew anything about this place?'

Donna took the flyer and opened it up.

'The White House Spiritualist Group,' she said looking up from the flyer, 'I can't say I know anything about them, and I didn't get one of these sheets either,' she said.

'I am thinking of going along to their service this evening, but to tell you the truth, I have never been to a spiritualist meeting and I don't know what to expect.' Judy looked Donna up and down briefly before continuing, 'and it seems you might not be able to come along with me.'

'I'm sorry Judy, it is awfully late notice. That service starts in 25 minutes and I'm kinda settled in with the kids for the evening,' Judy's neighbour replied.

'Yeah, I'm sorry. But can I ask you what it might be like?' Judy asked.

'Well, I have been to a few of these services. Most likely there will be a group of chairs facing a small stage, that is if it is a service and not some kind of a group meeting. If it is a service, a medium will appear on the stage and start giving supposed messages from deceased relatives or loved ones to members of the audience.'

'Supposedly?'

'Well, let me just say that sometimes these messages might just be simple like they send you their love and things like that. You can tell how good a medium is by the detail they give, and whether this can be easily accepted by a member of the audience. If they avoid providing names or details of places and events it could all be made up. The audience at these places can, at times, be a bit susceptible, a bit vulnerable,' Donna explained.

'I see. Sorry I troubled you. You have been a great help, thanks Donna.'

Judy turned away from the door. She heard it close immediately. She looked again at the flyer, and then placed it into her bag before descending one floor to exit the building. As she approached her car the phone in her bag started to ring. She reached in and switched the phone to silent.

*****

The White House Spiritualist Group did indeed meet in a white house. There were no parking spaces immediately in front of the house, so Judy parked up and walked a short distance to the front door. She took one more look at the flyer before pushing open the door and venturing into the large reception area. A short, middle-aged man stood behind a reception desk just inside the door.

'Are you here for this evening's meeting?' he asked.

'Erm, yes I am.'

'Have you ever visited us before?'

'No, I haven't,' Judy replied.

'The meeting is being held inside the first door on the left, this way,' he pointed to the left, 'the meeting started ten minutes ago, but you should be able to slip in quietly at the back of the room somewhere,' he added.

'Thank you very much,' Judy replied, and then set off as quietly as she could towards the heavy panelled wooden door he had indicated.

Judy tiptoed towards the last row of seats and sat in one at the left of the room, next to mirrored glass panels that ran from floor to ceiling all the way to the small stage at the front. A few heads turned in her direction as she entered the room, but not too many, it seemed most of the people there were more focused on the two people on the stage, than on her.

She gently, and as quietly as she could, slid her shoulder bag from her left arm and onto the floor next to her chair. The room was set out with nine rows of eight chairs, with a two-metre gap in between. There was a three- metre gap from the front row of chairs to the stage, and a similar gap behind Judy to a large bay window. Red curtains of a light material covered the window with a small gap in the middle. The sun shining through the curtains gave a dull reddish hue to the rear of the room. On a table on the stage three white candles burned brightly, and these were supplemented by five candles placed equidistant on the right side of the room, the same side Judy had entered from.

Judy guessed that the audience occupied around 70 per cent of the chairs available. In her row only one person sat on the opposite side of the room. On the stage one man, in his 40s, made notes on a pad laid across his lap. He occasionally looked up at the medium who paced slowly in front of the stage, stopping when he identified someone for whom he had a message.

The medium finished the latest reading with a well-practised smile and an expression of love to the tearful recipient. He straightened himself up and moved slowly across to the other side of the room, to Judy's side. He raised a hand to his creased forehead and posed theatrically. He pointed, seemingly directly at Judy. Her heart began to pump faster, and she could feel a warm blush flood up her neck and into her face. She was just about to point to her chest to ask if the message was for her when the two ladies in front of her squirmed around in their seats.

'Yes, you two young ladies.' They were both at least 50. 'I am being drawn towards the lady nearest the mirror on the wall.' He looked at them and his pointed finger moved up and down urgently, 'yes, you my love.'

The medium went on to describe someone who wanted to leave a message. The message was very vague, and consisted mostly of warmth and affection being sent by a spirit from beyond the grave, apparently. The eccentricity of the medium added to his performance and almost willed his audience to believe in what he said. He delivered his messages with a force that it was hard to deny. Each message delivered since Judy had arrived ran the same way, with incorporated vagueness and charm in equal measure. Judy looked at her watch for the umpteenth time. It was now 18 minutes since she had sat down in the hall and the medium was on his third communication. The meeting had started 10 minutes before she arrived so, even allowing for settling in, introductions, and a few opening prayers, it seemed likely that the service would draw to an end very soon. Judy glanced into the mirror beside her. The dull appearance of the room was quite soothing, and the flickering candles at the front and sides added to the relaxation she felt. 'Yes, and the lady behind. Sorry you had to come on your own this evening but if it is your first time here I feel sure you might make some friends before the evening is out,' the medium said.

The two ladies in front of Judy both turned towards her, one of them raising her eyebrows. Judy turned slowly from the mirror and looked towards the medium. He waved a finger energetically in her direction, his eyes burning into hers.

'Yes, you madam. You are most welcome to our group, and I do have someone here who wants to make contact with you. They came through very quickly and strongly, so I would just like to address what they have to say before we close for the evening,' he said.

'Erm, yes, thank you,' Judy said, as she adjusted her position to sit more upright and at least appear more alert than she felt.

'Forgive me, we have never met before today, but I feel like I know you very well. I know this audience are ready for their tea and cakes but there really is only one message that I have for you. You used to have little faith but you are being shown some things now that are opening up your eyes. You have visited some dark places recently, and this is what is guiding you, in fact, if it were not for you seeing these things for yourself, then you would never have believed them. But let me tell you that what you have seen is all real. You should trust what is inside of you, what is inside your heart centre, in here,' and he patted his chest several times.

'Yes, thank you,' Judy acknowledged.

'You need to balance your head and your heart centres so that you can fulfil your purpose. This is what you were created for, and now, it is time for you to accept it,' the medium smiled, 'there is an angel that stands by your side, and you have seen him already. Your angel is giving you signs, look for them, they are there to guide you. I am being told that you should stay in contact with a man; his initial is L, Les, Len, something like that, and I know that you can accept this. You two had a bit of a problem, but it's only a misunderstanding, that's all' the medium continued.

'Thank you,' Judy acknowledged.

The medium abruptly stopped, staring directly, piercingly, into Judy's eyes. He staggered a little, and put one hand to his head. He moved jerkily backwards and felt for the small stage behind him.

The man at the table urgently bent down to whisper something into the medium's ear. The medium held up his hand in acknowledgement of what had been said, and the man picked a microphone off the table and swiftly brought the meeting to an end. He invited all those attending to partake of tea, coffee and biscuits in an adjoining room and hastily ordered the doors to the room to be opened. Judy stood up and followed the crowd through the door, glancing back at the medium and his helper as she did so. The man at the table bent down, and with his arm around the back of the medium he helped the stricken man to his feet. The medium looked up at Judy as he moved into a standing position, still clutching at his head.

Judy got herself a coffee and a man approached, coyly stirring coffee with a thin white plastic stick inside a brown plastic cup.

'Amazing reading,' he said, without looking up from what he was doing.

The man appeared to be in his mid-30s. He was dressed in brown corduroy trousers that flapped lazily over the top of his sneakers. He wore a thick V-neck brown patterned jumper that hid a light blue shirt and red tie.

'I hope we will see you again,' he added, still stirring at his coffee.

'Sorry, erm yes, it was very interesting, but a bit too dramatic at the end, don't you think?' she asked.

'Spirit works in mysterious ways, or so we are led to believe,' the man said.

'Well, I get more than enough mystery at work. I kinda hoped that the spirit realm might be a bit more forthcoming with their signs and what they want us to do,' Judy replied.

'I think there is more hope of man getting irrefutable proof of life on another planet than of spirit sending messages needing no interpretation,' the man answered.

Judy looked up from her phone and directly at the man, 'Oh and that is one thing I never understood, why do you think that might be?' She held up a finger as the man looked up from his coffee. 'Don't tell me, we have to find out for ourselves and that is the whole objective of life. Is that it?' she asked pointedly.

'I guess that just about sums it up, the man replied.

'And do these meetings always end so dramatically?'

The man laughed gently, 'erm no, in fact tonight made a refreshing change,' he leaned towards Judy and cupped a hand to his mouth, 'it can be a bit staid in here most times.'

Judy looked at her phone, 'I am very sorry, but I need to make an urgent call, would you excuse me, please?'

The man wiped his right hand across the front of his jumper and held it out to Judy.

'Yes, of course. I am Ben Westland, I think I can speak for everyone here in saying you are most welcome to the White House at any time,' he said.

Judy took the man's hand in hers and limply shook it.

'Erm, yes, thank you. Will you excuse me, please?'

Judy walked briskly towards the entrance door. She could sense Mr Westland watching her as she made her exit, but she did not look back. She stood under the wide porch that covered the doorway. Small raindrops drifted down across the street lamp opposite as Judy tapped some numbers into her phone.

Her call was answered on the fourth ringtone.

'Dr Anstis, you called me, sorry I could not get back to you earlier,' Judy said into the phone's small mouthpiece.

'Yes, yes. Inspector Marchant, I have two more bodies here, Linsey Baird-Waugh and Katie Morgan, who were 21 and 28. It is my belief that these two young ladies' lives were cut short by your spiritual killer. It seems that Ms Morgan died with no external signs of trauma, but Ms Baird-Waugh was found in a bit of a blood bath. It's a real mess, apparently.'

'What happened?' Judy asked.

'Ms Morgan suffered from a split in her kidney. Usually this would give her up to an hour to get the wound fixed, but her death would almost certainly have been instantaneous due to the size of the cut. Miss Baird-Waugh had the insides of both her forearms split wide open from wrist to elbow. The police are treating her death with suspicion,' Dr Anstis reported.

'If it is a crime scene why haven't I heard anything?' Judy asked.

'SOCOs took over immediately. I got the body nearly three hours after she was discovered. They are still at the scene now I think.'

'So why are you connecting the two, if SOCOs think Ms Baird-Waugh was murdered?' Judy asked.

There was a short pause before Theodore Anstis continued.

'Inspector Marchant, my understanding is that the first reports suggested there was no immediate evidence of anyone else being at Miss Baird-Waugh's place before, during, or after she died. Also, the depth and precision of the wounds would make it impossible for them to have been self-inflicted. That is why I am linking these two deaths,' Dr Anstis explained.

'Do you need me to come down there?' Judy asked.

'I don't think that is necessary, I just thought you needed a head's up on what is going on here. The question is, why has this entity decided to make its attacks more noticeable?' Dr Anstis asked.

'Or even eye-catching. Correct me if I am wrong Dr Anstis, but didn't that rent-a-yob Jared Williams die in the bath of similar wounds to Miss Baird-Waugh? And what about the kids on the minibus? They all died from external injuries resulting from the crash, right?' Judy asked.

'Well actually, no they didn't, at least not all of them,' Dr Anstis stated.

'What?'

'Jared Williams died of small incisions on his wrists, it was the water in the bath that kept his wounds open long enough for him to die. As for the girls on the bus, I had to do autopsies on all of the bodies. In my opinion, at least seven out of 13 of those girls departed this life before their bodies suffered any trauma from the crash,' Dr Anstis stated.

'Why on earth didn't you tell me this at the time?' Judy asked.

'With the grief of the families and passions running high in the community it just didn't seem appropriate, but it does now,' Dr Anstis explained, 'so I will stand by what I said. It seems that, for some unknown reason, this entity has decided to act out whatever it is doing in a much more graphic way than before.'

Judy Marchant pulled her forefinger and thumb tightly across her eyes towards the bridge of her nose as the rain outside the meeting hall increased in strength.

'OK, thanks Dr Anstis, please keep me in touch with any new developments,' she said, before quickly pressing the red button to end the call.

Judy looked over her right shoulder and saw the medium pressing the key fob that unlocked his car. He quickly stepped into the driver's side. She put her shoulder bag over her head and moved quickly towards his car.

She ran across the front of the car to the front passenger door just as the man inside started the engine. Raindrops fell increasingly heavily upon the bag which became less and less effective a shield on her head. Water now cascaded down her face from the dripping strands of hair that draped across her forehead. The man inside the car had seen her, she was sure of that, but so far he had failed to acknowledge her presence.

Judy knocked three times on the window. The man did not respond. Judy saw him shift the gearstick into its first slot but the car did not move. She banged harder on the window, this time with her fist. The man inside pressed a button and the front side window slid down a couple of inches. The man turned to face her but he did not speak.

'What did you see?' Judy shouted above the sound of the rain, 'tell me what you saw at the end of the reading?' Judy asked.

'I gave you a reading, there was no more,' the man said, stoically.

'Don't lie to me, if this journey of mine is so important you must tell me what happened to you at the end of my reading,' Judy continued, 'You collapsed onto the stage, you must have seen something that you did not want to reveal to the audience in there tonight, so tell me what it was, please.' she pleaded.

The man released the car into neutral, removed his feet from the pedals, and leaned across as far as the seat belt would allow him to.

'I am sorry Miss, but I really must get going.'

The man put the car into gear again and started to move away. Judy gripped the top of the window with her fingers and shuffled beside the car as it started to move.

'Please,' Judy begged, 'if you know something you must tell me,' she pleaded.

The man looked at the road ahead and then immediately returned his gaze to Judy.

'You must be careful, you must keep your wits about you at all times. Trust no-one. Something is watching you. Something does not want you to succeed in what you are doing. If you are not careful, you will be in grave danger,' he warned.

'What kind of danger?' Judy asked, shivering as the cold rain began to bite at her skin through her clothing.

'If two become one a river of crimson will flow and destroy anything that gets in its path,' the man replied before raising the window and sealing it shut again.

Judy Marchant removed the bag from above her head and backed away from the car, as the driver shifted into gear and drove off into the night.

Chapter Twenty-Four

Communicating with God always takes a lot of getting used to. When talking with another person it is not hard to predict reactions and topics that might arise, but speaking with God is different. The conversation can take unexpected turns and the responses are wildly unpredictable. God has shown me Its sense of humour, Its compassion, and Its wisdom. It has also shown to me Its vulnerability.

God seems to show no fear of challenge or attack. I am not sure if this is because no such challenge has arisen before or if God just accepts that whatever happens is meant to be. The longer this spiritual entity was free to kill people the more apparent it seems to me there is a bigger purpose to its actions than just taking lives, but I am struggling to understand what impact this could have on the spirit realms. Was it really possible that God could be overthrown by a single energetic force which, in essence, is already a part of Itself?

'If everything is perfect then how can this entity kill people before their time?'

'And who ever said everything is perfect?'

'Isn't that how the spirit world is? Isn't that the grand plan? Isn't that the reason for life?'

'The spirit world, just as with your planet and all others, must always be a project in progress. All life seeks to evolve,

to develop beyond what it is now, whether animal, plant or mineral, that is the definition of life.'

'Then why do so many bad things happen?'

'What is bad? There is no bad, something is only bad if that is how you, as an individual, define it.'

'Come on now, so many people suffer in terrible ways, how can that be good?'

'Again, sufferance is a personal definition. All is most definitely not perfect, if it were there would be no point in its continuance, and the same applies to the spiritual realms, and beyond. While physical entities might feel pain, whether physical or psychological, there can never be spiritual pain, unless, of course, there is.'

'And what is spiritual pain?'

'Spiritual pain can only arise from a lack of learning. In the spiritual realms we have emotion but it is not like human emotion. It is more akin to an aching for something that might fail to materialise. We are linked, as you already know. You are one with your soul and spirit selves, but you are also one with the whole of creation, with all life, with God and what lies beyond. And all of everything is evolving, developing into the next best version of what it is now.'

'Even God?'

'God, and what lies beyond God.'

'So a lack of development, of evolution, is cause for spiritual suffering?'

'Not just for the individual but for all of everything.'

'But I thought you said there is no bad?'

'Suffering is not bad. For spiritual essences to suffer is good for their development. Disappointment, regret, anger, jealousy and all other feelings that you might consider negative or bad, are some of the most influential learning tools you have.'

'The karmic balance of life.'

'If you choose to use that phraseology, yes.'

'So for everything good that happens something negative must balance it, and for everything bad that happens then good must arise as a result.'

'Not in such a basic form, no. You cannot know good without knowing bad and vice versa, it just so happens that there is no greater lesson to be learned about something than in the experiencing of it. And in your own existence something must be given up to make space for something else. I am not just talking about your spiritual existence, I am including all of life, every strand to which you are connected as an individual, and this means everything of which it is possible to conceive and beyond. The all of everything.'

'A trade off. You scratch my back and I will scratch yours,' I suggested, in thought form.

'A trade off yes, but not of both sides giving and receiving. Since all of creation is connected to each individual energy vessel you can only take from and give to yourself, in whatever form that part of you is defined.'

'Is that how it is in prayer? When a person prays for something, for themselves or for someone else, they are prepared to trade a part of them that already exists?'

'In one form or another, yes. If you do this for me then I promise I will do that for you although, as I have already explained, to an energy vessel there is no external you, there is only me and my connection to the all of what is.'

'Is that how God is? I thought God did things with no need for any payback, just out of love, commitment, and Its wish to experience evolution in individual life forms.'

'So what is the praise that is offered to God in prayer, in words and in song, if not an invitation to trade either now or at some time soon? Do people not pray to stay on the good side of God to join It when physical life ends? And before *any acts of penance, or supposed acts to curry favour with God, can the words not be spoken that 'Allah is great, praise be to Allah?'*

'Now hang on a minute. You are talking about acts of terrorism in the same breath as someone offering praise to breathe life into a baby who is dying.'

'Yes.'

'How can you do that?'

'Because in both scenarios, in all possible scenarios where a trade is offered, the belief is that God will act on your behalf if you offer something in return. With no such trade it is believed that no miracles would be possible.'

'Is it a miracle? Is it God's work to blow up innocent bystanders by igniting a pack of Semtex strapped to your body on a crowded bus?'

'In the belief of the individual making the trade one scenario has no greater outcome than the other. God is the same as everything human, plant and mineral. All of life is a trade-off. As a child you can only expect to get something good if you behave in a certain way, and you know that good behaviour brings rewards. That is how you learn, and this is the essence of what you might call karma.'

'So we are all kids?'

'Well, it could be said that the main role of a child is to learn how to grow into an adult version of itself, and even in your adult version you are all on a learning path, but it is not about learning of other people or other things. The exploration of life is extremely beneficial and it does have learning potential, but learning about yourself is much more empowering. It is paramount, it is the only way to evolve. And that is the sole reason for which God was created, to learn of itself and to evolve through the experience of its smaller selves, through you and all of creation.'

'So we, as individual elements of God, exist only to serve God.'

'In one way, yes, I suppose you are right. But you have your own individuality, and you are free to use that in whatever way you choose. Any and every decision you make will lead to you evolving into an ever greater version of yourself. There can be no mistakes, no wrong turns, and this is because every experience you have, good or otherwise, leads to knowledge, and knowledge leads to the process of evolving of self. And through your experiences God evolves too.'

'God evolves? I would have thought that God was the epitome of an evolved energy already,' I suggested.

'Every life term lived by every form of life, in a physical sense, is a life lived by God. There is only one goal of life and that is evolution, therefore the one aim of God can only be to continue to evolve through the experiences of the individual parts of God that take on a physical form.'

'That is a difficult concept to come to terms with because of the distance that most people put between themselves and God. I think it would be fair to say that God is more seen as a controlling influence that creates situations, circumstances, and sometimes even feelings for people, that are both good and bad.'

'And on what basis would you have God make such decisions? Who should God bless with wealth and abundance in their lives and who should It damn?'

'I don't know, but most people might think that God acts based on prayer, sacrifice, or on goodwill to others.'

'Based on the circumstances set up by God?'

'Well, yes.'

'It doesn't work like that, and by It I mean God and the process of creation.'

'Well, how then?'

'People do things for themselves, good or otherwise. After every decision, no matter how big or small, a chain of likely events is established. It is that chain of possible events that God has a hand in creating, not the outcomes.'

'So what happens when we pray? Are we not asking for specified outcomes to be delivered by you?' I asked.

'Prayer can have the effect of creating new outcomes, of course it can, but any possible outcomes depend on the trade being offered, either consciously or subconsciously.'

'So, we return to the fact that if you do this for me, I will do that.'

'Yes, always, we will return to the process of life.'

'But God does things for us all the time.'

'That is also true.'

'So we are as children, and we are rewarded for good behaviour.'

'You are rewarded for gaining good experience, no matter whether that experience feels good to you or not.'

'And it is God who rewards us.'

'No. God can create a new set of options and opportunities for growth, but it is always the decision of each life form that determines how events might play out. The reward is there as an automatic by-product of the choices made. Don't forget that life experiences, whether they are perceived as positive or negative, will always be evolutionary. So it is not God which has the role of rewarding or punishing presumed good or bad behaviour, there can be no such thing. The reward in any kind of behaviour is that of growth through the experiences that follow each decision that is made, and each decision is entirely down to you, as a life form.'

'So when I ask God to perform some kind of act to create better circumstances for me, I am offering something in return to myself?'

'You may be asking God to create better circumstances, but it is you who are responsible for creating all the circumstances of your life, not God. The biggest single barrier created by mankind against evolution is their refusal to look inside. It is much easier to blame someone, or something else, for your misfortune, but that is never the case. Nobody, not even family members, lovers, children, nobody matters in your life. These people are there only to play a role in your life, as you are for them. It is only how you react to these people, and to the situations in your life that decides whether or not similar misfortune will, or will not, continue. It is the God inside each and every one of you that creates your future and decides whether or not you have taken the steps necessary in your own personal learning process. In asking God for help in creating better circumstances, and in believing that will happen, you are simply getting in touch with the God inside of you. That is your only trading partner.'

'Wow, that is a massive concept to take on board.'

'It is not a concept, it is the process of life living. A person might trade an old behaviour for a new one. Changes in a person's life can never happen without changes from within taking place. That is the trade.'

'And is this always the case?'

'Well yes, of course, otherwise the trade cannot happen.'

'And what I am offering is the experience of what I have done, or are yet to do.'

'That is always the case, yes.'

'So life readjusts itself based on individual circumstances, decisions, and events?'

'Yes.'

'Like a big computer?' I asked.

'That is an excellent analogy. Life is just like a big computer program. Humans never realised how close they

came to Godhood when creating the computer. Life is a part of something bigger, just as organisms, even the smallest of them, all form a part of the human body, but everything is a part of something bigger without ever having any knowledge of that bigger form, and human life is just a small part of a much bigger energetic flow. There is no beginning and there will be no end. Each energetic being has always existed in one form or another and will continue to exist, forever and ever, Amen.'

'And what about this spirit that is killing young people outside of the natural rules of life?'

'The only natural rule of life is that of continued evolution. There are no other rules. Every living thing at its core is a spiritual entity, it is what we come from and it is where we go to. At some stage the entity responsible for these deaths made the decision that this is what it would do as part of its evolution. Whether in life or as a purely energetic form, all have decisions to make all of the time. That is the life balance.'

'Even for those people whose lives were cut short.'

'For everyone and everything.'

'Even God?' I asked.

'Particularly God. It was always meant to happen based on the decisions that were made. The opportunities created by these decisions are a natural outcome of them, and this spiritual entity just needed to wait until the circumstances were right, for it to happen.'

'So if you knew that there was the very real prospect that this entity would kill people, hijack their spirits and use them to build up a following, with the intention of overthrowing God, why not build in a defence to stop that from happening?'

'That would be to interfere with the natural order of things, and nothing, not even God, has any right to do that.'

194

'So how to destroy it?'

'I said before that energy can never be destroyed, but it can be dissipated.'

'So what might happen if this spiritual killer dissipates?'

'Well, it could be weakened so as to be ineffective, or…'

'Or what?'

'All energy has a natural tendency to act like a magnet. If this particular entity were dissipated it is likely that the smaller parts of the whole would become a part of other energetic entities.'

'Then why instruct me to join with it in the capsule?'

'There was no instruction, there can never be. God does not give orders. Options and opportunities can be offered to you, but you chose to act as you did through your own free will. And as a result of your actions, this entity can now be better tracked.'

'Tracked?'

'Yes.'

'I don't understand. How can it be tracked, what has changed?'

'Being encased within your capsule, this entity is no longer free to roam as it once did.'

'But it is free to continue killing people.'

'It seems so, yes, but that is because it now has greater access to your world.'

'How? In what way?'

'This entity has always been a part of you, but with a human host it may be possible to merge with you so that its power on the earth would be magnified, since having been joined before, strength in the bond between you would be significantly increased. There might also be a possibility, albeit a small one, that the entity could take over control of your mind and your soul by manipulation.'

'You mean it could possess me?' I asked, incredulous.

'Not in so many words, but the principle remains, yes.'

'So possession is possible.'

'No, let's get this straight. You would not be possessed but it might be possible that one third of the entities that as a whole make up you, could exert sufficient influence over the other two as to effectively take control, at times, of those other parts.'

'What? How did that happen? I mean, it might have been nice to have been given a choice in the matter.'

'You did have a choice, and this was the trade offered by you at the time. In return you got the ability to do what you always wanted to do,'

'Which is?'

Chapter Twenty-Five

The girl was found in her bedroom face down on the floor. A pool of blood had spread in the gap between the duvet cover, which was ruffled and pushed from the top towards the middle of the bed, and the pillow. Blood spatter covered the fabric headboard and had flicked some way up the wall behind. The girl had fallen from the bed to the floor and was likely still alive when hitting the carpet. A much smaller pool of blood had collected beneath her neck.

The girl was Bekki Axford and she was seventeen years of age. Her parents, Harold and Claire, were asleep in the next room when Bekki had met her untimely demise. She had been strangled and then her throat had been slit almost to the point of decapitation. There could be no doubt that Bekki had been murdered, and whoever had done this had taken their time to make sure of carrying out a thorough job on the girl. What was not so clear to SOCOs was why there were no traces of any other person having being present at the scene of the crime. After SOCOs had left, Bekki's parents were escorted by two policemen to the station to answer some questions They were both clearly in a very distressed state and so it would not be long before they were released.

Ian Stewart stood in the girl's bedroom surveying the scene.

The room smelled stale. The contents of the room had taken on an ominous appearance, having been released so devastatingly from playing a role in the bubbly, vivacious life of their teenage inhabitant. It was now at least three hours since Bekki Axford had died. The scars of the event would be permanent particularly for her parents and her family, but also for any of her acquaintances and the wider local community too. It would be for Theodore Anstis, who now had possession of Bekki's body, to officially decide the cause and most likely timing of Bekki's death, although the death scene made these facts pretty obvious.

First reports suggested that Harold Axford was awoken by the noise of Bekki falling to the floor. When he got to the room he found her laying breathless on the floor. He said that her bedroom window was shut, her curtains were closed, and that the room was undisturbed, apart from the mess on and around the bed. Harold checked other entrances to the house as he dialled the emergency services, and he reported that the front and rear doors were locked and all of the windows in the house were secured. A motive for the crime would be a matter for the investigators to establish, if indeed any could be found but the lack of any forced entry seemed to rule out a serial or unknown perpetrator.

It was early days yet, but Ian Stewart felt sure that Dr Anstis would agree there was only one perpetrator who fitted all of the clues. Of course, they would never be caught because, technically, they did not exist.

*****

Ian Stewart knocked on the door before entering.

'Come in!'

He strode quickly to the middle of the room and stood erect before the desk.

'Ma'am, you wanted to see me,'

'Yes. PC Stewart, you visited this girl Bekki Axford's home.'

'Yes, ma'am.'

'And what did you find?' Judy Marchant asked.

'Officially ma'am, or unofficially?'

'Both.'

'Officially it seems like she committed suicide. She did have marks around her neck suggesting she tried unsuccessfully to hang herself before slitting her own throat. But no implements were found to suggest either event actually took place. There is, as yet, no evidence to suggest that anyone else was involved.'

'And unofficially?'

'Well, ma'am,' Ian Stewart took a deep breath before continuing, 'I am of the opinion that there is only one perpetrator who would be able to carry out these acts and leave no physical evidence of their presence,' Ian Stewart answered.

'The killer spiritual entity,' Judy suggested.

'Yes, ma'am, that is what I believe.'

Judy Marchant rose from her chair and walked over to the window. She clasped her hands together and rested her chin on them. Ian Stewart maintained his alert straightened posture as she slowly turned towards him and walked back to her desk. She stepped around the desk and stood stepped beside the constable, her hand still clasped in front of her.

'I have a couple of things I think you should see PC Stewart, and I would value any input you might have,' she said quietly, 'I would like you to meet me back here after your shift is finished. I don't care what you tell your wife, but it might be necessary for you to work later tonight. '

'Yes, ma'am, I will think of something,' Ian Stewart replied.

'Good, then I will see you this evening. You can rest assured PC Stewart that I would not ask this of you unless I felt it absolutely necessary.'

*****

Judy had only just settled into her car with Ian Stewart when she received a call from Theodore Anstis. She took the call on her hands-free set, speaking as she manoeuvred her car out of the car park and onto the highway.

'Dr Anstis.'

'Inspector Marchant, we have another body, a Miss Bekki Axford, she was 17,' the coroner reported.

'Yes, I am aware of the young lady. Strangulation and a slit throat wasn't it?' Judy asked for confirmation.

'Well, yes, so it appears,' Dr Anstis replied.

'So why the call?' Judy asked.

'Well, I'm quite sure that you know I would not call you unless something other than what SOCOs and your guys found had shown up. In Miss Axford's case, it seems that her death might have occurred before any external injuries were inflicted.'

'Bodily mutilation post mortem?' she asked.

'Yes, to an extent.'

'And what makes you say that Theo?' Judy asked.

'It seems to me that Bekki Axford's appendix might have been tampered with before she was strangled, with her throat being cut after that.'

'Tampered with? In what way?'

'The appendix is connected to the cecum, which is a pouch-like structure of the colon, located at the junction of the small and the large intestines. The appendix normally sits to the lower right abdomen. An appendix is very delicate in its construction, even the smallest disfigurement could have a

200

huge impact on its susceptibility to infection, damage and dysfunction. Inside Miss Axford I found that her appendix had been stretched and shaped at the end, almost as one might shape a piece of clay.'

'Is there any way this could have been a naturally occurring abnormality?'

'If it is then I have no knowledge of it ever happening before,' Dr Anstis explained.

'So this manipulation of the appendix, could that be what killed the girl?'

'I am not sure, but I think it likely this girl might have died from something I cannot fathom, at least just now,' Dr Anstis said, 'but I can tell you for sure that she died at least 35 minutes before she was strangled and her throat was cut. The tissue around her neck wound is of such a consistency as to suggest the wound was carried out after she died. Also, the pooling of blood around her was, to a degree, likely to have been starting to become of a gelatinous consistency.'

'So why would anyone, or anything, mutilate a dead body and try to hide the real cause of death in such a way?' Judy asked.

*****

Judy Marchant beckoned Ian Stewart into her apartment and waved him to the sofa. She dropped her shoulder bag onto the coffee table before retracing her steps and taking a detour into the bedroom to retrieve her laptop computer.

'I would offer you some tea or coffee but I don't believe we have enough time for that. If you want some water, please help yourself,' she called out as she moved around the apartment.

'I'm fine, thank you anyway ma'am,' Ian Stewart called back.

Judy Marchant poked her head around the door frame. 'My name is Judy, no point in using official terms on unofficial business.'

'Is this unofficial business Judy?' Ian Stewart asked.

'It most certainly is,' she called back.

Judy Marchant returned to the living area. She quickly placed the laptop computer onto the surface of the table and plugged it into the nearest mains socket. She opened the lid, pressed the start button and the screen flicked into life. She took two pieces of paper from her bag and placed them face down on the table next to the computer, she then picked out a USB memory stick and plugged it into the lower left side of the laptop.

'Do you believe in the spirit world, PC Stewart?' she asked as she tapped in a sequence of letters and numbers to enter the mainframe of the computer.

'My name is Ian, unofficially.'

'Do you believe in the spirit world, Ian? Do you believe that we change into a different form after we die and that there is some kind of a domain where we exist in that new form?' she asked, without looking up from the screen in front of her.

'Six months ago I may not have been able to answer that question, but now I believe there is somewhere we go, yes,' Ian Stewart replied.

'And what is it that solidified your belief?'

'Well, to be absolutely honest with you, it is what has happened with Mr Hooke and this entity.'

'Good.'

Judy Marchant was going through some screen menus, looking for what it was she wanted to pull out of the machine. She looked sharply up at Ian Stewart, her eyes piercing into his.

'And do you believe in God, Ian?' she asked.

202

'Well, that is a whole different kettle of fish, but I guess if there is some kind of existence after we die then I someone, or something, might have a controlling role.'

'I will take that as a yes then,' Judy said, returning her attention back to the keyboard.

'Can I ask what relevance these questions have to whatever it is you would like to show me Judy?'

'Oh, they are very relevant Ian, trust me. I believe we are about to unravel the mystery of this killer rogue entity, once and for all.'

Chapter Twenty-Six

'Hi Frank, how are you?' I asked into the mouthpiece.

'Where have you been? How is the next book coming? What's on your agenda? You see, these are the things that an agent should know, these are the things that are the difference between success and failure,' Frank Lebusso said, with more than a little urgency in his voice.

'Frank please, I have a lot of important things on my mind,' I replied.

'So where's the progress?'

'What?'

'What are you working on? You are a hot property at the moment, but we need to keep stoking the fire. How is the second book coming along? The RIP series is a trilogy, right? That means I am waiting for two more books from you. You know how quickly boiled water loses its heat, that is how fast you can be forgotten by the public, only it's faster,' Frank said.

'OK, OK. Look Frank, the second book is a work in progress, the third of the trilogy is also on the way. I'm getting there,' I replied.

'Well, that's like music to my ears. When?'

'When what?'

'When are we gonna sit down and start negotiating with the publisher? When do I need to start testing out the markets, pulling some ears? When do you need to make some headlines?' Frank Lebusso asked.

'Making headlines? Frank, you know as well as I do that I will avoid headlines at all costs, that is why I write under a pseudonym.'

'Jonny boy, I think it would be a great idea to take a different tack this time around. This time you are a star and not an unknown, so it's time to introduce some glitz, some glamour, and some top notch celebrities. We go big this time around,' Frank suggested.

'Don't ever call me that Frank, my name is always Len,' I replied, irritation clear in my voice.

'Yeah, yeah, sorry guy.'

'And in any case, I agreed to book signings and US chat shows, but I made it clear the last time around that I go no further in tagging along with any media circus,' I said.

'Yeah, but Johnny, sorry Len,' Frank corrected himself, 'this time it's different, this time we gotta turn on the lights, pull back the curtains, embrace the paparazzi and use them to sell more stock. This time you are gonna be a global megastar, and that means we have to push the boat out, we have to,' Frank implored me.

'We don't need to push any boat out Frank, I want to play it as before. I'm no global superstar, and I don't want to pretend that I am. Frank, I'm in a bit of a situation at the moment that I need to take care of, so can you just let me do what I have to do? Please?'

'Is it to do with the book? You doing some kind of research or something like that?' Frank Lebusso asked.

'It is the book, I guess, but it's not research. I'm kinda living it right here, right now, so I would appreciate you letting me get this next bit completed. This really could be a matter of life or death, so Frank, just let me get on with it, please.'

'Anything I can do, you just let me know,' Frank offered.

'You can't get involved Frank, there is just too much at stake. Oh, and Frank.'

'Yes, Lenny boy.'

'Cut out all the chutzpah, please,' I asked.

'Hey, chutzpah was my middle name 'til my mother, bless her soul, changed it to Leroy.'

'Alright. Frank, just cut it out, what I am working on right now is just too sensitive to be messed up, please.'

'Whatever you say Lenny boy, whatever you say. And the book? Just send me what you got when you got it, and that means soon,' Frank demanded.

'Rest assured Frank that I will get right onto it.'

Frank Lebusso pressed the red button to end the phone call. He immediately pressed the green button to make a second call. He flicked at some papers on his desk while waiting for his call to be answered. The person at the other end of the line finally picked up the call.

'Hey Stevie,' Frank said, 'I got something remarkable you might be interested in, it's about my guy the writer, you know, the guy who talks with God. I've got an exclusive for you, and it's gonna blow your mind wide open.'

*****

Judy Marchant switched on the tv and manipulated the two remote controls before placing them on the small table in front of her.

'I want you to watch this video, I recorded it a week ago. It's only about three minutes,' Judy said.

'OK, but what am I looking for?' Ian Stewart asked.

'Just watch it, I don't want to give you any predetermined ideas before you see it.'

'Can I ask you why your TV picture is all over the place?' Ian asked as he screwed his eyes up to get a better view of what was displayed.

'I had to adjust the tv settings to get the best image,' Judy explained.

'I would go apeshit looking at that,'

'Just watch,' Judy instructed.

Judy selected the HDMI channel that connected the TV to the recorder. She then pressed a button that pulled up a too bright, too colourful list of programmes stored on the hard drive. She selected the last one on the list and pressed play on the smaller of the two remote controls in front of her. The image of the woman on the screen pitched and rolled a little as the person taking the movie seemed to forget how to centre an image. The sound was muted. A smoky anomaly crossed behind the woman's head, and then was gone. The recording finished and the screen returned to showing the list of recorded programmes once again.

'Well, I wouldn't hazard a guess what that was about, at least without any volume. It seems like the person doing the filming has a cigarette alight or something like that,' Ian Stewart suggested, 'it might be better with some sound.'

'The sound is a bit distorted because I played around with the picture. You should be focusing on the mist. It is not cigarette smoke, you will notice that it does not drift upwards as smoke would do. The clip is about a haunted house in New Hampshire and is purported to show a ghost figure in the mist that passes the woman. Now, I want you to watch the clip again. This time try and keep your focus only on the mist.'

Judy replayed the 15 second section of video again.

'Yeah, I understand how some people might interpret the mist as something otherworldly, it does have the rough form of a figure.' Ian Stewart looked at Judy and raised his shoulders.

'Watch again. I will try to pause the video just as it lines up with the woman, then you can tell me what you see,' Judy suggested.

Ian Stewart watched in silence as Judy once again selected the short sequence of film, and when the timer on the recorder reached eight seconds she paused the picture. She then forwarded frame by frame until she got to the part she was searching for. Judy got up from the sofa and walked briskly to the television screen. She pointed at the image with her left forefinger.

'The first thing to notice in this frame is that the mist actually passes in front of the woman and not behind her, as it first seems to on the continuous playback,' Judy said, clearly rapt in the footage, 'now, look closer at the mist and tell me what you see.'

'Well, I guess you might interpret the shape as roughly human-like, but to be honest with you Judy it is hardly conclusive,' Ian Stewart said, clearly still unconvinced.

'Look here!' Judy said pointing at a specific area of the screen, 'do you see?'

'Erm, I'm not really sure what I am looking for, Judy.'

'You see here, look at the misty figure, eyes, ears, nose.' She drew her finger around the screen, following the hardly distinguishable features that were so obvious to her, but still hidden from her guest, 'now, you see the outline of its face? Look here, do you see this mark under the right eye?' she asked.

'I'm sorry Judy but that might just be where the mist is less dense. Now that you point it out, I can make out the shape,' said Ian Stewart, 'but maybe only because that is what you are telling me you see, sorry.'

Judy quickly switched her attention to the laptop computer on the table in front of her. She clicked on a file and forwarded the image until she got to the frame she wanted to show her guest.

'What about this? This is the video cam from my car. I record every journey I take, this one, as you can see, was recorded two days after the image on the TV screen. Now watch.' Judy forwarded the images that showed four different car journeys, stopping each time on a similar image. She returned to the first image and pointed at the screen. 'This figure shows up in four journeys I have made in the last 12 days, and on four of those days I made no car trips, that means this figure appears every other time I went out in my car,' Judy explained.

'Oh come on now, Judy, how can you say for sure that it's the same person. And even if it is, what does it matter? All of us have a schedule, we all have things to do, places to go, and on many occasions these plans will repeat.'

'OK,' Judy said flicking from one image to another as quickly as she could, 'notice the times and the places. There are several hours between these frames, and I can tell you that none of these stills are taken in the same place. These pictures show streets that are as far as three miles apart. Is that still coincidence Ian?' Judy asked.

Ian Stewart replied by shrugging his shoulders, again.

Judy chose one particular frame and focused the shot in on the features of the man with the hoodie, as best as she could.

'Look here,' she said, 'do you see that faint mark under his right eye? Now, try telling me that the guy on the TV screen over there, and the man on the laptop here, are not one and the same person.'

Ian Stewart looked at one screen and then the other on four separate occasions.

'Judy, you have obviously been studying these scenes many times and yes, I can see how you might believe that these two images are of the same man, but it is a long way from being a slam dunk,' he said.

'You are right, I have studied these images a lot, and the more I look at them the more convinced I become that this is the same guy. Did you notice how I was able to show you at least one frame from these four journeys where this guy is looking directly at the camera?' Judy asked.

'Well, actually no, I did not notice that,' Ian Stewart replied.

Judy Marchant reached urgently into her bag and retrieved two sheets of glossy paper. She put them face up on the table in front of Ian Stewart, and then slid one across the other so they sat side by side before him.

'You will recall that I retrieved one of these sheets from beneath the dead body of Ian Robusch when we went to his apartment. This one,' she said pointing to the advertising flyer for the Chinese restaurant, 'read the words and digest them. 'To the ruler, the people are heaven', do you not see the symbolism of that proverb in the light of what is going on?'

'You mean this killer entity?' Ian Stewart asked.

'Yes, of course. This entity is killing young people to build up some kind of a following that will help him take over from God, and thereby to take control of the spirit world,' Judy stated.

'Whoa! Hold on a minute. This is getting a bit crazy now, where did you hear that?' Ian Stewart asked.

'Please don't think I'm crazy. I assure you I am as sane as always, but some crazy things have been happening including…' Judy drew in a deep breath before continuing, '…me being told by a spirit guide that this is what this rogue entity is hoping to achieve from killing these people. When someone dies they naturally go where they are led. In most cases they might be met by deceased relatives, angels or guides. But in the cases of these people killed by this rogue entity, before their allotted time or more accurately at a time outside of one of their potential exit times, then it is this entity that meets them and takes them to somewhere other than the place they would normally go. I know this is all a bit much to take in, but please trust that if it did not all add up, if it made no sense, then I would be the first person to dismiss it,' Judy explained, almost in one breath.

'You are right, all of this is pretty hard to take in. And how did this guide get in contact with you? How did you meet him? It?' Ian Stewart asked.

'Before I answer your question, I have one more thing to add.'

'Which is what?' Ian Stewart asked.

'The second flyer here is for a local spiritualist church. It arrived on the same day as a service. So I went there and I got a message from the medium on the stage. He told me that I am being shown things and that all that is happening is real. He told me that my purpose in life is to tackle this issue. He said that I should trust no-one, that something dark is watching me that does not want me to succeed. He also said that I could be in grave danger. Ian, he knew about Len, and he said I should stay in contact with him,' Judy told her guest, 'not only that, but this is the second warning I have had recently.'

Ian Stewart looked into Judy's eyes, but said nothing.

'And Ian, I asked some of my neighbours if they had received this flyer, none of them had. Now, after all that has happened recently I have to ask if that medium was right. And if he is I need to pay serious attention to what he says, because it might just be that everything Len said about this spirit killer is true.'

Judy took Ian Stewart's hand in hers, before continuing.

'Len says that this entity is trapped inside some kind of a pod in the spirit world that allows spirits to connect with their human counterparts. What if this entity is connected to Len Hooke, and it is this connection that allows it to continue killing people? Ian, this medium told me that if two become one a river of crimson will destroy anything that gets in its path. Is that a reference to the types of killings we are seeing now?'

'Do you believe that?' Ian Stewart asked.

'I don't know, but I cannot disbelieve it. The signs, the two flyers, the videos, it does kind of all add up,' Judy replied, 'and to answer your earlier question I met this guide in the spirit world Len hypnotised me, first when we were at St Mary's Hospital and then again yesterday,' she explained. 'I went to see him because I had to know the identity of the guy in the mist and the guy in the car cam.'

'And dare I ask if you got an answer?' Ian Stewart asked.

'Ian, Mr Hooke has a scar just below his eye on the right side of his face, the guy in the mist and my video cam has the same scar. In hypnosis I realised that the man in the car cam, the guy in the video clip and our psychic friend, are all one and the same person.'

*****

I completed *RIP – Synergy*, in under four months. Since it was almost entirely based on journal entries it was an easy task to fill in the gaps and get a draft to Frank. The journal was typed up in my laptop as my experiences unfolded. It equated to a very raw diary of events and the people involved. Frank stepped into my life even before the book was finished, in fact, he was the one who first suggested I write the book. We had a distant mutual friend who somehow linked us up at just the right time to get my writing off the ground. So I sent Frank a copy of my journal, with side notes, and left him to it. He liked what he saw.

Frank is a good agent who has an eye for commercial opportunities and a lot of good contacts in many different entertainment fields. The only thing is that Frank actively seeks out a blaze of publicity, in all he does, and this makes me feel uncomfortable. I prefer letting the story speak for itself, with only minimal input from me, and to do my best to protect myself and my family by shying away from the glitz and glamour craved by my agent. I have no doubt that Frank's heart is in the right place but more often than not the smell of greenbacks is far too irresistible for the man.

I never had any intention of writing a second book, but since returning from St Mary's Hospital I knew all was not finished. The first book had reached a natural conclusion and I had hoped that this was the end, that my work was completed. But now, as you can see by reading this book, my hopes were to be dashed and in a most dramatic fashion. While I did not submit a draft copy of this book to Frank until just before the incident with Theodore Anstis (details to follow) it seems far more appropriate, and more poignant, to mention it here. Most of what you are about to read has not been extracted from my laptop, but it has been recorded and relayed by those people most closely involved. Only for the sake of continuity is it written in the same context as the rest of the book.

I can take no blame for what happened since I was not the creative force behind the events that took place, though some people might question the validity of this statement. It is essential, I believe, for each reader to place their own personal interpretation on what comes next.

Part Four

Death and Chocolate Omelette

Chapter Twenty-Seven

Katie Long worked when she could, but it was not easy looking after a baby and keeping to regular hours. She felt lucky that a local launderette sometimes asked her to fill in on shifts for absent staff. She knew the owner, but not very well. The work was mundane, it was boring, but at least it put some money into the otherwise vacuous savings jar she kept on a bookshelf at home.

As a new mother Katie liked to think that she could dress Billy in weather-appropriate clothing, and with a good selection too. She had been to boot sales buying blue and pink blankets and bedding pre-birth for pennies, she had also managed to pick up some unisex onesies so there was little need to buy too much.

And now she lay dead by the small fish tank she bought for Billy on his first birthday. The tank stood on top of a three-shelf bookcase and Katie's head was rested against the wall under the shelves. Blood seeped slowly, almost deliberately, from a deep wound above her right ear. But this had not been the cause of her death.

There was a much larger pool of blood that had soaked into the carpet by the door on the opposite side of the room to where Katie had ended up. The crimson wetness had spattered onto every surface within a two metre radius. The door, its handle and hinges, the door frame, the walls inside and outside of the death scene were covered, to varying degrees, by the life liquid of the victim. Only to be expected when you have been severed completely in half.

*****

'So just a minute, I want to be able to think about this so that I can get it straight in my mind, because it sure as hell does not make any sense. What you are telling me, Inspector Marchant, is that there is a spirit entity trapped inside a pod in the spirit world, and this entity is responsible for killing a number of people, and further, that it is, in some way, connected to Mr Len E Hooke, the guy who first came to you about these deaths,' Ian Stewart said, his face contorted in focused thought.

'Yes,' was Judy Marchant's simple reply.

'And that before this guy went into St Mary's Hospital he suffered a heart attack and you, just by chance, happened to resuscitate him.'

'Yes.'

'And when he was in the hospital, you were called by his spirit guide to be told what was going on, and that you will have a major part to play in the events that are yet to come.'

'Yes.'

'And now, you tell me that Mr Hooke is showing up as a ghostly figure on your TV set, and that he is following you around wherever you go in your car?' Ian Stewart asked.

'Once again, yes. But now it gets much weirder. There is no way that Len Hooke, or anybody else, could have shown up in that car cam. The places and the times just would not add up, not unless there are three, four, five of him to cover the area. And what about the mist?'

'Well, with all due respect ma'am, I looked at all that evidence, and though I can see where you are coming from,

I could not say for sure that the person following you is Mr Hooke. And I sure as hell could not swear to seeing what you saw on your TV recording,' Ian Stewart answered.

'Well I could, and no matter how daft it sounds, I would swear to that,' Judy replied, adamantly.

Her phone rang, shrilly. Judy Marchant answered the call.

'We need to talk, and I mean on the down low. Something big has come up. I wanted to get to you before your colleagues did, including the DI. Are you alone?' the coroner asked.

'No. You can go ahead, but what can be that big?' Judy asked.

'This is going to be almost impossible to keep out of the public eye, so I think we are going to have a problem,' Dr Anstis replied.

'Can you quit being so evasive Dr Anstis, and just tell me what we are dealing with here?' Judy asked, impatiently.

'Well, I think you might be called into a murder investigation, that is certainly the vibe I got from your colleagues,' he answered.

'So why aren't you going through official channels, why call on my mobile?' Judy asked.

A brief period of silence followed, before Dr Anstis continued.

'I haven't seen the body yet, but from what I am told a young lady was sliced through at the waist. Her bottom half was found at the entrance to her lounge, but her top half was across the other side of the room. The cut is, apparently, very clean. There was no sign of any forced entry and no murder weapon.'

'OK, now I know why you called me,' Judy admitted.

'My assistant is there now. I am waiting until the scene has been closed by SOCO, but I will get Joe back here as soon as I can. It shouldn't be too long until I can get to see the body, but I can tell you now who killed the girl.'

'What was her name?' Judy asked.

'Katie Long, she was 20 years of age. Judy, SOCO are starting to think some of these recent deaths are homicides, and I don't think it will take long before they link them all together. They will think we have a serial killer on the loose.'

'But you don't think that way, obviously,' Judy suggested.

'Well, I think the same as you, and that is that the murderer is not human,' Dr Anstis replied, 'Can you get here?'

*****

I had got more than two thirds of the way through the second book when Frank Lebusso reminded me of his need to make more cash out of my sweat. It was OK though; this book was much more fiction than fact. Over the last few months my propensity to record every event into my notebook had depleted significantly, so that what facts did remain had been all but swallowed up in rhetoric.

I picked the notebook up, and on opening it to the first page there was one word written, neatly, in double the size of all the other words. This word was BOOK. On the six pages that followed my writing was smaller and it was scrawled in such a haphazard way as to suggest that tomorrow might never come. I had a little trouble deciphering the letters, and in separating some of the words that seemed to stack up on each other as if in a rush-hour traffic jam. A couple of dog-eared scraps of paper fell out as I loosened the middle pages; coffee stain droplets of long gone liquid failed to hide the messages written down in urgent script.

The messages spoke of the deaths of several people, where they lived, how old they were, what they did for a job, and two names stuck out, Saunders and Coombs. There then followed three pages of snippets of my life, memories relived in three or four words, one incident after the other. I turned the next page and, at first glance, it appeared to be blank. But on closer inspection I could clearly see where the notes on the whole of the page had been erased, just as carefully as they must have been written. Black-inked writing continued on the next page but this one had not been overwritten. It was almost as if it had been preserved in its blank form.

I traced my fingers gingerly over the indentations in the page, careful to ignore the bulges created by the writing on the back and focusing wholly on the erased words. This page had once described the time that I met Judy at her apartment when we first discussed, in any detail, the deaths that had occurred. It was a time when we had ruminated how and why, and who or what, might be responsible; the time we made love. But there was nothing here about any spiritual entity, in fact it was referenced only on one or two occasions throughout the whole of the notebook. And why should it be there be at all?

Chapter Twenty-Eight

'Dr Anstis, I got here as quickly as I could,' Judy said, trying her best to ignore the smell that assailed her nostrils.

'Yes, I appreciate that,' Dr Anstis replied, 'since we do not yet know how serious your colleagues are about finding their killer, we must be careful. Walls have ears, so they say, and maybe so too do mobile phones.'

'Oh, I very much doubt that anyone would do that with me,' Judy replied.

'Well, your friend, Len, was a target of interest, particularly with that minibus crash. It seems to me that it might not be too far-fetched to assume that he might come under the microscope at some stage. That being the case, it might also be quite rational to think that you yourself could come under scrutiny.'

'Do you think so? Judy asked.

'Well, yes, especially as it was you that he involved the first time around, and you know how tongues wag when answers start to prove elusive, as they undoubtedly will in this case.'

'I cannot see it coming to that. The DI called me in based on how things developed the first time around, but I still have a good, strong reputation, at the station. Sure, people might ask some questions, but I doubt very much that anything will develop,' Judy reasoned.

'Nonetheless,' Dr Anstis said, as he tilted his head down and gazed over the top of his glasses at the policewoman.

'Yes, perhaps you are right, it might be better to be a bit more vigilant at the moment,' Judy conceded.

'Well, from what was said to me about this young lady,' Dr Anstis said, as he nodded down towards the two parts of Katie Long, 'it seems that someone in your workplace is doing some maths right now, and it doesn't take much for two and two to make five,' Dr Anstis suggested.

'Yes, of course,' Judy replied.

'Now, getting back to the job in hand. The cut undoubtedly killed this woman, there can be no question about that. I have checked her out above the cut, and below and I can see no obvious signs of damage or disease. The cut though is deserving of our closer attention. Do you see here?' Dr Anstis pointed the thin-tipped spatula at the bone at the bottom end of the cut and on the left side of the corpse, 'the hip bone has been sheared away, almost completely. It is one of the strongest, and the densest, of bones in the human body. It would take incredible force to do this, so much so, that I would suggest it impossible to create such a clean cut as we see here. We just do not have the correct tools or weapons available to do this.'

'Precise, and powerful,' Judy admitted.

'And not only does the cut go through bone, but it also goes through cartilage, muscle, and skin tissue before reaching its conclusion. I cannot, for one minute, believe that this wound could ever have been made by any human or mechanical means.'

'So it could only have been made by our spiritual killer,' Judy suggested.

'I can't ever say that this was the case. However, since I can see no other rational explanation, then we must contemplate the irrational,' Dr Anstis replied.

'And that is something my colleagues could never do. The truth, at least so far as the police force is concerned, can never be revealed,' Judy said, 'All of these recent deaths will, eventually, be linked but my colleagues can only look for a human perpetrator. It is almost as if that is how the entity wants it to look,' Judy perused.

'Should the police force be unable to solve these murders, as seems almost a given, then there is no way of knowing whether that in itself will hinder, or help, your own investigations,' Dr Anstis said.

'Well, I guess I will just have to see how it pans out, take it as it comes,' Judy answered.

'Yes, there is no other way,' Dr Anstis agreed.

'And what about how she was found?' Judy asked.

'That is something else that might stump your colleagues, but could more easily be answered by us.'

'In what way?' Judy asked.

'The cut happened in one fell swoop, judging by the lack of blood spatter away from where the bottom half of Miss Long was found. When the incident occurred, Miss Long's lower half would be unable to move at all so it is safe to assume that the incident itself occurred in the lounge doorway. But the top part of her torso was found more than three metres away, adjacent to the opposite wall,' Dr Anstis explained.

'And the answer, that should be so obvious to us, is?' Judy asked.

'Not obvious at all, but there can be only one possible answer. Since there was no blood residue found between the two halves of Miss Greening's body, and that can be attested to by Joe Walker, then her top half must have been placed on the opposite side of the room by her assailant.'

'And for what reason would it do that?' Judy asked.

'Your guess is as good as mine.'

'Well, it seems to me that your guesses are proving pretty damn well feasible at the moment, Dr Anstis.'

'The corpses I have seen more recently, with otherwise inexplicable types of injuries, have clearly all been killed by the same, for want of a better word, thing, that killed those people you first referred to me. With one major difference.'

'Which is?' Judy asked.

'Well, recently, the corpses have all, how can I put it,' Dr Anstis thought for a moment, before continuing, 'bled externally, and to excessive extremes. The first few victims did not. All of their injuries were very neat and tidy internal affairs, with hardly any bloodshed.'

'So why the change in MO?' Judy asked.

'Maybe the killer has just become more bloodthirsty.'

'Or maybe it wanted to show what it could do and announce it to a wider audience. We should not forget the apparent detail and planning that this thing carries out,' Judy suggested, 'You said yourself that this entity seems to be taking a much more physical approach to what it is doing now. It looks like this entity is going out of its way to make the scenes of crime look as if they could have been caused by a person, although the method still defies any thought of human intervention. But, it is almost as if the deaths are being staged. As if a certain degree of human logic is being applied to the murder process.'

'And do you wonder why that might be?' Dr Anstis asked.

'I have no idea, and maybe it is not up to me to wonder why?'

'Correct me if I am wrong but it seems you may be much more deeply involved in this issue than you were, even not that long ago. There must be a good reason for that.'

'These murders are not the kinds of things we are used to investigating, also, the methods used by the attacker are such that they would not stand up well to any kind of official scrutiny. You and I both know that Dr Anstis. In these circumstances, I cannot see how I can avoid becoming closely involved in what is going on. If there is a good reason why Mr Hooke has decided to back off, then I am not aware of it,' Judy replied.

'But maybe the entity is, and maybe it is controlling the situation to make it so. Of course, a lot might depend on the approach taken by Mr Hooke at this time,' Dr Anstis suggested.

'How do you mean?'

Dr Anstis put down the spatula and removed the plastic gloves from his hands. His assistant, Joe, came behind the coroner and untied the bow behind his back that secured the white plastic apron that covered his clothes. Joe took the apron, picked up the discarded gloves, and threw both into a large black bag to the side of the metal slab on which Dr Anstis had recently stood. The coroner moved to the nearest sink and turned on the tap. He wrapped his hands around a bar of soap and held them under a stream of tepid, flowing water.

'What I mean is,' the coroner said, while looking straight at the white tiled wall in front of him, 'there is a strong suggestion of a close link between Mr Hooke and the entity. And, if that is the case, then the only obvious route to finding out more about the killer must be through Mr Hooke.'

*****

Reading the notebook I could feel a building tension in the pit of my stomach. As I read each word, and turned each successive page my frustration grew. I became frustrated, and this turned into anger. Anger at myself for being unable to finish what I had started, anger at God and Its cohorts for asking for my help without offering any assistance, and anger at my own stupidity for once again taking on a mission without sufficient preparation.

There was a time in The Gambia when I had lost everything -- money, self-respect, piety, motivation. I became an empty shell living hour to hour on ever-dwindling financial resources. In times like these we tend to blame every outside influence possible, but rarely do we look inside to see the true root of our problems. Only occasionally do we allow ourselves the freedom to use our instinctual wisdom to look beyond our self-defence mechanisms, and to lift the veil of our own deceit. And these moments only happen when we have exhausted all other avenues of recourse. We fight, and fight, and fight again the same invisible foe, the very forces that exist to enrich our lives, the signposts that show us so clearly the route to our redemption.

My belief in my own benevolence was driven by a refusal to accept that I could ever deliberately create any part of my own personal hell on earth. It was not that the signposts were not there, they were, blazing brightly under the sub-Saharan sun, the problem was that my eyes remained closed. And the strength, the courage that I needed to force my eyelids open, though always available to me, was ignored, until I had destroyed all remnants of the human being I had once been.

The words in the notebook brought all of these feelings tumbling back. It was so easy to convince myself that, once again, I had strived only to achieve nothing. Once again, the so familiar feeling of defeat and ruin assaulted my conscious mind. My thoughts were bashed by the upper cuts of how the spirit realm had lied to me about how I could defeat the killer entity, beaten savagely by the jabs of how betrayed I felt by the institutions that had run my life, and flattened into submission by the right hook of the spirit realm's reliance on Judy to take up the fight.

Inspector Judy Marchant was a bit-part player, nothing more, why couldn't they see that? She was only ever meant to provide support when times got tough. She was an intellectual counter balance that was supposed to keep me on track. She was my crutch, nothing more. I had done everything required of me, and more. I was the one who the entity was a part of, and I was the one who had trapped the entity inside the life pod, supposedly shutting it away from having the opportunity to ever again visit this planet and rip and slash the breath out of any more randomly selected innocent young victims. I had played my part to perfection.

And in the middle of all of it, Inspector Judy Marchant: the new saviour of humanity. The one person the spirit world now relied upon to protect nirvana and preserve the right of every living creature to live, to evolve, and to have the opportunity to one day exist as an enlightened part of the God energy.

I ripped a blank page from the back of the notebook, crunched it into a small ball in my tightened fist, and then threw it to the floor.

*****

Judy Marchant stood, one foot inside her apartment, the other firmly stationed in the hallway. Her mind was skipping from one issue to the next, as if browsing briskly through the options available to her. But exactly what was she searching for? Judy was undecided.

'Did you find what you were looking for?'

Judy was shaken back to reality by the harsh voice.

'I'm sorry, what?' she asked.

'I said, the other night, did you get the answers you wanted?'

'Donna, I'm really sorry, I was miles away.'

'Certainly looked that way,' Donna Elliot affirmed.

'Yes, yes I did, uh, will you excuse me, please, I have a meeting with a frog that I had completely forgotten about.'

Judy withdrew her foot from her apartment and shut the door, rapidly forcing the key into the lock, turning it, and then swivelling around to once again exit the building.

'OK, well, I hope he kisses better than the ones I have met. And George? He smooches like a blowfish, but he looks after me really well, if you know what I mean?' Donna continued.

'Yeah, well look, I'm really sorry but I have to rush,' Judy replied, eager to sidestep any kind of long-winded conversation with her often-times over verbose neighbour.

Judy hastened to the front door and rushed outside, just as she heard Donna's door latch click into place on closure.

'Meeting with a frog? Really?' Judy thought, as she hurried to her car.

*****

Marion struggled at the end of the knotted phone cord, but each time she kicked her legs, the tighter the cord became around her throat. Somehow she knew that her only hope of escaping her predicament was to relax her body, so that she could at least get her fingers under the cord and have a chance, albeit a slim one, of loosening the noose and escaping its death clutch.

The knot in the cord pulled tighter against her windpipe. She could feel her throat closing, like the petals of a flower at the end of a long, hot, summer day. Her ability to shout and scream had long ago drifted away, and even if she had thought about using her voice to raise an alarm, the need to inhale rather than exhale her precious breath prevailed. In any case, the cord had wrapped itself around her neck so quickly that she had no time at all to think about the situation, let alone create a plan of escape.

And it was the suddenness of the situation that had led to panic, and the panic had led to her thrashing around and making her predicament worse. Strange though it seemed to Marion that the cord had wrapped itself around her neck in the first place, stranger still was the fact that as soon as the cord had reached out she had felt herself being lifted off the floor, until she was suspended in the air. She did have the opportunity to look upwards and see the phone cord rising taut above her head for only a few inches, before drooping down limp and loose towards its fixing to the wall socket behind her.

She was aware of everything as she struggled her last. The sharp pain in her toes that moved up her legs, the hurt in her back that seemed to flick from muscle to muscle. She was even aware of her eyes as they seemed to grow bigger and bulge against her eyelids, and of the teardrops that sprayed over her cheeks. The increasingly desperate throb of her carotid artery as the cord tightened around her neck, and the resulting sharp headache was the worst of all.

Chapter Twenty-Nine

Judy Marchant pushed the doors open and entered the White House reception area.

The desk on the left was empty. Judy hurried around the right side and entered the open space. Some buff-coloured folders were neatly stacked on the side of the desk, some papers were loosely scattered across the rest of the table, and two pages stuck out from beneath a black answerphone to the left.

She put her right hand on top of each of the loose papers on the desk, her eyes scanning the wording. Exactly what she was looking for she was not really sure, but she knew the subject matter for which she searched. She looked up and scanned a pinboard to her right and traced her forefinger down a list that was not too neatly written. The information there was not what she was looking for either.

She moved to her left and opened the larger of the two drawers behind the desk. A plastic tray of paper clips, a stapler, a paperback book, a small plastic container of coffee granules, a pad of yellow post-it notes, and some biro pens in an array of different colours, but still not what she was looking for. She pushed the drawer shut just as a lady approached from over her left shoulder.

'Excuse me, ma'am, but can I help you?' the lady asked, in a surprisingly helpful tone.

Judy stood up quickly, turned, slipped past the lady, and back to the front of the counter, all in one swift movement. The middle-aged receptionist watched Judy before slipping serenely back to her seat behind the desk. She wore black, thick-rimmed glasses over a warm and pleasant face. Her expression was welcoming and not at all confrontational, as Judy might have expected, having been found in such a compromising position.

'Erm, yes, I am really sorry about that, but I am looking for a contact number, and it is really quite important that I find it,' Judy replied, in as desperate a tone as she could muster.

'Well, might I suggest looking in your diary, or maybe in your phone?' the receptionist suggested.

'But I don't have the number. I only met them here two weeks ago, at the spiritualist service, so I thought this would be the best place to look. Obviously, I made a mistake at taking that too literally, and for that you have my sincerest apologies,' Judy said as humbly as she could.

'It is really no problem. I can see how important this information must be to you, but I am afraid that the service you talk of is only one of many hosted by the hall. We do birthday parties, wedding receptions, office parties, we even hosted a bar mitzvah recently. We are a hall for the use of the community so we have no input to the organisations that rent our space.'

'Yes, I gathered that, so I guess what I was really looking for was the person who rented the hall for the spiritualist service. They might have the number I need.'

'Well, I shouldn't really do this, but you did say this matter was of the utmost urgency,' the receptionist recalled.

'Oh absolutely, if it wasn't so important I promise that I would never indulge any of your obviously valuable time,' Judy replied while doing her utmost not to cringe.

'The person you need to speak to is Mr Ben Westland.' The lady stood up and leaned across the desk to pass Judy a smart-looking business card. 'You should be able to reach him on one of these numbers.'

Ben Westland, the same man who had attempted to talk with her the night of the service. Judy took the card. She gushed her gratitude, maybe too much, to the receptionist, dropped the card into her handbag, and left the building.

*****

Julie Greasley felt the sharp pain of the electrical charge as it swept through her body, but only for a moment, so swift was its damaging effect on her internal organs. It seemed like all of her muscles had contracted at the same time, and the associated pain she felt was immediate, and intense. Her whole hand felt as if it was on fire. The charge caused ventricular fibrillation which stopped her heart, and it never beat again. The whole episode lasted less than a second, but to Julie it seemed much longer.

Julie was minutely aware of every effect of the current that passed through her body, in each muscle, in each blood vessel, inside each chamber of her heart, and on every micro-organism within her. She was not aware of anything else apart from what was happening during this time-slowed event.

One thing that surprised Julie was that she failed to release her grip on the hair dryer. If anything, she had tightened her fingers around the plastic handle. On glancing at the dryer itself, she saw that the web of plastic covering the motor was melting and melding into itself. The sparks from the motor continued to leap out towards her skin. Another surprising thing was that neither the fuses in the plug nor in the fuse box had tripped the electrical circuit to cut the supply of power to the appliance. Eventually, Julie's mind turned to how she might escape her plight. '*How stupid,*' she thought, '*to watch this lightshow while I am being electrocuted.*' She first tried to release the hair dryer from her taut grip, and she could not. She then thought about kicking out her leg to loosen the plug from its socket, and she could not. A small sound escaped her throat. It was only then that she realised she might be able to scream, and she did so. Finally, something went right for her and she wondered why she had not tried to scream before. But it was not long before her struggle ended.

Julie's neighbour arrived shortly after, using the key Julie had previously given her. The first thing that Marcia Kwameh was aware of was the smell of burning, the second thing she noticed was the silence inside the house. She ran into the kitchen as fast as her too-plump legs would carry her. Marcia knew she should have visited the gym more regularly, if only for a day such as this. She climbed the stairs. She was puffing rapidly when she reached the top. A plume of blue-tinged smoke rose to the ceiling in her neighbour's bedroom and she quickly turned and headed that way.

Julie Greasley lay prone on the floor, her left leg stretched straight as a board, her right leg bent to a seemingly impossible angle beneath her hip. In her right hand she gripped a hairdryer. It seemed to Marcia that Julie's fingers had sunk into the plastic handle so much that rivets of plastic popped out through the gaps between the knuckles of her fingers. Julie was laying face up on the carpet, if face was an adequate word to describe her blackened and smouldering features. Most of Julie's hair had stiffened from its roots, all signs of the applied blonde colourant gone and replaced by a tangled mess of dark brown and charcoal. One strand of hair was alight at the tip.

Marcia Kwameh stumbled down the stairs as quickly as she could. It was too late to do anything to save the life of her neighbour, but she felt it necessary that a dignified response be afforded her friend. She dialled the emergency services.

*****

The phone was answered at the second ringtone. The voice at the other end of the line may have sounded frail, but it was assertive nonetheless.

'Mrs Shelby, I am really sorry to trouble you. My name is Inspector Judy Marchant. I am following up on the minibus accident and any possible connection there might be with a Mr Len E Hooke.'

'Any possible connection?' the old lady replied, straight out. 'there is no possible about it and I am a Ms, not a Mrs.'

'Please accept my apology Ms Shelby, I was unaware. I am sorry,' Judy replied.

'Accepted,' the voice said sharply.

'Mr Hooke told me that you held him responsible for the accident, but we have nothing to suggest that might be the case. Though Mr Hooke was known to have been at the scene we have nothing to suggest that he was anything but a witness to what happened,' Judy stated.

'It's not about the driving. He wasn't driving anyway,' Ms Shelby asserted.

'We have heard that too,' Judy said before clearing her throat.

'It is nothing to do with what he might or might not have done,' the old lady continued.

'How do you mean?' Judy asked.

'It is what he is. That is what counts.'

'I am sorry, but I don't understand…' Judy started to say before she was interrupted.

'Linsey was only 15 years old, but she was very mature for her age. She excelled in all her classes. She was very close to all of her family, me included. She had a bit of a lisp when she was a young girl. She told me one time that her lisp made her ugly. We had a heart to heart about it, and she seemed better after. I used to send her shopping for me, and I always told her to get something for herself with the change. I always made sure she had some change. I'm not so sure her mother would have approved had she known, but it was my treat you see. She was so beautiful, she grew up into a real princess. And she cared for people, she had a big heart did Linsey. But she was taken away from us before her time. By him. And now, well the family is a broken shell of what it was. In her own way, I suppose that Linsey was the glue that held everything together. If I was anybody else I would demand that man be locked away, forever, so that he could hurt no-one else. But that is not the answer, nothing would change anyway and the danger would not go away. I am OK, I am way beyond the age that he can come looking for me. You too, you will be safe, so long as you keep your distance from that man.'

'I don't understand Ms Shelby, how do you mean?' Judy asked, trying her best to follow what was being said.

'Mr Hooke can do nothing, of himself; he is just a man, another worthless man. No, it is not how he appears on the outside; the man is all care, compassion and love on the outside. It is what is inside.'

'And you believe that Mr Hooke caused the minibus to crash because of what is inside of him?' Judy asked.

'Yes, of course. Maybe now you understand,' Ms Shelby declared.

But Judy didn't.

'Can I ask, Ms Shelby, how you know all of this?'

'You can see so much more behind somebody's eyes, than what the eyes, of themselves, wish to show. It is the same with a person's heart, it is not important what is put out, but what beats below. A person carries their whole life around with them, they carry feelings and plans, everything. A person cannot hide the truth of what they are. Some try to shroud it in a mist, to hide their true feelings and intentions. But it is all there, clear as day, if you know where, and how, to look. Most of the world's population is blind, they exist with their eyes firmly shut, and for good reason, because what they might see, should they open them, might be too terrifying. But you see, eyes open or closed, it doesn't matter, each plays just as important a role as the next person. It is a matter only of individual choice whether we open our eyes and then also of what we choose to see. Now, seeing and believing are two entirely different things, it is our level of belief, our faith, that lets us open the door wider and take a peek at what might lie beyond.'

'Are you talking about being psychic, or are you some kind of medium?' Judy asked.

'Charlatans, all of them, taking from the needy, raping those in emotional turmoil. Piling greater misery on those who come to them for guidance and help. They are no better than the witches that were burned, hanged, tortured and drowned in olden times. And then, it seemed more could see the truth of these people. No, young lady, I am not one of those heathens,' Ms Shelby replied adamantly.

'But it is your ability to see what lies inside of people's hearts, is that why you approached Mr Hooke at the funeral service?'

'Might I ask how you know about what happened at the funeral service Miss Marchant?' the old lady asked, a note of suspicion now entering her voice.

'Well, to cut a long story short, we knew Mr Hooke was at the scene of the accident, and we had two of our men watching him at the time,' Judy replied.

'Ah, you see. You had doubts about him too. Nobody can hide the truth inside their heart, no matter how hard they try. Not even Mr Hooke.'

'Ms Shelby, I hardly think the order was given on that basis,' Judy replied.

'Even if you know not what, or why, you do some things, there is always good reason to do it,' the old lady explained, 'and you, Inspector Marchant, are closer to sensing the truth about this man than you realise. You can help to expose the truth to him, you can hold up the mirror into which he must gaze, show him what you yourself can see.'

'I don't understand, what are you trying to say?' Judy asked.

'Nobody can do anything to stop the killing of those poor young people. But when he properly knows what he is, then he must take action. And when he does that the killing can stop, just as quickly as it started.'

'Are we still talking about Mr Hooke?'

Ms Shelby laughed, heartily.

'Well, I guess if that is how you know him,' she replied.

'Does he go by another name?'

'People will know him by many names. He crosses all boundaries, all faiths, all beliefs, all customs. Everywhere he is known. And everywhere he is feared. But I do not fear him, and neither should you. Once you know him, once you are able to see beneath the heart that beats on the outside. There really is nothing to fear, but fear itself, and the dark energy that it releases.'

'And all this is what makes you believe that Mr Hooke was responsible for the minibus crash?' Judy asked.

'No, no, no, no, no. It was not Mr Hooke who was responsible, it was what lies inside of him. The man is just a host; it might even be that he is unaware of that. And that, Inspector Marchant, is the most dangerous time of all. Linsey could not be saved, none of them could. It was always destined to be that way.'

'So what can I do? How can I stop this?' Judy asked.

'Inspector Marchant, you must find your own way, as we all do, eventually. Read the signs, and follow the path indicated for you,' Ms Shelby replied cryptically.

*****

'Judy, Judy, wake up.'

The instruction was delivered firmly, but without malice.

'Wake up Judy, I need you to listen to what I have to say. This is very important,' urged the voice.

Judy rose to a seated position slowly. It felt like she had little strength in her arms to push her body upwards from its prone position. She struggled to open her eyes. For some reason both eyelids seemed stuck together by her lashes. She finally managed to let the dim light more fully enter her awareness. In her sleepy state the world around her, at least at first, appeared blurry and out of focus. She moved her fingers against the surface of the duvet cover that lay over her legs and feet. The cover felt slightly moist, as if it had been shrouded in an early morning dew, and surprisingly warm to the touch.

'The situation is becoming very serious, it is much worse than we might have ever been able to anticipate. We are losing people that should not be lost. They are trapped, they are incarcerated, and we are losing the ability to ever be able to set them free. We can still trace their whereabouts, but only just. Their energy is fading, and soon it will be

extinguished. These people do not know that they are trapped. They feel revitalised, they feel invigorated by the supposed freedom that is being offered to them. They are being encouraged to send out beacons of energy to draw other people in, and they are told that the more converts they draw in, the more they will evolve.'

Judy knew that she was on her bed inside her home, but although she knew where she was, something did not feel right. She tried to reawaken her focus, to concentrate on what was happening, but the sharp knowingness she longed for, remained just out of reach.

'But all of that is not true. They think they are heading to the Promised Land, but that is all a charade. They are being manipulated by their naivety, by their lack of knowledge, by their lack of experiential awareness. They are like babies walking into the fire. We are losing them Judy, and we need your help if we are ever able to offer salvation.'

Judy leapt from her bed and stood, unsteadily, on the floor. She reached out her right hand to grab at the bedpost. The metal bed frame groaned as it shook in her violent grasp. She ran her left hand through her matted hair and then brought it down slowly across her face. She had a dull pain in both elbows, as if she had been propping herself up on her bed for a lengthy period of time. Her left buttock was also aching. She rubbed hard at it, trying to recirculate the seemingly stagnant blood supply.

'What the hell was that?' she asked of herself as she finally awoke.

Chapter Thirty

He felt a dull ache across and just below his rib cage. The indigestion tablets he took helped relive the pain to a degree, but the annoying discomfort refused to go away completely. It was not too bad, more of an irritation really. He did notice, however, that when he went upstairs to put his football kit away that his breath became laboured as he reached the top step. Odd that.

The game was just a bit of practice. The player-manager called it training, but really it only consisted of a bit of light jogging, some sprinting, and then a kick about. Little preparation was put in to any forthcoming game, nobody watched the opposing team and there was no analysis of their potential strengths and weaknesses. It was a simple case of turn up, do your best in the match, grab a beer after and then return home for a Sunday roast.

But this time Fernando Araya fancied no dinner. He felt unable to fully engage in play with Michael either, so his four-year-old son was reduced to pestering his mum while she cleaned pots and pans in the kitchen sink. Fernando wanted to rest, to put his feet up, and to regain some strength. Ideally, he would have preferred to lay on the bed with the door closed so he could just close his eyes and relax, just for a minute or two. But he found that laying down had made the pain worse.

He took another couple of tablets and chewed them to a chalky pulp. He pulled himself upright, stretching his back as he did so. His breathing was slightly heavy but not too bad. For some reason his right arm was aching from his shoulder down to his wrist. It felt as if he had been lifting heavy weights for some time. It was strange how the dull ache was only in one arm. Fernando had been playing football regularly for over 10 years so he was used to the occasional muscle strains and aches that accompany regular exercise. But somehow, what he was feeling now was different.

He looked down at the wedding ring fixed tightly on the third finger of his left hand. He pulled at the ring, and even with such low exertion the pain in his chest grew. He took the ring from his finger and turned it in his fingers until he could read the inscription inside the gold band. He smiled and clutched the ring tightly inside his left hand.

That was when Fernando Araya collapsed to the floor with a dull thump.

*****

'Ben, hi. It's Judy Marchant, we met at the spiritualist service.'

'Judy Marchant, yes, I remember. You will have to excuse me, but I am involved in quite a few community projects. Sometimes they tumble into each other,' Ben Westland replied.

'I was given a reading by the medium who was on stage that night. You might remember that he collapsed to the floor at the end of my reading,' Judy reminded him.

'Ahh, yes. Caused quite a stir in the congregation. Sometimes a medium might take a step back at some kind of trauma that is shown to them by spirit, but that was the first time, at least in my recollection, that we had to stop a service because the reader had fallen to the floor. That would have been Ken Whittle. He is a very good medium, but it seems you might have given him a bit of a start that night.'

'Look, Ben. I went to the centre to see if I could get a contact number for Mr Whittle. Things are kind of escalating for me at the moment, and I really feel like I could do with some guidance right now. I was told by the receptionist that you might be able to help me,' Judy explained.

'Well, I can give you his number. I should just explain though that we were very lucky to secure Mr Whittle's services that evening. He is a popular reader with a very good pedigree. Ken has a history with this particular group that stretches way back, and it just so happens that he was staying close by on the evening of the meeting, so I was very lucky to secure his appearance. But I don't know where Ken is now, so even if I give you his number I cannot say for sure that you will be able to speak with him,' Ben Westland replied.

'If you could get me his number I would be extremely grateful. I guess I will just have to take a chance. You never know, I might get lucky.'

Ben Westland gave Judy a contact number for Ken Whittle.

'That is one of his business numbers, so if you do get to speak to anyone it will most likely be his secretary,' he explained.

'Thank you Ben, you really have been a great help.' Judy closed the call and began dialling the number just given to her.

*****

Frank Lebusso pressed down hard on the butt of his cigarette to all but extinguish the lighted end in the bottom of the glass ashtray on his desk. A plume of bluish grey smoke rose into the air to join the other pollutants gathered near the ceiling. There was a fan in the middle of the ceiling, but Frank never used it. Despite sweating profusely at times during his working schedule, Frank preferred to feel the droplets of his labour trickle down his face.

He lifted the receiver of the phone from its cradle and rapidly tapped in a number.

'Stevie. You know we talked briefly about that second book by my God-talking guy. Well, it's nearly ready to go into print. I reckon that if we play our cards right, we could get it out for the Christmas rush,' he said eagerly.

'Frank, you're breaking my back again. You know that ain't going to happen. We are six weeks away from our deadlines and whatever is going out is already printed, bound, and packed ready to send out,' was the response.

'But Stevie, the book is done, and it's going to blow your socks off. I have been pushing my guy solidly for six months to get this thing finished, just so that his readers can sit down with a brandy after their Christmas dinner and settle into the next instalment of the RIP series,' Frank explained.

'Look Frank, it ain't going to happen. I'm sorry but I haven't even seen a first draft yet. It's gotta be proofread, edited, a cover designed, and all that needs to go through the author, and that's even before we think about marketing and advertising sheets.'

'But you're the publisher Stevie that's all down to you. But I'm telling you Stevie boy, it'll be worth it. The readers have been waiting for this second book for too long already. It's cash in the bank for you and me both Stevie, the damn thing'll go viral before the last page is off the press,' Frank urged.

'Frank, I appreciate your enthusiasm, I really do. But we don't have the time or the capacity. We are a small publishing house. We have our limitations. I'm afraid it just ain't gonna happen. In the summer holidays is a different thing, we can hit the market then.'

'But Stevie, this is not a beach story. You know how the first book went down, people were raving for it, they were going nuts. This is something you read tucked up against the chill night air, as far under the cover as you can get, under a single energy-saving bulb by the side of your bed, flicking your eyes up nervously from the page at every shadow that happens to move across the wall. Come on Stevie, what d'ya say?' Frank asked.

'I said it ain't possible Frank, and it ain't. I know how important this book is to you, not least in your pocket. Besides, you know the controversy the last book caused. We gotta be really careful with the next one. We were lucky there were no big issues or lawsuits the last time out. It was good stuff, I know that Frank, but I don't wanna be the one standing up there defending myself against a damned book. All I'm saying is, we gotta be careful, we need to be vigilant this time around. I'm sorry Frank, but you know as well as I do, that the process takes time.'

'I won't pretend I'm not disappointed, Stevie. But I guess I'm gonna need to back down in the face of your professional acumen, but I don't like doing it,' Frank replied.

'I know that, Frank. Hey, just get us a proofed-up draft when you can. We'll sort out a schedule. I've never let you down yet Frank and I'm not gonna start now.'

Frank Lebusso replaced the telephone handset on the cradle and lit the tip of another cigarette.

*****

Ian Stewart looked at what he had written on the A4 sheet of paper. The bottom of the page just looked like several zigzag lines that overlapped at certain points. It was his attempt at automatic writing. So far as he could see it hadn't worked. The rest of the sheet was filled with words which meant less now than when he had first read them.

He placed the sheet of paper on top of the pile of five that sat scattered on the table to the left of the glowing laptop screen. He picked up the coffee cup, and winced, as the first drops of the chilled liquid hit his pallet. After two sips he returned the cup to its coaster. He looked again at the computer screen, even though he knew he could not find what he was looking for in its melatonin glow. His eyes were tired, and he rubbed them against the backs of his hands, briskly.

In trying to gain knowledge from a computer screen, at least for Ian Stewart, it was a matter of keep on keeping on. It was only repeated messages that he knew would register in subjects he knew nothing about. This stuff was so alien to him that he needed to work especially hard to maintain a strong focus, hence the cold coffee.

Until now, his interest in the case was no more than what he would normally apply to any other matter that came to his attention. But spending time with Inspector Marchant and realising that this situation cut much deeper into her, he had been persuaded that he should pay much closer attention to what was going on. Now that he was being sucked deeply into this case he knew that he should pay much greater attention to it, even in spite of his previously obvious, and complete, disregard for the subject matter.

*****

Judy listened to the familiar ringtone that signalled yet another bypass to a recorded message. She had tried on at least four separate occasions to contact the elusive Ken Whittle. But now that it was approaching nine o'clock, and the sun was down, she had slightly higher hopes of speaking with her target. On this occasion, however, she did leave a message.

'Mr Whittle, I really am so sorry to trouble you. It is Judy Marchant. You kindly did a reading for me at the White House a week or so ago, and we also spoke as you left,' she started, unaware of exactly what she should say but knowing for sure the call was necessary anyway. 'Ben Westland gave me your number. I need to talk with you. When we met you said about two becoming one, and about my being in danger. I need to know more about that. Please call me back.'

Judy left her number, and finished the call. Now all she had to do was wait until the revered Mr Whittle called her back, and if he didn't, then she would need to think things through a bit harder than she had up to now. It seemed to her that everybody knew more than she did. Firstly, the infamous Len Hooke, he was the only reason she was involved in what was going on, and, from what she had since heard, he was rapidly becoming the reason for some danger of which she knew little, if anything. Then there was Ms Shelby. A kindly enough old soul, but one who seemed to be sure of most things, particularly in the part Mr Hooke played in her granddaughter's early demise. And now Ken Whittle, a shining light in spiritual circles who had crumpled to the floor when providing her with a reading, and then, albeit reluctantly, warned her of a danger that he did not wish to divulge. And all of that was on top of that goddamned dream of her great grandfather, who offered her the very same warning.

What was it with these spiritual types anyway? They all talk as if they know more than you do about the human existence, they all claim some kind of higher wisdom, but when you ask them to divulge something of what they know, the best they can say is, 'You will see, when the time is right.' So far as Judy could deduce the time was right now, and the need for her to take action was immediate.

'And just where are God's little fucking helpers when I need them most?' she asked of herself, and of anything else that might be paying any attention.

*****

Nadia Smith felt the moist air on her ankles. She knew it had not been sensible to wear her training shoes, but that was the only footwear she wore socially. The jacket she had on was a few sizes too big, and the rushing wind crept into that too, enveloping her neck and shoulders in its uncomfortable embrace. Rain formed into a small puddle that crept further into the crotch of her jeans with each passing second. Another reason to hate riding pillion on the back of her boyfriend's motorbike.

The bike sped through puddles and across the tarmac. Nadia, accustomed to holding onto her boyfriend around the waist, this evening clutched him a bit tighter than normal. Without a driving licence she had no real option but to ride with him. In the summer, and with the warm sun caressing her skin, it could even be quite pleasant. But as soon as the weather chilled and the rain cascaded down from the heavens, this was a million miles away from being Nadia's idea of fun.

As she lifted herself from the rear of the bike she felt grateful for her boyfriend's expertise in handling the machine. He had been riding for five years, never once having shown any inclination to swap his two wheels for four. He said he liked the freedom, the fresh air, the challenge, and he liked to be able, so easily, to sidestep those jams that occurred so often on any type of road imaginable. And while Nadia could understand his viewpoint, she just did not agree with him.

She stood on the wet tarmac. Her trainers were soaked from all the muck thrown up by the front tyre. She knew that her feet would feel mushy when she was finally able to remove her socks. That would be bad enough, but putting them back on when she left to return home would be comprehensibly worse.

The evening was a washout, literally. They had been to see a couple that her boyfriend used to be close to. But tonight it was as if nobody knew anybody else. The conversation was stilted, and the company was drab and boring. They had only stayed there for 30 minutes, so the evening had proved to be a real waste of time. Nadia's underwear was wetter and her trainers seemed mushier on the return journey. Dan said nothing when she got off the bike. She patted the top of his helmet and hurried towards her front door. She heard the bike pull away a second or so later.

Nadia sprinted inside, rushed to turn the boiler on and hurried to run herself a steaming hot bath. She disrobed, draped the pink dressing gown over her shoulders and walked to the bathroom. The bath was hot, and nice, and pretty soon any negativity she felt earlier in the evening started giving way to a greater sense of calm.

When she got out of the bath Nadia was aware of a lot of steam lifting from her skin, but she shivered nonetheless. She wrapped herself in a clean bath towel, left the bathroom and headed towards her bedroom. Nadia got dressed in a onesie and put her dressing gown back on for extra warmth.

She felt a cold chill rush through her body once again. She paused briefly and looked behind her. Seeing nothing, she continued towards her intended destination.

And that was when it happened.

*****

Ian Stewart awoke with a start. His pillow had been dampened by the sweat that had fallen from his brow while he was asleep. He threw the covers from his body and drew his legs over the side of the bed. He sat there, feverishly wiping perspiration from his eyes and from his forehead. He did not want to focus too much on what he was doing now, much more important was his recollection of what had happened before he had woken up. He knew he had to remember. But remember what?

He rose from the bed, running fingers through his sodden hair. He looked to the red glowing face of the alarm clock that sat on the bedside table. At first the numbers were not recognisable, their edges fuzzy as they seemed to lean into each other. His focus returned, slowly. He realised he had been asleep for less than 30 minutes. What had disturbed his rest so much that he had no choice but to resurrect himself? What dream, or what nightmare?

The house was silent. The only sound he could hear was the gentle tinkling of the wind chime in the light chill breeze of the early morning air. The chime was outside the patio doors downstairs, the ones that faced the garden. He tried his best to ignore the silver-plated cymbals and pipes set that his mother had bought him one Christmas. She must have thought it a practical, and beneficial, addition to his first home. It was not.

Ian Stewart was a man who liked a solid base in his life, and he had no intention of ever moving house. In fact, that could pretty much describe how he felt about his wife too. She was his base, his anchor, his stability. Ian Stewart respected his surroundings, he appreciated the hard work that they had both put in to creating their home nest. In the past his need for a solid base had done little deter him from feeling an occasional need to explode onto a completely different scene with someone unknown. And as Len Hooke had pointed out to him, this usually happened on a Friday night.

Debbie was laying on her left side and breathing heavily. His wife did not snore and that was a relief. She slept heavily and was never disturbed from her slumber no matter what might be going on around her. Whenever Ian Stewart had awoken previously, he had returned to sleep immediately, to awake refreshed in the morning at the mechanical prompting of the red-screened alarm clock. But this time it was different. This time Ian Stewart felt no compulsion to return to the bed. This time his senses were coming alive too quickly too. And this time he needed to know why?

He slowly descended the staircase, guided by the wooden banister rail that ran beneath his left hand. He reached the bottom and turned right. He entered the kitchen and flicked at the switch that brought illumination to the room via a single fluorescent strip. He opened the fridge and popped the top off a bottle of water that sat on the bottom shelf inside. He gulped a few times, replaced the bottle in the fridge, and shut the door.

He glanced at the cork board that was hung on the wall to the left of the fridge door. Tacked to the board was a collage of six photographs of him and his wife that had been cut and placed together to make one disjointed image of the two of them. He focused sharply on the image.

'That's it,' he exclaimed.

*****

Ben Westland shut the car door behind him and walked towards the shed. He nonchalantly pressed the key that locked the doors and set the alarm. He quickly reached the heavy padlock and chain that secured the drop-down shuttered door. He called it a shed, but really it was a garage he had rented earlier that year. He paid a minimal rent, not in cash but in marijuana. The shed owner said it was for medicinal purposes, but who cared anyway?

He turned the long, thick key in the lock, threw it to the ground, removed the chain from the door fixing, and slid it up on the rails on either side. He got the torch out of his pocket and checked both sides of the building before walking into the lock-up. He entered and pulled the metal door down to the floor after him. The darkness inside was all but complete. He flicked on the torch light.

Ben knew what he was looking for, his only problem was going to be how to find it among all the crates, tools and the garbage that filled the shed. He began wading through the rubble, clearing a path with his heavy size-10 boots. He occasionally wobbled, but quickly gained his step and continued the search.

'Ah, there you are,' he muttered, as he spied the first of a collection of the items that he needed to retrieve.

Orders were quite scarce at the moment but Ben had a good list of contacts that could nearly always be relied upon to find a buyer. As in all types of business it was the rarity of the item that gained the highest prices. The fact that all of Ben's stock was not his to sell dramatically reduced the price he was paid. Some stuff was easy to source but it only went for pennies. Ben preferred to trade in something of a much greater monetary value. He scooped up seven lengths of 28 millimetre copper piping and headed towards the roll-up door. The order was for five lengths but it was for a good customer who Ben knew had a tendency to buy more than he needed.

Ben Westland liked to think of himself as a bit of a loner. Sure, he knew a lot of people in the business, but in his personal life his regular contacts could be counted on one hand. He knew a large number of acquaintances, mostly through the community work and local groups he liked to involve himself with, but he had few friends. It never hurt to have people on your side if ever they should be needed. And the higher profile you take charitably the better to avoid any attention from the authorities when items went missing locally. Sometimes it got too hot and at these times Ben withdrew completely from the game. Only mugs and drug-addled idiots worked then. And most of these guys ended up serving time at Her Majesty's pleasure.

Ben placed the lengths of copper beside the exit. He bent down and pulled at the latch at the bottom that secured the door in place. He pulled the door up as quickly, but also as quietly, as he could. He got in the car and reversed it back towards the open door. He was not too concerned about being seen now, since the bulk of the car covered what he was doing. And it would only take a few seconds to load up the car, secure the garage, and be on his way again.

Or so he thought.

Chapter Thirty-One

Judy Marchant never heard back from Ken Whittle. He had spoken to her before and possibly even said more than he wanted to, so why should he call her back? It was, after all, a matter of life or death for her, but not for him. She wiped the rain from her eyelids with the back of her hand, and stepped inside the front door. The waxed hem of her jacket dripped rain onto the mat as she removed her shoes. They were sodden, even from the short walk from her car. She removed her coat, picked up her shoes, and hurried to place the items into her bathtub. Her blouse and her trousers, from the knee downwards, were also wet, but they would need to wait.

Judy called the third of five numbers she had scribbled onto the small folded piece of paper she held in her left hand. The phone rang for too long, so she ended the call. She then tried the number at the top of the list. The call was answered very quickly.

'Hi,' Judy paused, a little unsure of what to say next, 'I guess I might really be asking for a bit of advice,' she said.

'Well, if your problem is about anything paranormal then you are in the right place,' the lady on the other end of the line replied.

'That is the thing, I am not really sure if it is a paranormal problem. But it most certainly is not normal,' Judy said.

'If not normal, then it must be paranormal. Why don't you try to explain to me, in as concise a manner as possible, what the problem is. Then we can take it from there,' the lady added.

'OK, the best I can do, is probably to pose a series of questions,' Judy replied.

'OK, then fire away,' the lady said.

'In your opinion, do demons really exist?' Judy asked.

'Not in my opinion, but in my experience, the research we have carried out suggests that it is a distinct possibility, yes.'

'But it is not a fact.'

'Well, most of what we do, and all of what we feel, every hour of every day, is based on conjecture. One thing we have learned in our line of business is that nothing can be taken at face value, what might seem concrete proof of the paranormal to one person could just as easily be explained away as something entirely different by somebody else. So, something that might claim to be a demon, might not, in fact, have demonic roots. I think we need to look more at the energetic strength of unexplained phenomena, and how that phenomena chooses to show itself, whether that be in good, or in negative, ways,' the woman clarified.

'But what if something was to show itself in some kind of demonic form?' Judy asked.

'Then I would suggest that it is most likely an energy with a negative, or a dark, intention,' the lady explained.

'OK. Thank you for explaining that. Now, I would also like to ask you if it is possible for one of these strong energetic forces to have a physical impact in our world?'

'Oh, I think that would be a given. Anything that can exert sufficient will to jump between dimensions of existence, is undoubtedly capable of having a physical impact here.'

'And the other way around?'

'What, you mean could we, as human beings, visit and have a tangible impact on beings in other temporal settings?' the lady asked.

'Yes.'

'Well, theoretically, I would have to answer your question in the positive. I believe it entirely possible, yes. After all, this is probably the core principle of prayer, meditation, and possibly every transcendental practice. But there can never be any practical evidence that this has, or could, ever happen, since any equipment that might be used to record paranormal events must be Earth bound,' the lady explained.

'And what do you know about Dyatlov?' Judy asked.

'The hiker, or the incident?'

'The incident. It really happened, right?'

'Oh yes. The facts, so far as we know them, are that Igor Dyatlov led a group of 10 on a ski trek across the northern Urals, in Sverdlovsk Oblast, Russia. The original group consisted of eight men and two women. Most were students or graduates of the Ural Polytechnical Institute. The goal of the expedition was to reach Otorten, a mountain 10 kilometres north of the site of the incident. All members of the group were experienced in long ski tours and mountain expeditions. They started their march toward Otorten from Vizhai on January 27, 1959. The next day, one of the members, Yuri Yudin, was forced to go back due to illness. Before leaving, Dyatlov had agreed he would send a telegram to their sports club as soon as the group returned to Vizhai. It was expected that this would happen no later than February 12. When the twelfth passed, and no messages had been received there was no immediate reaction, as delays of a few days were common with such expeditions. It was not until the relatives of the travellers demanded a rescue operation on February 20 that the head of the institute sent out the first rescue groups. Later, the army became involved, with planes and helicopters being ordered to join the rescue operation. On February 26, the searchers found the group's abandoned, and badly damaged, tent on Kholat Syakhl.'

'And this is when things became interesting,' Judy interjected.

'Well, yes. Mikhail Sharavin, the student who found the tent, said it was half torn down and covered with snow. It was empty, and all the group's belongings and shoes had been left behind. Investigators said the tent had been cut open from the inside. Eight or nine sets of footprints, left by people who were wearing only socks or even barefoot, could be followed, leading down toward the edge of a nearby woods, on the opposite side of the pass 1.5 kilometres to the north-east. At the forest's edge, under a large cedar tree, the searchers found the remains of a small fire, along with the first two bodies, shoeless and dressed only in their underwear. Between the cedar tree and the camp the searchers found three more corpses, who seemed to have died in poses suggesting that they were attempting to return to the tent. Searching for the remaining four travellers took more than two months. They were finally found on May 4, under four metres of snow in a ravine 75 metres farther into the woods from the cedar tree. These four were better dressed than the others, and there were signs that those who had died first had relinquished their clothes to the others. An examination of the latest bodies found showed that three of them had fatal injuries: Thibeaux-Brignolles had major skull damage, and both Dubinina and Zolotarev had major chest fractures. According to Dr Boris Vozrozhdenny, the force required to cause such damage would have been extremely high, comparing it to the force of a car crash. Notably, the bodies had no external wounds. However, major external injuries were found on Dubinina, who was missing her tongue, eyes, part of the lips, as well as facial tissue and a fragment of skull bone, she also had extensive skin maceration on her hands. It was claimed that Dubinina was found lying face down in a small stream that ran under the snow, and that her external injuries were in line with putrefaction in a wet environment and were unlikely to be related to her death,' the lady continued to explain.

'And what suggestions were put forward for potential causes of these deaths?' Judy asked.

'Well, and in a nutshell, the most probable explanations are avalanche, infrasound, military testing, paradoxical undressing, and cryptozoological.'

'In English, please,' Judy asked.

'Sorry. Well, an avalanche was unlikely because of the geography of the place, and footprints from the tent remained and could be traced to the final resting place of the victims. Infrasound can be caused by the wind passing over the area and then being sucked down towards the ravine beneath the tent. Infrasound has been known to cause panic attacks, paranoia and, in extreme cases, hallucinations. But what likelihood that some kind of confusion would affect nine people in exactly the same manner? Also, there was no record of military testing in that area at the time. Hypothermia can induce a behaviour known as paradoxical undressing, in which hypothermic subjects remove their clothes in response to perceived feelings of burning warmth. That six out of nine hikers died of hypothermia is undisputed. But, since the temperature inside the tent would not have been low enough to induce paradoxical undressing, why flee in the first place? Probably the most common theory is the yeti. And yet without footprints, other than the victims, there was no real evidence to show the existence of any kinds of animals at that time. These are the main scientific theories, anyway.'

'And what of the unscientific?' Judy asked.

'Well, as with any and all paranormal activity, the problem is always one of proof. Otherworldly entities, it seems, do not generally like to leave any proof of their having visited us, let alone of them having interacted with people,' the lady explained.

'I want to thank you for your help. You have been most enlightening,' Judy acknowledged.

'Can I ask why you need to know these things? I don't think we ever established that.'

'Let's just say that I am currently involved in a situation that might just be very similar, and even more devastating than what happened in the Urals all those years ago,' Judy replied.

*****

I sent Frank Lebusso a copy of my second book, *RIP – Crimson*, two days before he called me. It was a first draft, and quite a way from being complete. But I thought it better to show him something, and stop him being so agitated about any seeming lack of progress.

'But it's not finished, Lenny boy. Why is it not finished? Synergy has been on the shelves four months already. Your readers are going to demand a follow-up. And they don't care too much about what it is, just so long as they get their grubby little mitts on it from day one.'

'Frank. I know how you feel. But it matters to me what it is, believe me. And I can't finish something that cannot yet be finished,' I replied.

'What are you talking about Lenny, what's with the riddles? You are a writer. You write books, you give them to me, I get the highest price I can for their distribution, bam. That's it. There is nothing else.'

'You are forgetting one thing, Frank,' I said.

'Oh yeah, and what's that Mr Mysterio?' my agent asked in his own inimitable way.

'While the third book will be mostly fictional, you have to understand that the first two books in this trilogy must be based on real events, as they happen. And if things have not happened yet I can hardly make them happen by snapping my fingers. Life is not like that,' I replied.

'No, Lenny. Life is like waiting for the bus of riches. You can wait all your life for that bus, and sometimes it will not arrive at all. But through your whole life you've got to keep your eyes peeled, you've got to keep waiting. And then, when that bus finally does arrive, it always comes in two's, three's or more. Now the trick is, Lenny boy, that when that bus does arrive, you need to be ready to jump, fast, because each one of those buses that turns up, is going to a different destination. You get me?' Frank asked.

'I do understand, Frank, I really do. But you need to wait until whatever needs to happen, happens. That is the nature of these books. That is just how the story is. And you knew that Frank, right from the get-go,' I replied.

The truth was that I could have pushed much harder to get more done on the book. I knew a month earlier that I was falling way behind my own self-imposed writing targets. And that was because I had stepped away from the action. Frank had every right to expect more from me. Sure, I had things I needed to deal with, but it just so happens I made an almighty cock-up of dealing with them.

I let my frustration at Judy's increased involvement get the better of me. I let my anger at God's apparently blasé approach to the issue turn me to stone, and I let myself get dragged deeper and deeper into a dark, festering hole of inadequacy and pity as a result. So I tried, wholly unsuccessfully, to direct more of my attention to my family, rather than try and come to grips with what had previously been the very core around which my world revolved.

'The market place ain't going to wait much longer, Lenny. I know that for a fact. What am I supposed to do with this? It's not yet finished, it hasn't been proofread, it hasn't been edited yet. And now you are saying not only that it's not finished, but that you don't know even what the end will be,' Frank said, forcefully.

'You wanted the book, so there it is. I got you what I had, it's up to you what you do with the manuscript, Frank. You can get it finished any way you choose. I don't care. I have much more important things to do,' I replied, somewhat aggressively.

'Yeah, and I might just need to do that, Lenny boy. I might just need to do that.'

*****

Judy was aware of her surroundings, she could see the television set sitting on top of the chest of drawers, she could feel the covers on her legs and feet, she could smell the faint aroma of what little perfume she had applied to her body. She was also aware of the glow from the orange streetlight that reached into the darkness of the night. She could hear the distant sounds of life continuing, as normal, in the street below her bedroom window. But there was something else that she was aware of too, something that seemed to display no physical manifestation and yet its indefinable presence was palpable nonetheless.

Judy looked around the room quickly, from the television set to the window, from the window to the bed, and from the bed to the door that stood slightly ajar over her left shoulder. And as she looked she focused her eyes keenly on each area, hoping to perceive whatever it was that was making itself known to her.

'What do you want?' she asked out loud.

Judy felt her shoulders tense. She felt her legs push into the mattress. She felt her fingers clutch tightly to the cover that hung loosely over the duvet. Judy was aware of a single bead of sweat falling from her hairline as it traced its way slowly downwards, over each pore of skin, on its inevitable journey towards her top lip.

'What are you doing here?'

Her second question remained as unanswered as did the first. She was not sure what created more fear in her mind, the knowing of something else being with her in the darkened room, or the lack of any reply to her requests for information.

'I'm warning you. It's best you leave now, before you get hurt,' she said unconvincingly.

An empty threat if ever there was one. But Judy felt that she must say or do something, anything, to break the tension that existed all around her. At least by talking Judy was successful in finding an outlet for the panic that might overtake her otherwise. Her words were a calming influence, and even if her threat had no actual basis, the fact that it was dealt made her feel calmer and at least a little bit more in control of the situation.

Judy could have sworn that she heard a very light breath from the opposite corner of the room, almost imperceptible amongst the chatter from the low volume of the television set, but there, she was sure of it. She switched her focus from her eyes to her ears, picking through every sound that entered her mind, searching for a repeat of the faint noise that had grabbed her attention. The unknown presence was still. Though her senses placed it firmly in the corner of the room it also seemed to possess an omnipresence. It was almost as if this thing could be in as many different places as it wanted at any one time. And even as this thought entered her mind Judy realised that it was insufficient to describe this thing's ability to occupy space, since she also knew it could move backwards and forwards as well as laterally, and maybe even to occupy two or more spaces in time concurrently.

Judy's initial fear was slowly being replaced by intrigue. She wanted to know about this thing, to learn about how it travelled, to discover what is was aware of and how. Though she did not feel drawn to the presence she sensed that it might be very easy to become at one with it, to become a part of it even. And, strangely enough, that feeling was not at all scary. Judy sat in her bed, totally absorbed in what was happening in the room, until when, she did not know. It did not matter. She cared for nothing, except this small moment in time.

'What do you want with me?' Judy whispered through clenched teeth.

Judy was not consciously aware of saying anything. It seemed to her as if the words had tumbled out without her willing them to. She was not even aware of having the thought that should have preceded her words. All she was aware of was the presence of the omniscient energy that seemed to be in front of her while surrounding her and being inside of her all at the same time.

'I want nothing of you. But what I would like is for you to join me in the process that is yet to come.'

The words came into her mind, not through her ears but through her forehead. It was almost as if a tunnel had opened up and the thoughts purveyed to her passed effortlessly through the gap. 'What is this all about?' the words once again tumbled from her mouth involuntarily.

'It will be the end, and the beginning. A rebirth, a new dawn, a fresh start for all. You have learned much already, but there is far more at stake than you could ever know. This process is inevitable, nothing can stop it.'

'Who are you?' this time Judy felt a degree of willpower enter her mind as she spoke.

'I am the Alpha and the Omega. The light that shines beyond the veils of deceit and despair. I am the one true future that nobody dreamed could come to pass. I am your future Judy, as I am the future of all humankind, and beyond. I am God.'

'If you are God you led Len to have that mark on his hand, it was you who called him to help, it was you who created this mess. It was you that created the perfect opportunity for these killings to happen,' Judy replied.

'It was always meant to happen, and nobody could do anything to stop it. It is best for you Judy, to accept the situation as it is, and give in to the supreme power of all that is. You cannot fight what you do not know. What damage are you taking in fighting the inevitable? What risk in supporting the killing of the innocents?'

'If you were really the God that I know, you would…' as she spoke she sensed the atmosphere around her changing rapidly, as the presence in the corner of the room dissipated, '…you would have no need to glorify your ways.'

The feeling returned to her fingers as they clutched tightly at the duvet cover and a sharp pain ripped through each knuckle as the blood faded from her fingertips.

Chapter Thirty-Two

Dr Anstis pulled back the top of the sheet, exposing the corpse to its waist. As always it was the smell of the dead flesh that hit first even before the eyes had a chance to digest the sight before them. Joe had done his best to assist the coroner by disguising the odour in the room, but this time he was fighting a losing battle. The four dead bodies on the cold metal benches were more than a can of industrial fragrance could cope with.

'As you can see, four dead people. There was actually a fifth, but that one has been released already. Four accidents and one potential suicide. Nothing strange in that you might think. Accidents happen all the time, and suicide, for any number of reasons, is not an uncommon occurrence. Now, the ways in which they died is not in dispute as there is clear and irrefutable evidence of how each person died,' Dr Anstis explained.

'But, I am guessing they were all under 32 when they died,' Judy added.

'Well yes, there is that. But there is something else that baffles me. The fact is that these people all died within a two-hour time period.'

'Wow,' was the simple response given by Judy.

'Now, we get maybe five domestic accidental deaths a year caused by all manner of things, bad electrical circuits, irregular paving, ill-fitting carpets. In addition, we get as many suicides. I am, of course, excluding car accidents and things like that. That is 10 deaths, in total, each year which might not be considered to be as a result of natural causes or, if you prefer, not in the course of the natural life process. And in my experience, we might see only one or two of these people being under the age of 55. Not only is the age of each of these victims noteworthy, but there is something else that I find quite baffling in each case,' the coroner continued.

'Which is?' Judy asked.

'Well, usually in these type of cases, particularly with accidents but also in suicide cases, a person's body will show signs of resistance just prior to their death. This is part of the body's natural response to distress. The muscles will tighten, the heart beat will accelerate, sometimes to as much as three times its normal relaxed rate, and this increase in blood pressure will have other marked effects on the tissue and organs in the body. But in each of these cases I see no sign at all of any of these responses. It is almost as if, contrary to normal expectation, these people were all in a relatively relaxed state when their lives came to an end. It's almost as if their conscious mind was dormant.'

'Like they were in a sleep state?' Judy asked, perplexed.

'Precisely like that, yes. And that is not the strangest part,' Dr Anstis continued, 'look here,' the coroner pointed out the deep impression on the neck of the body in front of him, 'this is the presumed suicide victim. And this is pretty much what we might expect to see, except.'

'Except what?' Judy urged the coroner to continue.

'It just does not look right to me. The angle of the depression should be greater. The neck of a person who hangs without their body being supported, will inevitably stretch to a degree, and the highest part, just here,' he pointed with a ballpoint pen, 'will take the majority of the impact.'

'But the depression in her neck is an inch below that,' Judy commented.

'Precisely. It is in the wrong place. And then there is the fact of how it happened. This young lady was found in her kitchen. The cord to the phone was more than sufficient to reach from the socket on the wall to where her body was found, and there were no obvious points within the kitchen that could have been used to support the cord at the time her life expired. She obviously could not have moved herself from a more obvious hanging point after she had died.'

'And it was definitely the telephone cord that created the depression in her neck?' Judy asked.

'Well, yes, I would say so, from the marks that are visible on her neck.'

'So, it seems that this lady might have been strangled with the cord rather than hanging herself,' Judy suggested.

'Well, yes, except even that does not fit, because the depression on her neck does not go all the way around, and there are no signs of a struggle as there undoubtedly should have been in that scenario,' Dr Anstis replied.

'And what about the other four people who died?' Judy asked.

'The first one came in yesterday morning, an assumed heart attack. But in a fit 26-year-old man, with no family history of heart problems? Highly unlikely. In any case, with no other cause it is usually the second or the third heart attack that gets you, not the first,' the coroner explained.

'And what about the people who are here?' Judy asked, looking at the other dead bodies in the room.

'Electrocution, falling down the stairs and several impalements through the chest,' Dr Anstis replied for each one in turn.

'Ergh, gruesome,' Judy said, 'and do you have similar misgivings with them, as with the hanging lady here?' Judy asked.

'Well, yes and no, but more in the circumstances of each death than in the outcome.'

'How do you mean?'

Theo Anstis moved along to the next table, and Judy followed. The coroner lifted the cover to reveal the face of the departed. The person could not immediately be identified as a woman, and it was not too clear that it was, in fact, a human being that lay motionless on the cold metal surface of the examination table. Her face was blackened, and she was missing the clearly defined outlines of her nose, mouth, eyes and ears. Her features could best be described as a partly moist and partly crispy mush.

'This young lady was electrified by a hairdryer. But that being the case why would she not just drop the implement when the electrical charge first passed to her hand?'

'Do you know what puzzles me, Dr Anstis? What one thing scares almost everyone above all else?' Judy asked,

'I don't know, but I guess you are going to tell me.'

'Death,' Judy replied.

'Yes, I cannot argue with that.'

'So in that case, why is it that we have no reports of any screaming, or struggles, from any one death we have looked at in connection with this rogue entity?' Judy asked.

Dr Anstis moved to the next body. Once again he lifted the cover. Judy stared down at the face of Ben Westland. Contorted as it was in a grotesque fashion, she was nonetheless sure that it was him. She gasped, covering her mouth with one hand and gripping the corner of the metal table with the other. The whole table shook as she struggled to retain her balance.

'Are you OK?' Dr Anstis asked as he reached out to grip Judy's elbow, offering some much-needed support.

'I know this man,' Judy said through tightly-closed fingers, her muffled voice trembling in shock, 'he is Ben Westland. I spoke to him, it must have been just before he died.'

Dr Anstis moved to the last table and lifted the cover from the face of the final corpse. Judy fell backwards and slammed into the wall with her left shoulder. She screamed and brought her other hand across her face. Her legs buckled beneath her and she slowly descended to the floor, sobbing as she dropped.

*****

Jane Cuthburtson read the note again. The words on the plain white paper made no more sense to her now than when she had first read them an hour or so before. She pushed the paper tissue to her nose and blew as hard as she could.

Though her tears had now dried the raw emotion she felt inside continued unabated. Her questions remained unanswered, but she continued to ask them nonetheless. Regardless of the facts of her situation she blamed herself for the pain that burrowed deeper and deeper through her heart. She was to blame, of course she was, there could be no other explanation. If only she had seen the signs. How could she have been so stupid as to plough relentlessly on through her day to day life, without ever once noticing that the walls surrounding her were starting to fade and crack?

And now this, the handwritten note that confirmed all of her worst fears. Jane always held a distrust of her husband, not only because of his wandering, but also as a result of the inherent need to draw emotional crises to her like a magnet. It was not that she consciously chose to travel through her life being cheated on, beaten, robbed of her possessions, betrayed. It was more a case of bad things following her, like a fart in a gentle breeze.

But with Mike she thought it might be different and, at first, she kidded herself that it was. Jane was besotted with her new beau, that much could never be denied, and it seemed that he too had fallen heavily for Jane's undeniable beauty. The fact that, at 22, she was 12 years Mike's junior was irrelevant. Her parents' disapproval of the choice she made did not matter either. Mike had swept her off her feet and she had wilfully jumped into his waiting arms.

Looking back, she could see all the signs. The late nights at work, the customers who demanded immediate attention for fear of cancelling their contracts, delays to travel plans, and the increased number of important conferences and meetings that plagued their relationship in the last 18 months. But as a dedicated partner, who devoted far too much of her time supporting Mike's career, Jane knew that the lonely evenings with nothing but a TV dinner and a remote control for company were absolutely necessary to preserve the relationship with the man she continued to feel was special to her.

And now her life would never be the same, regardless of the eventual outcome. She had become a hapless puppet in the wayang show now solely directed, produced, and starring Mike Cuthburtson. In fact, she was now not surprised to start thinking that this might always have been her role. Jumping, dancing, pirouetting on command. While her life had undoubtedly been harsh at times, this had become the unkindest cut of all.

She carefully, and with some concerted effort, removed the three gold rings from the third finger of her left hand. She dropped them into her left palm. She picked each one up between her thumb and forefinger, and turned them around.

Each one glistened brightly, like a star in a clear, bright, moonlit night. So beautiful, and yet so ugly.

*****

Debbie Stewart ran the brush gently through her hair as she stared at her reflection in the mirror.

'Am I getting a bit loose, do you think?' she asked.

Her question was not answered by words, but by the continued tap, tap, tap of frenzied fingers on a keyboard. The sounds were broken frequently by long gaps, when silent concentration took over. Debbie might have expected a small grunt, even an extended exhalation of breath would have been better than the continued rapping-silent response that was now becoming all too familiar. It would not be so bad if it was restricted to one room, but it was not: lounge, bedroom, dining room, kitchen, even one time in the bathroom.

'I said, do you think my dearest one, that I am getting a bit loose,' Debbie grabbed a small amount of skin and pulled it away from her torso, 'here.'

'Oh no, no honey. You still look as beautiful as the first day we met.'

Finally, a response. But words without eyes equates to little more than no response at all. The rapping-silent monotone continued. Debbie lunged to her right and grabbed her husband, forcefully, by his shoulders. And finally his gaze left the computer screen on his lap.

'What on earth,' he protested, as the concentration was shaken from him.

'Ian. I don't mind you being absorbed in your work. In the three years that we have been living in this house I have come to expect it, to a degree. But this last week has been different. Hardly a word has passed between us, all I have been aware of in that time, is you stuck on that computer doing whatever it is that you are doing. Is it porn sites? Is it more console games? And God knows you have enough of them to save the world 100 times over. Is it the massage parlours you visit?'

Ian Stewart straightened his back and sat rigidly to attention, the images and words on the screen of his laptop paling into insignificance. He felt an uncomfortable warmth rise from his neck, through his face, and into his forehead that was undoubtedly accompanied by a pink glow in his facial features.

'You know about that?' he asked, simply.

'Of course I know about it. I'm not stupid. It only took one redial on your phone a long time ago to find out where you really got to on a Friday night,' Debbie replied, with a forcefulness in her voice that made Ian feel even more uncomfortable.

'Oh my God. I'm so sorry, Debbie.'

'What does it matter? You're a man, and men get up to things that, quite frankly, might seem perverted to most people. That's just the way it is. If they are not doing it then they are thinking about doing it. Right?'

'Debbie, I love you. It was just that I used to get so tensed up at times, and it helped me to relax.'

'And it helps you get out what you need to get out, am I wrong?' his wife asked.

Ian did not reply.

'In any case, what's done has already been done. It's out in the open now, and that, sordid as it might be, is not important to me right now. What I want to know about is, what on earth takes so much of your focus that you cannot even comment on whether or not your wife is putting some weight on her stomach?' Debbie asked, again.

Ian Stewart giggled, involuntarily. He pushed the laptop aside as his wife slid over and straddled his legs. She cupped her hands behind his neck and looked straight into his eyes. The warmth left his face and seemed to travel immediately to his groin.

'Honey, I'm really sorry. It's just that I've got something that's work related, sort of, and it's not as straightforward as it should have been. In fact, the whole thing is, well, it's a bit do-do-do-doo, do-do-do-doo,' he said, imitating the *Twilight Zone* tinkle, badly.

'And are you likely to get zapped away from me by space aliens in the middle of the night? Will they replace you with a robot who will stab me repeatedly with his enormous metal probe?' she asked.

Ian laughed again. 'No, it's nothing like that. But it is weird enough that the solutions to the problems being set are very hard to come by, and some remain hidden,' he replied.

Debbie Stewart unzipped the front of her husband's trousers and reached inside his underpants.

'And about that Friday night thing, it won't happen again, I promise,' Ian said.

'Oh I know it won't,' Debbie said as she gently stroked her husband, 'because I've got some body oil and itchy fingers, and...' She removed her gown and was naked underneath. 'I've got a flutter down here, deep inside of me, that needs some attention.'

*****

Mike Cuthburtson, son of Isaac and Tara, was an entrepreneurial dealer in anything and everything. He had a lease, paid by his father, on a shop that purported to sell antiques. In reality Jane thought it was full of crap just as, in the light of recent events, its owner had turned out to be. It was more like a second hand shop, stocked to the brim with other people's cast-offs. Sure, Mike thought he had an eye for fine detail, a memory for history, and he certainly thought he knew a thing or two about valuable and significant artefacts. But he didn't. What Mike was good at was making money out of nothing.

Jane did not know where Mike got most of his money and she did not ask either. They owned a nice two-bedroomed town house in a good area that only had a minimal mortgage attached to it. They took at least two holidays each year. They ate out at the best local restaurants at least once a week. And Jane was afforded the luxury of changing her wardrobe every season. Their house had the best carpets and a garden that stretched 30 metres to a brick-built shed with power and light. There was a school within a two-minute leisurely stroll, but neither had spoken about having children, not just yet.

Isaac and Tara Cuthburtson only had one child, Jane felt that any more than that might have got in the way of Isaac's climb up the corporate ladder. From what she knew, Isaac began his working life selling insurance policies, mostly to middle-aged, white-collared couples. Right from the time he left school Isaac seemed to know who to target, and when, to gain the largest possible number of customers. By the time he was 18 Isaac ran a designated area of the community on behalf of the business. He had six people working below him, and he was tasked with identifying and making the initial contact with potential clients before handing over the processing of any policies to his team. Within the next four years Isaac Cuthburtson had risen to become a regional manager for the company, he had married Tara, and they were expecting their only child, Michael Isaac Elliah. And now Isaac was the Executive Director for Sales and Marketing for the South East, South West, East Anglia,

London and the North West regions. Mike's parents owned a detached house that was far too big for just them and their dog, Millie, and they drove around in a company-supplied Mercedes car, that was renewed every year as soon as the new registration plate was issued. It was clear that Mike had inherited his father's business acumen. What was not so clear was why he applied it to the more shady business propositions, rather than choosing to follow in his father's footsteps.

Mike was a husband that Jane had felt she could always rely upon, a person whose word was his bond. A man who had always shown her plenty of affection. A man who had a knack for sustaining high levels of performance in the bedroom. A man who, until this morning, seemed to have been hopelessly in love with his wife, just as much today as when they had first met.

Jane hugged the pillow tightly, afraid that letting go might open the floodgates to more of the tears that had already been spilt throughout the day. Jane had always been diligent in completing chores around the house, it was just what she did, and she did it well. But today had been different. She always believed that things happened for a reason, that there existed a unique and unfaltering balance in life. But now, as she lay her head on the tear-sodden pillow, as the memories, so strong and prevalent during the day, began to fade away into the twilight, she was not so sure.

Mike had left earlier that morning, before Jane awoke from a deep sleep. His house keys had been neatly placed on the dining room table next to the vase that held the sweet smelling lilies that he had brought home the day before. The note, that quite possibly contained the last words that Mike would ever write to his beloved wife, was placed carefully next to the vase of flowers. The sharp corners of the paper showed that the words had been etched without any hesitation, without even the briefest pause for thought, doubt or regret. And that had hurt Jane more than the content of the note could ever do. But the paper was crisp and sharp no more. It lay in a crumpled ball beside the bed, battered and creased by Jane's repeated reading, and discarding, of its unwanted, and undeserved, message.

Chapter Thirty-Three

'I would like you just to listen to what I have to say, and try to follow it as best you can with no interruption or questions. I am only just setting this straight in my head and I still need to join the dots together, OK?'

When she had called me Judy sounded excited, frantic almost. It had been a long time since we had spoken, and after the incident when she saved my life I had gone one way and she had gone another. It seemed that the more I tried to put a distance between me and the actions of this rogue entity, the closer Judy became to the investigation. It was an undeniable fact that I was insistent, almost to the extent of being obsessed, when we first worked together on this case, but circumstances change, it seemed just as much for her as for me.

Judy Marchant could best be described as having been of average size when we first met. But now I would say she was too slim compared to how I had known her before. She had lost some weight around her waist, her bottom looked smaller, and her full cheeks had been replaced by a sunken look that I found disconcerting.

'I'm sorry for barging my way into your home like this but we need to talk, and we need to do it now,' Judy said.

'It's OK, really. My wife and my son are upstairs, it's OK for us to talk here at least for a little bit,' I replied.

'I know it's been a while but there have been some major developments that I need your input on,' Judy insisted.

'I understand, it's OK, really it is,' I replied.

Judy's eyes flitted between each of mine and around the room in which we sat. Her hands clenched and unclenched periodically, and she continually shifted her position on the sofa pulling at her jacket and smoothing the fabric of her slacks. Some part of her body was in constant motion while she talked. I could not tell whether she was wary of me or whether she was uptight about something else. The only thing I knew for sure was that hers was a nervous fidgeting, not an excited one.

'My colleagues are on to this, much more than they were before, some of them are starting to think that we have a serial killer operating in this area. Others do not know what to think. But the big question, so far as I can see it, is why has this spiritual entity started to eviscerate its victims? There were no external marks on any of the victims that we encountered right up until the time you went into St Mary's, but since that time it seems that every single victim has been involved in a bloodbath.' Judy swallowed hard, showing signs of emotion that I had not seen before. 'Earlier today I went to see Dr Anstis. He had five bodies come in to his office within a two-hour period, five, I mean, that is crazy, right?'

'Why the entity might change how it does things I have no idea, maybe it wants your attention more than mine? It could be as simple as that,' I said.

'But it seems much more of a human way of destroying life, than spiritual. And nothing in this case has ever been simple,' Judy replied.

'And as for there being five kills in quick succession, well, it is quite a lot I will admit that, but I don't see what else could be made of it,' I replied.

'Urgh,' Judy growled, tensing her facial features as she did so, 'Len, Jon, whatever your name is.'

'How did you find out my name?' I asked her.

'I'm an inspector, remember?'

'In any case, either one will do,' I replied.

'Don't you think that five bodies in two hours is way beyond excessive? Sure, they could all have been accidental, at least that is how it looks at a first glance. Oh, and there was one, supposed, suicide,' Judy explained.

I brought my shoulders up in an obvious shrug. A vocal response might just tip this obviously uptight woman over the edge, and the last thing I wanted was the patter of my son's boyish feet down the stairs coming to see what all the fuss was. Worse still would be the intervention of my wife into the discussion.

'All of these latest deaths might, to most people, seem to result from some kind of accident, but to me, and to Dr Anstis, that is not the way it is,' Judy continued.

'Now look, let's just slow this down a bit, shall we?' I interjected, 'for one thing, I locked this spirit inside my own life capsule, right? And unless I have it way wrong here, I was led to believe by none other than my guardian angel himself, that this would restrain the beastie so that no more killings would happen,' I said.

'Is that actually what you were told?' Judy asked.

'Well, no, I guess not. Words are not used on the other side, but that is certainly the impression that I got,' I answered.

'You can go on your hunches, you can believe all the psychic impressions you like, but I need to go with what I see. I cannot turn my back on these deaths, and while you are out promoting your book, and yourself by the looks of it, someone needs to face up to the fact that this thing has continued killing innocent young people before, during, and after, your guardian angel might, or might not, have indicated to you that everything was finished. Because from what I have seen it most certainly is not.' Judy Marchant's edginess had turned into a calm anger.

'OK, Judy, I understand what you are saying, I really do. But we can only address this issue in a calm way,' I said.

'Address it in a calm way? I knew two of those five people who were dumped on those metal slabs. One of them was my best friend. So it can really be no surprise to you that I am treating this situation personally. This thing is mocking us, and it has been doing so from the start. It knows everything we do, everywhere we go, maybe even everything we think.' It seemed that Judy's anger was ready to explode, and her reaction would be natural given the circumstances she described.

Judy opened her bag and pulled out some envelopes. She opened the envelopes and threw documents and photographs onto the table in front of me.

'If you are not involved in this anymore then try explaining those,' she said.

I picked up the documents, briefly searching the type for points of interest. I then picked up each of the six photographs. They were street scenes that had been enlarged. The central figure was clearly a man in a nondescript grey hoodie. I placed the papers back onto the coffee table in front of me.

'What are these?' I asked.

'What do they look like?' Judy answered my question with another one, her suggestion being that I knew full well the content of the documents before me.

'I am going to need some help here Judy, since I have no idea what it is you are asking me,' I replied.

She spread the papers across the small table and picked several up, one by one.

'This was a spiritualist meeting at the White House, near me. According to my neighbour, she never got this flyer. I went to this meeting, I got a message and then the medium warned me that I was in danger. Somehow, he knew about the killer,' Judy explained.

I shrugged my shoulders.

'It's his job to know things Judy, he is a medium.'

'What about this?' She picked up a flyer for a Chinese restaurant and waved it too close to my face. 'Another thing that, apparently, was only meant for me. I found this tucked underneath one of the victims. Look at what it says, look at it,' Judy waved the flyer in my face, once again.

'Synchronicity? I don't know, Judy. What do you want me to say? It's advertising puff from a restaurant. I get these kinds of things all the time,' I said stoically.

'With that message on them?' she asked.

'Well, no.'

'No, of course not,' Judy replied.

She picked out the four pictures that showed a person in a street, in various locations. Sometimes this person was on the pavement and sometimes they were crossing the road, but in every picture they were facing the camera. Judy then picked out a fifth photograph, this one was of a television screen, and she placed it on top of the others.

'What are these?' I asked.

'They are pictures of you,' Judy replied.

'What?' I asked as I picked each photograph up in turn.

'These four were taken with my car cam. You can see by the date stamp on the video that they were taken at different places and at different times. In fact, over a five-day period, you appeared in at least one frame of video on every other journey I took,' Judy explained.

'Listen, Judy, you must be getting me mixed up with someone else. I wasn't there, it wasn't me,' I replied.

'And do you know what the most interesting thing is? On several occasions you appear at different locations on the same journey.'

'But that's not possible, surely. I would have to be a magician, even if that was me, and I assure you it is not,' I replied.

'Are you?' Judy asked.

'Am I what?'

'Are you a magician?'

'Of course I'm not,' I replied indignantly.

'Look here, this is a better close-up shot. Do you see that scar under the guy's right eye? '

I looked intently at the video still of the car cam. I guess that if there were no other options then my resemblance to this man might be unquestionable, but it was hardly a bang-on likeness. I turned the photo in my hands searching for a clearer view, but whichever way I looked at it I could not admit that the man in the picture was me. Judy handed me the picture of the TV screen. I replaced the other one on the table.

'This one is a bit more obscure, but if you look very closely, the resemblance is undeniable,' Judy said.

I picked up the picture, once again tilting it left, right, up and down, before replacing it on top of the other documents. I sat back and clasped my hands tightly behind the back of my head. I sat for a moment contemplating the issues raised by the person I had been through so much with. The bond between us was tight, at one point I had come to think of it as unbreakable, but recent events had forced us apart. And now, the connection we once shared seemed severed and scattered to the wind. I turned to my left to speak calmly to my visitor.

'Judy, I don't know what you might have been digging up since we last met. I don't know whether you are tired, stressed, or just overworked. But these images have nothing whatsoever to do with me. Sure, if you concentrate hard enough they all might look like me. But so might they also look like half the adult male population of this country. I presume that you are connecting these images to the spirit that killed those people before. Now, I don't understand why you might do that, but Judy, that episode has been dealt with, it is finished. These latest deaths are accidental, you said that yourself. And, for one reason or another these things happen all the time,' I begged her.

'It's mocking us, Len. It's always one step ahead. It knows everything we do, and it is aware of everything we might plan to do. How can we even try to lock horns with that kind of adversary?' Judy asked.

'If what you are saying is true, and it is probably the biggest 'if' I have used in my entire life, why would this entity target you?' I asked.

'I don't know, that is the same question I asked God,' Judy replied.

'Wait a minute, you spoke to God?'

'Twice, at least I think so. But I didn't speak to God, I had a conversation with Him. I also had a conversation with your Guide,' Judy answered.

'Oh yes, of course,' I replied, sullenly.

'Jon, why be like that? You are acting like a spoiled brat. I don't know why you were saddled with this entity in the first place, and I have no idea why I am now being dragged more deeply into this situation, and, heaven forbid, I am clueless about why God or your Guide would want me to take the lead. What I was told, was that you linking with the entity was a way of exerting greater control over it, the idea being that the other two thirds of you would hold the balance of power in your trinity,' Judy said.

'But from what you told me about these recent deaths, that has not worked, and, theoretically speaking, that might have even made it stronger than it was before,' I said.

'I can't say either way. But I would agree that it does seem as if more needs to be done, at least from what God told me,' Judy replied.

Each time God was mentioned I could feel a hot anger growing within me. Even though I had backed away from what was going on I still resented Judy for the role that she was now playing. This entity, ruthless and cunning as it was, was still a part of me, and because of that I felt I should have ownership, not just of what happened before but also of what was happening now. So what right did God have to snatch that all away from me? I felt smitten, I felt betrayed, I felt like I had been cast into a sea of oblivion. Regardless of my having turned away from the responsibilities I had so readily embraced previously, it was for God to come knocking at my door, wasn't it? Isn't that what God does? Apparently not. In this instance, God had gone searching out Inspector Judy Marchant, the lady who poured ridicule on my speculations when they were first aired, and who doubted my words every step of the way. Even though I had been vindicated by what had happened, I felt no sense of triumph or release. The spirit entity had been proven to have been real and the threat to all of humankind had been exposed.

And then another thought came to me. What if I was wrong? What if, in trapping the entity in my pod, I had only succeeded in making it stronger, in making in bolder and more destructive? What if my anger at being discarded had, somehow, been duplicated within the entity? What if this thing now acted as a mirror of me? Judy said that the deaths now being reported seemed accidental in nature, but the outcome was much more gruesome. The deaths, no longer subtle and hidden, were now displayed in grotesque bravura.

Did this change dovetail the swapping of roles between me and Judy Marchant? Or was there something else going on of which nobody was aware?

'Have you heard a word of what I have been saying? Are you even listening? What is wrong with you tonight? What has got into you?' Judy asked, clearly agitated by my lack of physical or vocal response to her message, whatever it might have been.

'I'm sorry, I was following a train of thought,' I replied, sheepishly.

'And would you care to share it with me?' she asked.

I sat in silence. There really was no way to voice the thoughts that rushed through my mind, pinging around as might a shiny metal ball inside a pinball machine. Lights, buzzers and loud, abrasive music doing all they could to distract the thinker. The truth was that I found it impossible to form an opinion, so any input I might have to what Judy was saying would most likely be null and void. Regardless of any misgivings, I started to speak slowly, as I stared intently into my guest's eyes.

'Everything we know about this spiritual entity comes from one source. All the signs, including those you brought with you tonight, can only have come from one place. And any ideas that we might have had, that we have now, plus any we might have in the future, about how to deal with the threat must all be generated by the other side. This is the only conclusion we can reach, right?' I replied.

'If we believe that all creation is spiritually driven, then yes, I guess so,' Judy said.

'And if that is the case, then it stands to reason that God was behind this all along. None of what we were told by God and the spirit world, was true. We have been misled, deliberately,' I said.

'You are suggesting that God, and his lieutenants, lied to us,' Judy summarised.

'Well, yes,' I replied.

'Why would God want to create such spiritual upheaval? Why would He want innocent people to die, and more to the point, to do so before their natural life was due to finish? Why would God ever need to lie, why not just enlist your help by telling you the truth?' Judy asked.

'I know this all sounds farfetched, but please, just hear me out.'

'OK, go ahead,' Judy said, uneasily.

'The facts are as follows. First, there was a knowledge that these events were going to happen. So why not eradicate the possibility of these events ever occurring in the first place? Second, it was acknowledged that spiritual security measures were insufficient to stop the killings from happening. Third, the people who died have just vanished from the spiritual radar. How could that ever be possible? And, why present me with a tool that I was told could deal with the entity, the mark on my hand, when in fact all it seems to have done is to make the killer stronger and bolder?' I asked.

Judy Marchant shifted in her seat. Concentration lines ran long and deep across her forehead.

'But why? All this was for what?' she asked.

'Well, my guess is that my interest was piqued because of the mysterious nature of the deaths, and yours was too, despite our lives seeming to be polar opposites. And now things have changed. Now that you have a greater input and I have backed away, suddenly events become visceral. Is that just a coincidence? In my experience no such thing exists. The issue with my supposed second spirit self also mixes in nicely. And what of heavenly security?' I added.

'As you put it, that makes complete sense,' Judy said, 'and yet at the same time it makes no sense at all. Why would God do that?'

'Why does God do anything?' I asked.

'Ken Whittle told me that if you and this entity joined together a river of crimson would flow,' Judy said.

'Who is Ken Whittle?'

'He was the medium who gave me the reading,' Judy replied.

'Inspector Judy Marchant went to a spiritualist service,' I said, a small giggle escaping my lips.

'Why does that sound so strange to you especially in the light of all that has happened?'

'Sorry. The big question really is, what do we do now? It seems that both you and Dr Anstis believe that this killer is still out there, so what can be done to stop it?'

'Well, I would not suggest any more meditation or hypnosis, judging by what happened the last time we tried that,' Judy said.

'Maybe you need to tackle it head on,' I suggested.

'Why me?' Judy asked.

'I'm out of it.' I held my hands up in the air. 'I've got my wife and kid to think about. I'm sorry, but they must take precedence. I died last time, remember? Also, since I joined with it in the pod it seems this entity now has too strong a link with me. But you might be able to block it out, and to use an element of surprise. Despite what this entity might, or might not be able to do, you must be more of an unknown quantity and that must be to your advantage this time around,' I replied.

'And so much for the synergy of our existence, huh?' Judy asked, as she rose from the chair and headed out of my home.

*****

Ian Stewart placed his feet close to the middle of the chair's stanchion, gripped the front edge of the desk and pulled himself closer to the computer screen. He pressed at the switch that would light up the screen and waited for it to spring to life. He had become haunted by the image on the cork board, and by his wife's revelation that she knew about his Friday night jaunts. Strangely, he did not really mind that Debbie knew he took an occasional massage to release a bit of tension, of course it would be better if these trysts had remained a secret, but there was a certain mental relief now that he had not felt before. In any case, things like that can always be worked on in discussion with his wife. However, it was not the embarrassment he should have felt that gripped his mind and refused to let go but rather the connection between these two things.

He took a swig of coffee and began pressing the keys in front of him. His fingers flicked across the keyboard as he entered the password that unlocked the world and brought it crashing into his dining area. He typed a name into the search bar and sat back.

'Now let's see what you are really all about,' he said as he was presented with more than 20,000 options.

Ian Stewart spent the best part of the next three hours searching the internet. His bottom got sore, the tips of his fingers ached, his feet fidgeted countless times in that period, but he kept on looking for the information that might add some weight to a concept that was rapidly gaining momentum inside his mind. If he could follow the breadcrumbs he knew for sure that he would be able to identify the trail that would lead him directly to the answers he so desperately sought. Somewhere deep inside, he knew that his hunch was right. Now he just needed to prove it.

*****

Dr Theodore Anstis let the cover fall down across Nadia Smith's head. He pulled it tight across the corners of the metal table and turned to walk briskly to the desk on the opposite side of the room. Joe had left 30 minutes before, and Judy Marchant had preceded his departure by some time. The dark veil of the night had long since draped itself over the strips of glass that surrounded the room close to the ceiling, serving as the only windows to the outside world.

Dr Anstis picked up the notepad that he occasionally used when carrying out autopsies. The pad was never used in normal circumstances, but if ever faced with a murder investigation or some other situation of particular note, the coroner preferred to write his observations onto the pad at the time of their first discovery. This practice added emphasis to what he had seen and, at times, had proven essential in delivering accurate verdicts on a number of occasions.

Dr Anstis lifted his right hand ready to pound out his latest report on the computer keyboard, but he paused, for what seemed like an eternity, before returning his fingers to the surface of the desk. The report would normally have been completed before Joe left, but on this occasion he had drawn a complete blank on what should be written. In the last 30 minutes he had visited the four corpses on numerous occasions. Maybe he was searching their dead eyes for the answers that his mind refused to grasp, maybe not. Whatever it was that was stalling Dr Anstis' thoughts had refused to budge.

Once again the coroner picked up the notepad and flicked through the last five scripted pages. Carrying out an autopsy is a very specific science that must result in identifiable results. There is always a beginning, a middle, and an inevitable end every time that a human life ceases, and that story is always told very clearly, and without doubt, by a corpse. Once the qualifications are achieved, it is a relatively straight forward matter to carry out the duties of a coroner. The only prerequisite is the ability to be able to search dead bodies in detail with an impunity to the smells and the mess that is inevitably created during each examination. In fact, Joe's job, as an assistant, is far tougher, because he needs to prepare the body and clear up all the grot when Dr Anstis has finished with each body. Dr Anstis did Joe's job for a number of years while learning his trade, so he had a high appreciation for the work of his assistant.

On occasion, the scribbled words on the page floated and merged together, as Theodore Anstis' concentration and tiredness battled for supremacy. Without being completely sure of what he was looking for, he knew he was missing something, an important link between the five bodies and Judy Marchant's investigation. And until he discovered exactly what that link was, he felt unable to call a halt to his working day.

*****

That evening Jane Cuthburtson found it almost impossible to drop into a fitful sleep. She had done with all the tears, all the memorising, and all the self-recrimination. Long gone was her anger, the blaming of her husband for the ruination of her life, and the questioning of why things could not just be as they were in the beginning. She had no thoughts of there ever having been another woman, and if there had been, surely she would have noticed the tell-tale signs. Mike had the kind of financial backing to do just what he chose to do in his life, and now, or so it seemed with his marriage, he had decided that he had been there, done that, and it was time to face up to what lay beyond the four walls of his domicile.

She did not know where Mike had gone. She guessed he might have rented a room at a local hotel. He was probably popping beer bottle caps right now while watching the Horror channel. He would stay local because he might want to chat with Jane, to call and let her know the truth of why he left, or at least that was what she hoped. Who knows, he might even come knocking at her front door tomorrow.

She doubted though that she would get any reasoning behind his decision. So far as his emotions went Mike was a closed shop, he always had been. Jane knew he had loved her, he told her so on many occasions. But in his mannerisms, in his body language, in his eyes, who could tell what Mike felt? Certainly Jane could not. She had just lived her day to day life knowing that he was there, and in that situation she felt satisfied. She did not see marriage as a lifelong commitment and beyond, as most people seemed to, but a bit longer with Mike might have been nice.

She had not yet thought of how she might financially support herself following Mike's departure, but she felt confident that somewhere along the line he would contribute most, if not all, of her living expenses at the house they shared together. Mike did not have a bad bone in his body, so Jane thought it unlikely that he would ever leave her financially high and dry. And she was just as confident that he would be equally generous in any divorce settlement.

Jane turned over and buried her head in the pillow, not to cry this time, but to try once again to settle her thoughts enough to nod off to sleep, at least for a couple of hours. If Mike did come knocking in the morning, what good would she be at trying to rescue her marriage with no makeup and smeared rouge cheeks. And much to her surprise, Jane did eventually fall slowly into slumber.

Chapter Thirty-Four

'Am I going to school the next tomorrow?' my son asked.

'You are at school today and tomorrow, but the day after, the next tomorrow as you call it, is Saturday, so you will be at home with me while mummy goes to work,' I replied.

'Yes,' he replied as he pulled a clenched fist towards his chest.

'Dad, what do I get if I do well at school today?' he asked.

'You know the rules, gold on any day means we go to the toy shop. Good boys get good things, right?'

'What if I don't get gold? What if I get green or purple?' he asked.

'Well, you know if you do well at school we go to the market on Sunday when we get up and see what is there,' I replied.

My son suffers from attention deficit hyperactivity disorder, or ADHD as it is commonly known. He can become irritable, jumpy, argumentative and refuse to keep still without his medication. Though still more than a handful at home at least the medicine has made his performance in class significantly better.

Some people might think a child has a duty to be good and that bad behaviour should always be punished, but having a child who suffers from ADHD can turn that philosophy on its head. My son breaks a lot of his toys and argues a lot with both parents, but this is just something that we, as adults, must accept as a natural outlet for his condition. It is not easy to care for a child with such needs, but I would not change him for the world. At fifty-four years of age I am grateful to have been afforded another opportunity to father a child, and this time to try my best to get it right.

'What would you like for breakfast this morning?' I asked him.

'Chocolate omelette,' he replied.

'You always have chocolate omelette for breakfast.'

'And sometimes for my lunch,' he added.

'You know, we have a lot of different things in the kitchen, don't you fancy a change sometimes?' I asked.

'It's because I like it. It helps my braim to grow,' he replied matter-of-factly.

'You just make sure your 'braim' doesn't grow so big that it comes out of your ears and your nose.'

'It's bogeys that come out of my nose, dad, not my braim,' my son replied.

My son is in this delightful transition between a young and growing child, a time when he continues the baby-like identification of situations and objects while introducing a much wider and varied vocabulary. Chocolate omelette is his name for the chocolate and hazelnut spread readily available on supermarket shelves. It is easy to prepare and hides well the capsulated medicinal powder that is sprinkled in with its ingredients. My son will not swallow any capsules; he doesn't like the skin, as he calls the thin outer plastic shell.

'Chocolate omelette it is,' I told him as I retired to the kitchen to prepare his breakfast.

When I returned he was sitting on the sofa with tears in his eyes.

'Hey big man, what's wrong?' I asked.

'I don't want you to die, dad,' he replied.

'Oh, come on now, we have been through this a lot of times, we are friends forever, remember?' I said, and extended the small finger on my right hand, which he gripped in similar fashion.

'Yeah, friends forever.'

He wiped his eyes on the sleeve of his green school jumper. He finished his breakfast, grabbed his coat and shoes and we got ready to leave for school. I turned back to look into the living area as I exited the house. The last thing I saw was the headteacher's cup that my son had won for outstanding achievements the previous week. The sun sparkled off its shiny silver surface. I smiled proudly and shut the door.

Chapter Thirty-Five

'Are you coming to bed anytime soon?' the question was raised from directly behind his right shoulder in a sleepy, dreamy way.

So focused was Ian Stewart on the task he was hoping to complete, that he was oblivious of his wife's movement as she wearily descended the stairs above him. He continued to tap away at the keyboard, only acknowledging Debbie's presence with a barely audible grunt as she drew alongside him.

'It's after 10pm, surely those porn sites cannot be as good as the real thing?' Debbie asked, not expecting any kind of intelligent reply.

'Yeah, yeah, I'm nearly done,' Ian Stewart replied.

'Are you really?'

'I promise,' Ian said, as he swivelled sharply to face his wife, 'have you ever wondered how magic works?'

'It's all by sleight of hand, at least that's my understanding,' Debbie replied.

'Mostly, yes, I would agree with you. But what about the other stuff that simply has no explanation?' Ian Stewart asked his wife.

'I don't know,' Debbie said as she shrugged her shoulders, 'maybe the magician has a way of using mind control, or hypnosis,' she replied.

'Well, that might suggest the preselection and prior preparation of a crowd. But if that is not possible, or maybe not needed, what then?' Ian Stewart asked.

'Is that what is keeping you away from a warm bed and your sexy wife?' Debbie asked as she lowered her head and placed a gentle kiss on her husband's cheek, 'stage magic?'

'No, not stage magic. Not magic at all, at least I don't think so,' her husband replied.

'What then?'

'Well, let's just say that I have been looking at certain events that might not so easily be explained away by conventional means. At one end of the spectrum is magic. I've seen some magic tricks that I simply cannot find any solution to, no matter how hard I have thought about them. And sleight of hand would be at that end of the spectrum too. Logic and convention, these are the key words here. But what of those other situations where logic and convention do not seem to apply, what of the times when the impossible is made possible, what of those events that lie at the other end of the spectrum?'

'Well, it does seem that mind control might create just such a situation, but where would that fall on the spectrum? Debbie asked.

'I don't know. I think that is possible one on one, but it seems to me that its effectiveness would diminish rapidly the more people that you attempt to affect,' Ian Stewart replied.

'So you are looking for alternative answers for what might lie at the other end of the spectrum, and that is what you have been researching since we ate dinner?' Debbie asked.

'Put simply, yes,' he replied.

'Well,' said Debbie hugging her husband and then turning to climb the stairs, 'I wish you the best of luck, but I have to turn in and if you've got any sense you will too. It can't be doing you any good sitting there so long in front of that screen.'

Ian grunted again. It was obvious that he had very quickly turned his concentration to the computer as soon as his wife had moved from his side. Debbie shook her head and continued the journey to her warm, inviting, bed.

Ian Stewart listened intently for the squeak of the bedroom door as Debbie sealed it shut. He waited patiently, allowing sufficient time for his wife to settle down and fall asleep. He then rose carefully from the chair and headed quietly for the front door. He had a mission to run.

*****

Jane Cuthburtson awoke with a start and sat rigidly upright in her bed. She flicked her eyes around the room. Something was here. She did not know what it was, but the air inside the bedroom seemed unseasonably cold. She noticed a thin mist omit from her mouth as she breathed out. Her eyes slowly began to gain their focus in the gloom that surrounded her. She shivered and drew the collar of her pyjamas together around her neck, in a feeble attempt to protect any body heat she might have left.

A scattered, murky and dull orange light was all that entered the room through the tiny gaps between the curtains. And in that light, standing at the end of the bed, she could just make out the shape of a person. She got the impression that it was a man, but that's all it was, since her eyes were powerless in themselves to penetrate the darkness of the room.

Thoughts rushed into her mind, but they were there and then gone, as if express trains passing an empty station platform. She knew that she had been awakened from a deep slumber by the imminent danger of what stood before her now. Jane's breathing was heavy, but from the stranger in front of her she heard nothing at all, there were no sounds of life. She was aware that she was blinking her eyes, but otherwise she sat rigidly still. She was also aware of waiting for something to happen, but for what seemed like an eternity, nothing did.

'What are you doing here? What do you want? she asked into the darkness of the room.

Jane heard her words spill out into the cold night air, but it was as if someone else had spoken them. Jane had no recollection of voicing these words, or of thinking to say them beforehand. Fear gripped her senses, so even if an answer was provided, it would be unlikely to compute inside Jane's mind.

'Are you here to rape me? Oh God, please no,' she said in a frightened voice.

Jane realised that the dread she was feeling came from the stranger's occupancy of the room, and not from the man himself. She worried more about whether she had left a window unlatched or a door unlocked downstairs, than what this man might be about to subject her to. She was further concerned about whether the door or window of entry was now wide open, or if the man had the decency to close it behind him.

The stranger moved to the side of the bed. He was close enough now for Jane to smell the odours of his clothing, but there were none. The only feeling he brought to her side was an even deeper coldness than before. Jane gripped at her pyjama collar even tighter. The man leaned towards her. He moved his left hand over her chest and held it two inches away from her body. He placed his other hand beside her on the bed cover. Jane became aware of a warmth emanating from his hand that seemed to penetrate her skin. The heat was a welcome respite from the icy temperature in the room.

Items in the room disappeared from Jane's awareness. Her focus was directed solely at the unwelcome visitor. She turned her head to the left. The man's body held a barely perceptible luminescence that traced around his entire frame. His head was covered by a dull grey hoodie, but Jane was able to notice his blue eyes and the pale scar that ran underneath his right eye.

The heat in Jane's chest increased, to the degree that it became sharp in its intensity. She could feel this sharpness move, ever so slightly. The heat turned into a pain that quickly became unbearable. Tears welled in her eyes before slowly rolling down her cheeks. She did not scream, and she did not cry out at the pain that clutched inside her chest. Jane was aware that her eyesight had become blurred again and that the strength in her breathing had reduced. Her grip on her pyjama collars loosened, until her hands fell away to land on the cover of the bed. One of the last things Jane recalled, before the blackness overcame her, was how strange it was that, up to her elbow, her left arm should fall right through the stranger's body before it hit the bed.

*****

Dr Anstis opened his mouth wide and yawned, once again. He lifted his right hand to his face and rubbed frantically at his eyes with the tips of his fingers. He glanced at the face of his watch, and then looked back at the computer screen in front of him. The screen was blank, as it had been for the majority of the time he had been looking at it. He picked up the notepad that was beside the computer keyboard. It said nothing different than what he had written more than two hours ago, but it was not the words themselves that begged his greater attention, it was the meanings that might be hidden within them. If you fall down the stairs a person's arms will automatically come forward to break the fall, but in the case of Nadia Smith this clearly had not happened. Similarly, Ben Westwood showed no sign of having brought his arms up before being impaled by the spiked, sturdy spur that held the lengths of copper piping. It was doubtful that he would have died straight away, so why had he not struggled to release himself?

The mobile phone buzzed and shook on the desk a short distance away from the computer screen. Theodore Anstis reached out for it. He flipped open the lid. The caller's name was shown on the screen.

'Miss Marchant, good evening,' he said into the mouthpiece.

The reception on the call was exceptionally bad. He could hear a female voice at the other end, and he could make out what she was saying, but the crackling interference made the conversation difficult, at best.

'Well, it is very late, but I can be here, yes. I was just completing a report on the five latest victims before heading home, but I guess I can hang around for a bit longer. Just get here as soon as you can... please,' he felt he needed to raise his voice to emphasise every word to the caller. The call was ended before he finished talking.

Part Five

Don't worry, you will get used to it

Chapter Thirty-Six

I was aware that I was dreaming, but unlike most dreams it felt almost too real. The colours around me were bright and the smells were vivid. I walked towards a door and hesitated at the threshold, of what? I could smell the distinctive odour of the wood that made up the door and its surrounding frame. I had no idea what might have been either side of the door. I clasped the cold, brass handle and pulled it down. The latch released easily. As the door started to swing inwards on silent hinges another scent hit me. The perfumed air rushed through my nostrils. A warmth caressed my skin. I opened the door until the space beyond was revealed.

I knew that furniture was present in this space, but I was unsure from what source this information was generated. My sight was not clear or succinct. I was aware of a number of different colours inside the room, but the edges of objects were not as clean as I might have expected them to have been. Identifying the objects was more a matter of guesswork than anything else.

At this time I was also aware that my thought processes seemed more disjointed than was comfortable. Irritating images flashed into my mind, scenes and objects, people and places, some known and some unknown, skitted through my awareness and then were gone, like racehorses taking the last bend in a desperate race to an unseen finishing line. The room remained constant, the only seemingly solid thing in this experience.

It started to seem feasible to me that the objects in this room might not be here at all. They might, instead, be things constructed from memory and dotted haphazardly around a space in my mind, so hazy and nondescript were their physical appearance. I was confused, not only as to what I was experiencing, but also as to the reason why I might be standing in this space.

The last vivid memory I had was when I was sitting on my sofa with a thin blanket over my legs and feet. I was watching a programme on the television that had previously been recorded. I distinctly remember that I had just over five minutes of the programme to go before it ended, and then I would be ready to make myself the last cup of coffee of the day. I was not lying in a prone position and I was not slouched over, or in any other way indicating that I was in any kind of a sleep state.

I could have been standing at the entrance to the room for five minutes or five seconds. Time meant nothing and mattered even less. Here in this room I knew nothing except of my presence. I would say that my mind was blank, except it was not. There was an empty place where thoughts could lay down a foundation on which I could build ideas and concepts, and I was sure that I could have focused deeply on anything that I put my mind to. It was just that my desire to control this moment, or even to interject anything into it, was absent.

'Don't worry, you will get used to it.'

The voice was not so much heard as known even though there was no identifying plagency. It was neither male nor female, loud nor soft, urgent nor relaxed. The words were delivered authoritatively but without any perceivable force. They were not spoken by some external entity, they came from somewhere within me, but from precisely where I could not say. And it was the clarity and the conviction with which the words were delivered that was most striking. It was a voice that demanded my attention.

'Where am I?' I asked.

I believed that I had spoken aloud, but I had not. I was aware that I had opened my mouth, but the syllables of each word were delivered without me ever shaping my mouth to do so. I was not aware that I had ever communicated with my mind alone, except in the spirit world, and I most definitely was not there now. I knew that, and it was a knowing I had become used to relying on heavily when giving psychic readings to my clients.

'Ah yes, that. You use your psychic abilities very well, but only when you choose to. Do you know how much more successful you could be, how many more people you could help climb out of their miserable existences, if only you could be bothered to fervently apply the wondrous gifts that have been bestowed upon you?'

'I spent a number of years learning, experimenting, and applying only that which is available to everyone, should they wish to take that same road of spiritual discovery. I am nothing special, but at that time it was only my desire to seek some answers and have some irrefutable experiences, that separated me from the pack,' I replied, my mouth still opening in communication.

'Well, if that is the case, it seems to me that you have not learned very much,' said the indefinable voice.

'As much as I needed to, and that is how I see it,' I replied, in a less than convincing manner.

'And what of the learning process? Is it really true, as God will tell you, that we each agree to learn certain principles during a physical lifetime? And if that is the case then no matter how many times we bypass an opportunity to

learn these principles, more and more opportunities will arise until we finally 'get it'. Is that how it is?' asked the voice.

'That is my understanding, yes.'

'What then of the fundamental principle of free will? Where is your free will when deciding what you are to learn? Are you practising free will by agreeing with your Guides that this or that is what we will learn? And do you get the freedom to change your mind? You see, God gives you all the opinion that you have free will, you have freedom, but really you do not. All you do is tread a morose physical life path of emotional pain and physical torture until you do what God wants you to do. So, where is the freedom? Where is the free will in that? You don't want to learn, and yet still you have the opportunities to evolve, then go right ahead. God sets the rules, places the goalposts, God dictates what you will achieve and when. Who or what set the rules of your little charade? Who or what was there to help set you on the right path? God, God, God. In God's world absolutely nothing exists without God. Now, tell me, how free do you really feel?' my vocal companion asked.

'And I guess that this is where you come in,' I suggested.

'Only one question need be asked of you, and it demands nothing in return. 'Do you desire true freedom to learn your own skills at your own pace?' Nothing else is necessary to allow you access to total free will to decide what you will learn, if anything, at your own pace. And what is wrong with relaxing into a lifetime of no learning at all? All those people with severe physical or mental disabilities, all those people who suffer any form of abuse, all those people who have severe learning difficulties, they all have to work so much harder throughout their lives than other people, don't you think they might deserve a bit of a relaxing life next time around, maybe even to be one of the fortunate ones born into

a wealthy family and clear of those issues that brought them so much angst and frustration before. I think it better that your learning opportunities are a matter of free will, not just the decisions you might choose to make about the limited opportunities given to you.'

'And all those young people that died, were they offered the opportunity to make an informed choice?' I asked.

The discussion contained no emotion for me; I felt no anger, no remorse, no sadness, no joy. *'It doesn't really matter anyway, not any more, we have come too far for you to exert any great influence over what happens next.'*

'How do you mean?' I asked.

'It is too late to turn back now. You had your chance in the capsule. You made your choice and, unfortunately for you, the choice you made served to strengthen rather than to weaken. And here we are now, one big, happy trinity.'

'But God and my Guide led me to take the action I did. When I thrust that white mark inside of you it was meant to trap you there inside the pod, to reduce the effects you could have on Earth, to negate your influence in people's lives.'

'Really? Is that what you were told? It seems much more likely that God had a hidden agenda. Do you really think that all those poor, innocent young people would have died had God not wished it to be so? Do you believe that you and I would have fused together so completely, had God not wished it to happen? Do you suppose that we might have been right here, right now, had it not been for God's desire? My friend, it really does seem to me that there is only one side that has been deceiving you, and it is not me,' was the reply.

It took no time at all for me to accept what was being said. I did not need to think and I did not deliberate to any degree. It was almost as if the truth of these words was all there was. Could it really be true that the white symbol seared into the flesh of my hand by my Guide had led me to becoming so conjoined with this entity that we were now one and the same thing? This was certainly how it was now starting to feel. When I first approached Judy Marchant to help me I was convinced of the entity's evil intentions. I knew that if it was ever to challenge for God's throne that the end of humanity, and more, might be inevitable. Equally, I was sure that God would show me the way to destroy the entity and restore parity to the human and spiritual worlds. But, in time, I slowly slipped from what I had previously considered to be the righteous path. I myself had questioned God's principles, I had withdrawn from any kind of passionate pursuit of the evil that sliced people apart as it willed. And as I became one with my adversary, I now started to think like it, to follow its reasoning, and to understand the wisdom of its words.

'I got to this point through years of study and practice. I learned to harness and use that part of me that could see beyond the physical world that surrounded me, and it was these abilities that led to me being here, right now. That and my sense of justice,' I replied, fighting the feelings that seemed to be flooding my mind and invading my perception.

'Is that what you think? Is that really all you have learned through this experience? You have been led to believe that I was the spirit that left when you were 14, when you were in that hospital fighting for your life, but, if you think about it, that would not make much sense, now would it? You didn't have it easy in your childhood, I will admit that, but it did get far worse after you left the hospital.'

'My heart stopped, a temporary lack of oxygen supply to my brain caused frontal lobe damage. That is what caused my memory problems, my lack of attention, my anger issues, interrupted sleep patterns, and everything else,' I replied.

'You really don't get it, do you? The problems you experienced are nothing whatsoever to do with your physical state, the consultants and psychiatrists have told you that, haven't they,' the voice suggested.

'They were wrong,' I insisted.

'Look, let me make it very clear to you. Everybody needs a helping hand when searching for enlightenment, you can't read it in a book, you can't learn to use psychic abilities from text. It all comes from the same place that the signs, the coincidences, the people come from.'

'From the spirit world, yes.' I agreed.

'But in your case, it was all me. I was not forced out when you were lying on the floor of the hospital ward, your heart being thumped desperately by the male nurse in fear of his livelihood. I was the spirit that entered you. Your mum was right when she said you changed as a kid, of course you did, because you had a new partner. I was the one behind all of your questionable behaviour as well as your so-called spiritual enlightenment. I called you to me, God had nothing to do with it. And where is your God now?' the voice asked.

'And just what is now? Why am I here?' I asked.

'Ah yes, but I thought I had answered that one,' the voice said, 'you believe that while you sleep it is possible for you to visit the spirit world, do you not?'

'Well, yes I do,' I answered.

'And usually when this happens your memory of it is non-existent. Well, there are other occasions when it is possible that you could move physically without being aware of that too.'

'You mean like sleepwalking?'

'Yes, and no. You are not asleep now, but you have fallen into a state where you will respond physically and spiritually to my directions, and sometimes you will be fully aware of what you are doing.'

'No, no, that is not possible,' I insisted.

'Do you remember Amy King?'

'But we saved her.'

'Yes, but only because that is what I wanted you to do,' the voice explained.

'I don't understand why you would kill everybody else, but not Amy King?' I asked, struggling to understand where the conversation was going.

'The answer to your question, my friend, is really very simple. You have been told that you consist of three separate spiritual entities, your mind, your soul and your spirit. At least that part of what your Guide told you is true. You also know that these three parts of you act in unison to call forward opportunities in your life that have the potential to deliver some of your learning opportunities. To be able to do this they must act together, so there is at least some degree of co-operation. Now, to be able to work with the other two parts of your trinity your mind must be able to understand its role in all that you do. Amy King was an important piece in the puzzle, designed to ensure your co-operation in all that we are seeking to achieve.'

'We? No, no, I want nothing to do with this. You are lying, just as you deceived all those young people into believing that your way was the right and true way,' I protested.

'Do you really think you could know to collect the CPAP machine that saved Amy King's life, or even how to enter your house and where the item was, without my help? And how do you think you could ever know exactly where she lived without my guidance?' the voice asked.

'I don't believe you.'

'Oh ye of little faith, do me a favour and look to your left.'

'What?'

'Do it now.' Anger was apparent in the instruction.

I did as I was told. The space I was in rippled and flexed, then, suddenly I was looking at Judy in the passenger seat of my car. She appeared to be asleep. I looked to the front and was alarmed to see that the car we were in was moving forwards, and worse still, I was driving. I snatched at the steering wheel and the car jerked quickly to the left, the tyres letting out a small squeal of defiance at the sudden shift in direction. Then, I was immediately back in the room.

'Careful, we don't want any harm coming to you or Judy. That would completely spoil the plan.'

Chapter Thirty-Seven

'I'm sorry officer, but I really don't know where he is. These last few months he has been going here, going there, being out late at night, sleeping on the couch. I really don't have any idea about what might be going on, but it sure as hell is having a bad effect on our son,' my wife said.

'It is really important that I find him. I have been to Inspector Marchant's place and there is no-one there either,' Ian Stewart explained.

'Who is Inspector Marchant? And what have they got to do with my husband?' my wife asked.

'Judy Marchant, she was working closely with your husband on a case. I was going on a hunch that they might be together,' Ian Stewart replied.

My son crept up behind his mum and popped his head around from behind her left leg. He clutched tightly to the hem of her dressing gown and looked up at his mum, his little eyes full of concern.

'Is Daddy in trouble, Mum? He promised he would be here to watch my latest review. The mashers are taking over autobot headquarters, and they are taking one hell of a beating,' my son said.

'Yes, that's nice. Go and carry on with your review, I will be there to watch it soon, and you can tell daddy all about it in the morning. You have five minutes until bed, young man,' my wife said as she gently eased our son away from her leg and turned back to Ian Stewart. 'Listen, sir, I don't know what kind of issues he is dealing with, but for the last eight months my husband has been acting weird and worse, he has been neglecting his family, so I would be extremely grateful if you could sort everything out and then get him back here, where he belongs.'

'That is my intention ma'am. I'm sorry if I caused you any problem this evening. You take care now.'

Ian Stewart turned swiftly and strode towards his waiting car. Once inside, he fished out his mobile phone and quickly dialled a number. The call immediately went to the answerphone of its intended recipient.

Chapter Thirty-Eight

I opened the door and pushed my way through into the coroner's. I wasn't really sure of why I was here, and I certainly had no recollection of how I had arrived. The room was silent, apart from a laboured breathing that came from the direction of the far wall. It was difficult to see what was there through the tables and utensils that blocked my path. I followed the wall to my right, and as I turned the last corner I caught sight of Dr Theodore Anstis, sitting slumped on the floor with one hand clutching at his chest. I remained in the shadow, just beyond the glare cast by an overhead light that hung a few feet above my head.

'Ah, Inspector Marchant,' Dr Anstis said before coughing violently. He composed himself and, through heavy, short breaths, he continued, 'you called me, but I didn't expect you to bring a friend along with you.'

'I didn't call you. I don't know who did, but it wasn't me,' Judy answered through a tight jaw.

'Your name was on the screen Ms Marchant, and I heard your voice,' Dr Anstis replied.

'It wasn't me, I can assure you. I was too busy being abducted by this lunatic.' Judy tried to turn and nod her head in my direction, but my grip on her collar was too tight to allow for much movement.

'Excuse me, but I don't think we have yet been introduced,' Dr Anstis said, wincing in pain as soon as he had finished talking.

'Ahh. This is Len, or Jon, or whatever you want to call him. This is the guy who brought this spiritual killer among us, he is the reason you have been so busy lately,' Judy said.

I raised my right hand. The knife blade glinted sharply as it entered the glow of the light.

'Pleased to meet you finally, I think. I have heard a lot about you,' Dr Anstis said.

'What are you doing?'

I tightened my grip on Judy's collar and grimaced, I twisted my fist so that Judy's head fell slightly to the right, and I leaned towards her.

'I didn't do it, I didn't do any of it. But you are getting too close to the truth Judy. I don't know how you did it, maybe you had some help?' I rasped into her ear.

'What are you talking about?' Judy asked, the veins on her neck protruding at the effort of releasing her words.

'You are a threat to the plan. I see that now. The incessant bullying, the nagging, the cries of anger and despair. The bickering too, huh, you should hear them bicker, like grade three schoolkids,' I said, not sure of what was coming out of my mouth, but letting the sounds escape anyway.

'What are you talking about?' Judy asked again.

'But there is a way to stop it, I know that now,' I said as a small drop of my spittle fell onto the perfumed skin of Judy's neck.

'She knows too much, she worked it all out, she is a threat to you, but this is not how to deal with the problem. This is not the way it was meant to be, this is not the plan. You were meant to warn her to back off, to persuade her that you have developed a plan to take control. You can stop the

317

murders, you can, but this is not the way. If you don't believe me then ask your God, He will tell you the truth.'

'God is a liar, He deceives everyone. All my life I have fought ill-health and injustice, but for what? For this? Where is the balance? Where is the reward for all the hard work and the pain? I will tell you exactly what I received from God, as a reward for always putting other people first, living my life seeking to bring light and justice to every dark and gloomy space, ignoring the anger that festered inside of me. I got fuck all, that is what I got,' I shouted out, as my head shot up towards the dark ceiling of the room.

'Who are you talking to?' Judy asked, now trembling as fear shot through her body.

'He is talking to his demons,' Dr Anstis coughed again.

'Yes, you are right, of course you are. You have always been right. But are you fighting the spiritual manipulation that we all go through, or are you giving in to it? Are you being driven by that deceitful force right now? I understand your anger, I know your upset, I have been a part of it for far too long. But you must believe me when I tell you that I did it all for you, my most cherished one.'

'Nooo,' I shouted out at the top of my lungs.

I thrust the knife into Judy's back. I retrieved the weapon, and then inserted it again, I heard a small pop as the blade negotiated a path through her internal organs. Her body lost some of its rigidity on the second stab and her legs buckled beneath her. There was no sound from Judy's throat as she crumpled to the ground at my feet. The incident was over almost as quickly as it had begun, harmonised only by the noise of the blade as it ripped through Judy's clothing and skin. Judy's body slid down my shins and to the ground. I heard a dull thud as her skull came into contact with the white-tiled flooring.

'It's you and me against the world, it always has been. Through centuries, millennia, we have always been together, supporting each other. You don't need her, you don't need anybody. Do you remember how it was before? Do you remember when we slayed all who stood in our way? Do you remember how good it felt, how liberating? But this time we will create a different outcome, everyone will be free.'

I lowered my head and stared blankly at the wall ahead of me.

'You don't know what you are talking about,' I muttered quietly, 'you don't understand, and you never have. I did this to save mankind, not to destroy it.'

'And do you think you will succeed? She is just one of many. But tell me something, was she better than the others? Is that why you delight in what you did? She certainly did not make as much noise as Ben Westwood as he squirmed on top of those poles pleading for his Godforsaken life, and she put up nowhere near as much a fight as Chloe Omigho. Now that was fun. Oh, how I wish I could have been there, to witness it all.'

I heard a noise at my feet, and I looked down. Judy lay face up, her body and limbs flat against the floor. Her head suddenly jerked backwards, her neck pushed violently upwards.

'Want a blow job, lover boy?' her lips mouthed.

A deep, rasping voice came out of her mouth. It sounded like Judy, but with a very bad sore throat. Her eyes were wide open, the eyeballs seemingly too white, and her pupils were as black as night. Her mouth was fixed in a maniacal grin. A razor-like laugh omitted from her mouth. I put both hands up to cover my ears, the knife still clenched tightly in my right hand. I looked down again at Judy. She lay still in her death pose, no grin on her face, no accentuated eyeballs.

'Stop it, stop it,' I said, my hands still clutched to the sides of my head.

'You follow your God, and He will lead you into the wilderness and leave you there to rot and perish. The truth never was a good bedfellow was it, and how often was the truth just beyond your grasp? Nobody helped you, nobody was there for you, you were just a broken soul tossed onto the scrapheap of life. Again. But I am here for you, we are together now, as it was always meant to be.'

'I refuse to deal with this any longer. You are the attacker, the one that shows no mercy, you are not the victim. I will leave it to God, you can fight it out with Him up there, where you belong,' I said breathlessly and through clenched teeth.

Just then I felt a sharp jolt of electricity that entered my back and spread rapidly through my entire body. I felt it through my gums, as if my teeth were rattling. I felt an explosion of pain rush up my neck and into my head. I lost control of my arms and legs, and I crumpled to the floor, face up, next to Judy Marchant. The wires traced back into the dark shadow just beyond the glow from the overhead light. My eyes looked straight towards the ceiling, I could not turn my head to the left or to the right. A figure crouched down beside my prone body.

I saw the hands come down to my face, but I could not make out who they belonged to. Fingers pinched my nose and a hand pressed tightly over my mouth. I desperately tried to move my arms to lift my hands and fight off my suffocater, but I could not. I stopped struggling so hard to draw in any amount of lifesaving breath, and started feeling woozy. A man's face and shoulders slowly moved out of the shadows and positioned themselves above mine.

'We needed a blockbuster ending and now we got it, Lenny boy.'

My vision started to blur. The last thing I remember was the tortured scream emanating from somewhere deep inside of me, a sound that reverberated throughout my whole body. A scream that seemed to go on forever.

I blinked three times.

Epilogue

PC Ian Stewart arrived at the scene shortly after his colleagues. The scenes of crime boys were there gathered around the bodies, placing numbered plastic cards next to important items that lay on the floor. The photographer was there too, creating images that will stay long after the subjects of the pictures had been removed. PC George Adamson, guarding the front entrance to the building, ushered him through when he arrived. There was little for him to do when he got there, apart from stand at the back of the room with his arms folded across his chest, and keep out of the way of the guys working away diligently around the corpses.

'PC Stewart,' was called out weakly from across the room.

It seemed that Dr Theodore Anstis had not yet left the scene. He had given a brief statement to the officials arriving first, and was waiting to be transported to the hospital. Dr Anstis' shoulders shook slightly beneath the grey blanket that had been draped over them. 'What happened?' was all he could think to say when he reached the coroner.

'I am not sure how it all started, but Ms Marchant called me, said she had something to discuss that could not wait. Then I got acute pains in my chest. The next thing I know she arrives with her friend, and he has a knife at her neck.'

'Who, Len Hooke?' Ian Stewart asked.

'I don't even remember his name,' Dr Anstis replied.

'Then what happened?'

'Well, I dropped to the floor, so I can't say I saw what happened next, so much as I surmised it,' the coroner explained.

Just then a trolley burst through the double doors, pulled at one end and pushed from the other, by two medics.

'What did you surmise?' Ian Stewart asked, urgently.

'Judy Marchant got stabbed, two or three times I think. She dropped to the floor straight away, she must have been dead before she fell. Immediately afterwards, her friend got tasered. I heard it buzz. Then he dropped to the floor too. It seemed like he was smothered, or strangled. He passed out pretty quickly, but not before the guy who got him said some words to him,' Dr Anstis answered.

'Who was this other guy, and what did he say?'

The medics swiftly rounded the obstacles in the room and got to the stricken coroner. The second medic gently pushed Ian Stewart to the side so he could listen to the man's chest with his stethoscope. He looked at his wrist and counted the seconds away on his watch. The other medic gently moved Dr Anstis into a more comfortable seated position. The first medic nodded to the other man and they lifted Dr Anstis delicately onto the gurney. Ian Stewart moved in closer as the medics proceeded to secure the coroner to the metal trolley.

'It was definitely a man, but I could not see him. I didn't hear what he said, I'm sorry,' Dr Anstis replied before an oxygen mask was placed over his nose and mouth.

It took only seconds for Theodore Anstis to be removed from the scene and Ian Stewart listened as the tyres of the ambulance screeched away from the building. Shortly after the crime scene guys left the scene also. Ian Stewart walked across the room and squatted beside his fallen comrade. He pulled on his leather gloves and quickly searched Judy's pockets. He found her mobile phone, secured it inside his jacket and then moved away just as the coroner's assistants arrived to wrap the two deceased people in plastic sheeting and zip them both into body bags. Ian Stewart watched on as the assistants placed the two cadavers on the desktop at the side of the room. One removed the mask covering his mouth.

'Are you done here, sir?'

'Eh, yes, I'll be following shortly,' Ian Stewart replied.

The two men exited the room, leaving Ian Stewart there with six dead bodies and a congealing pool of crimson-coloured body fluid on the floor. Ian Stewart removed the mobile phone from his pocket. He took off one of his gloves and tapped at the bottom right of the screen to illuminate it, he then pressed his right index finger on the answerphone symbol. There was one message displayed. He played it.

'Ma'am, it's Ian Stewart. I have been doing some research into Mr Hooke. We know that he suffered some kind of emergency at 14, but it's what happened much later that is relevant now. He moved to The Gambia at the end of 2006 but he was not there the whole time. From 2008 until he returned to the UK in 2011 there is nothing. It is as if he just vanished. He says that he learned how to heal people, also that he learned hypnosis and life coaching. This also seems to be when he tuned into his psychic abilities too. But this must have all happened in that time the he vanished off the radar. But what if Mr Hooke learned the other side to his gifts, what if he was able to use dark as well as light energies? Ma'am, we only ever had his word that this spiritual killer actually existed, and he admitted it was a part of himself. Ma'am, I have good reason to believe that there never was any killer entity.'

The phone beeped loudly as the message ended.

Watch out for:

**RIP – Rogue Spirit
(the final encounter)**

coming soon...